Love You Anyway

A BUTTERCUP HILL NOVEL

STACY TRAVIS

FJP

FAST TURTLE
PRESS

LOVE YOU ANYWAY

STACY TRAVIS

Cover Design: Wildheart Graphics

Cover Photography: Lindee Robinson

Cover Models: Alexis Susalla and David Turner

Copyediting: Jenny Sims, Editng4Indies

CHAPTER

One

PJ

When I was a kid, I killed it at hide-and-seek.

It became my all-time favorite game, if only because it was something I could do better than my four older siblings. I loved outsmarting them by finding better hiding places. As the smallest, I could find my way into tiny spots where they never thought to look.

I always stayed hidden the longest, so I always won the game. Every time without exception. With several overachievers in the family, winning was everything.

It still is.

I didn't learn until much later that my sister and three brothers often intentionally "forgot" to keep looking for me once everyone else had been found. They'd move on to another game while I stayed curled up in a kitchen cupboard and eventually fell asleep.

I wonder now if winning is really in the eye of the beholder—or, in my case, the winner. As in, it doesn't matter if I won according to the universal rules of hide-and-seek. What matters is that I believed I won, and it gave me a few notches of the confidence I desperately needed as the youngest of five competitive kids.

In some ways, the game served me well. I can still fall asleep almost anywhere and in almost any position—in the car, on a plane, sitting up, or leaning my forehead on my hand at my desk. And I learned early on that I need to find an edge if I want to be noticed in our family.

The overachievers are still busy doing their Type A personality thing, and half the time, I wonder if they've forgotten I'm here.

I didn't understand the power of not being noticed when I was a kid, but I understand it now. It makes me much more aware of what's happening around me because no one is bothering me. It makes me hyper-observant and able to fix problems before they even become problems.

Like a helicopter sitting on a grass field amid the grape vine-yards, where it most definitely isn't supposed to be on a Wednesday morning. Or any morning.

At Buttercup Hill, our vineyard needs that field as part of our ecological diversity. We need a variety of plants—fruit trees, vegetable crops, flowers—so our grapes don't grow in a monocul-ture. Since we farm organically, having pollinators from diverse crops means we can do without pesticides.

What we don't need is the wind-producing rotors of a giant machine.

This entitled person's helicopter probably just scared off a week's worth of bees and bluebirds. It won't ruin our grapes in one day, but still…

Annoying.

Some people just have no awareness. Like the ones who sit in the car, scrolling through some social media feed, while someone else waits for the parking spot. Or standing in the grocery store waiting for the checker to put groceries into a bag instead of being a little bit useful and lending a hand.

Case in point, the guy standing in front of me at Sweet Butter, the café at our family winery, where I'd like to order my daily latte and get moving. It's already past nine, and I have a strong case of the Monday blues, wistfully recalling how nice it felt to sleep in yesterday, go on a long hike, and leave work behind for the day.

I don't have a lot of patience for a man who never seems to have ordered a cup of coffee before. "So the macchiato, that has less milk?" His deep rasp makes this question sound serious.

Meagan, a sweet kid from the local high school who works summers here, sweeps her dark bangs out of her eyes and stares up at him. I stand just off to the side and try to catch her eye, letting her know I feel her pain. But she stays focused on the customer. "It's smaller than a cappuccino, so yes."

"And the simple syrup, is that vanilla or something?"

"No, it's basically liquid sugar." She smiles, revealing a small gap between her front teeth. She's so much more patient than I would be. Good thing I'm not a barista at Sweet Butter because I'd have thrown a cup at this guy's head by now.

How hard can it be to decide? I wonder if he's new to coffee. Or life.

I fake a small cough. Maybe he doesn't realize anyone else is here as he asks Meagan to walk him through the entire chalkboard coffee menu. Maybe the sound of another human will startle him out of his oblivion, and he'll pick the medium roast and get on with it.

If he hears me, he doesn't budge. Not a flicker of acknowledgment in the broad frame that still mostly blocks my view of Meagan. "Hmm, okay. Maybe I'm making it too complicated."

"*You think?*" I almost say out loud. Fortunately, my inside voice prevails. I can't get much of a look at him from where I stand other than very broad shoulders that pull at the fabric of a frayed denim shirt. He's tall and lean and looks like an athlete. His dark hair is damp and smells vaguely of the rosemary and mint shampoo we have in the guest rooms at the inn. It's undergoing renovations, so there shouldn't be anyone staying there, but maybe they've opened a few of the rooms.

He leans a forearm on the glass bakery case, and his back muscles flex against his shirt. Tapping long fingers on the glass, he shifts from one foot to the other. His navy sweatpants hug his tight ass, and I try to stop staring. But it's hard.

I haven't dated in ages, and this man candy is a nice distraction on an average morning, even if he's cramping my style with his coffee idiocy.

"Okay, well, I'm open to whatever you think is best. Do you have a favorite?" I can hear the smile in his voice. Great, now he's flirting with the barista? We could be here a while.

"It's just coffee," I mutter. "It's not that hard."

That he hears. Casting a glance over his shoulder, he greets me with piercing eyes in a color I've only seen once before—in the clear blue-green waters of the Adriatic Sea off the coast of Croatia. Jacques Cousteau declared those waters to be the cleanest on the planet, and I don't doubt it, given that I could see the sea floor through sixty feet of water.

Even in the throwaway glance, this man's eyes look sharp, discerning. Like they don't miss a thing.

Ironic.

"Sorry?" It's more like the purr of an expensive car engine than a word.

His eyes roll over my face and down my body like he's assessing a piece of art at an auction, looking for its hidden value and its flaws. I offer the same perusal in return, noting the sharp line of his jaw under a couple days of scruff and the strong jut of his chin. And his pecs give the worn fabric of his shirt a run for its money. It just might rip if he inhales.

I hope he inhales.

No, I don't. Because I need to get my daily caffeine fix and get out. He's just taking up space and time in my day, and that's nothing but annoying. And spoiler alert: this auction item has no flaws, at least none visible to me. This man is absurdly gorgeous, which is a red flag in itself.

Warning, contents may not accurately reflect their packaging.

Spoiler alert—in my experience, they never do.

I could clear my throat and pretend that what he heard was an errant noise without any meaning. But I don't have much of a filter before my first cup of coffee, and he's made me wait longer than usual for mine.

"It's just...pick something. Anything! You can't really go wrong when you're just talking about combinations of beans and hot water and weird milks. It's all just coffee. It's not astrophysics."

He turns the rest of the way around to face me. I expect an irritated glare because I've butted straight into his coffee business, where I have no reason to do so. The hard line of his jaw and the heated flash of those blue eyes make it clear he's done his share of glaring, but that's not how he's looking at me. Not exactly.

He seems more...curious. Tilting his head to the side, he studies me like I'm an interesting new species. Or a bug he's about to squash with one fist.

"Not astrophysics, eh?"

My cheeks flame, and my brain fires, ready to explain astrophysics to the knowledge-impaired, even though my only real knowledge of the subject comes from *Astrophysics for People in a Hurry*, and I'm in more of a hurry than most people.

His eyes roam over my face, where I know my bottom lip juts out because I'm just that exasperated in anticipation of the coffee I really need. Right now, it's the only thing that will allow my brain to understand what's happening before me.

He brushes a hand through the wet strands of hair, which looked perfectly tousled a moment ago and looks even more so now. Then his lips part, and he exhales a long breath. "Slangry?" he asks.

My mouth opens, then closes again. I intend to answer, but I have no idea what he means with his question. "Um..."

"Sleepy and angry?"

"Um..." If I'd finished the drink he's denying me, I'd have a better answer.

"And I'm what's standing between you and caffeinated salvation."

"I…yes, exactly," I admit. From his confident perusal of me and his large stature, he looks like someone who's accustomed to being right. No reason to begrudge him. Except that he's annoying.

He takes a slightly exaggerated step to the side and extends his hand, ushering me to the spot he just occupied in front of Meagan. "By all means." The gesture reeks of smugness, like somehow he thinks he has the upper hand even though he's the one who doesn't have the basic skills to order a drink.

I'm "slangry" enough that I don't have the wherewithal to tell him where he can shove his *means*. I smile at Meagan and order my usual latte with oat milk, bristling at the quiet chuckle I hear beside me.

"Oat milk. I didn't even think of that," he says. I'm tempted to ask him what rock he crawled from behind when he's clearly never seen a half-caf, two-shot, caramel skim macchiato like a normal person. He beats me to it by telling Meagan, "Her coffee's on me."

Now I'm stunned.

First of all, my coffee is on the house because my family owns the café, which is a part of Buttercup Hill vineyards. We've been family-run since my grandfather started the winery with one strain of grapes several decades ago. Our father grew it into an empire, and some big shots invested money in it. Now we distribute to stores and restaurants all over the world. The story is printed on placards all over the property as a kind of homey origin story that guests love.

I'm not stunned because I expect him to know all that. It's that I can't think of the last time someone offered to buy me a cup of coffee. A part of me likes the gallant gesture, even if it's coming from this strange man who's been cock-blocking my caffeine until this moment.

"N-no. You don't have to do that," I tell him, not intending to explain why he doesn't need to pay.

"I insist. And I'll have what she's having. Sounds like she knows what she's doing," he tells Meagan. With that, he whips out an Amex Black card, swipes it through the machine, and walks past me to sit at one of the tables while he waits for Meagan to make our drinks.

I should be happy to be done with him and even happier to hear that luscious sound of beans grinding, which means I won't be "slangry" for much longer. Instead, I'm annoyed again because this man has walked over and sat at the one table by the window where I always drink my latte.

Always.

I'm not a rigid person. I get along with others. You don't grow up as the youngest of five siblings without knowing how to sit in the middle seat of the car and make do with the orange popsicle nobody wants. I am nothing if not accommodating and easy to be around—once I've had my coffee.

But I do have this one daily ritual. Each of my siblings has one. We all live on the two-hundred-acre property that houses our vineyards and winery—as well as the inn and two restaurants. Part of how we've managed to live and work so close to one another is that we each have our roles and habits and give each other space.

Archer, the eldest, likes to run at the crack of dawn, so his whole morning routine is a mystery to me, someone who prefers to stay in bed until it's light outside. Similarly, our middle brother, Jackson, has some need to get to his office at four in the morning or something ridiculous. I don't cross paths with him on the way to work…ever.

Beatrix, my older sister, is a little more normal in terms of waking hours, at least, but she has an espresso machine in her office. That leaves Dashiell, the youngest sibling, save for me. He tends to go out most nights, sleep in most days, and he never cooks. That extends to making a cup of coffee. He's in charge of all the hiring around here, and I've never known him to schedule a meeting before ten in the morning. If anyone, he's who I'd expect to see in the café.

This brings me back to the man in front of me, sitting at my table. He's not someone who works for us. The winery's tasting room isn't open yet, so there's no real reason for anyone other than my family or an employee to be here.

I stand in front of him, realizing I've been here for a minute at least without doing anything but stare. He doesn't seem bothered. He's probably used to women gawking at his pretty face.

He meets my gaze with the same steady curiosity as before. Maybe he's missing a few marbles.

The sound of steaming oat milk calms my frayed nerves a bit, and I tell myself that I just need to get my coffee, inhale the entire cup, and be on my way. That would be the best idea.

Instead, I point at the chair, dwarfed by his large frame. He has an arm slung over the wooden backrest and sits facing sideways to the table. "I normally sit there."

It's ridiculous. I know I'm being ridiculous. If he's a guest here, that's all the more reason for me to let him sit wherever the heck he wants. I don't know what's come over me this morning, except that he's thwarted my morning routine twice in a matter of minutes, and I'm not handling it well.

He points at the chair on the opposite side of the table. "Join me."

"Join…?" His words make no sense. I wasn't inviting myself to have coffee with him.

"Ready," Meagan calls from behind the counter, and the man pushes up from his chair and saunters over to retrieve our two lattes. As tempted as I am to shove myself into the chair while he's gone, I'm not quite that unhinged. He glances back as though checking. I nod and cross my arms, though I'm itching to drop my derriere into his seat.

He hands me my drink before sitting in the chair opposite the one that I'm guarding like a pro hockey goalie. "Better?" he asks, starting to arrange chess pieces from a box on the windowsill. He places them expertly into the proper squares, barely looking down. Not his first time.

I nod and feel my weight hit the wooden seat just before I bring the cup to my lips and take a long, soul-satisfying sip. Something clicks in my brain, and I return to full functionality. I take in a much more complete picture of what's happening before me, namely that a man I don't know is setting up a chess board at the table where I usually sit.

Not wanting to be rude to a guest, I look at the pieces. The hand sitting in my lap twitches, wanting to make an opening move. The other one clings to my cup for dear life, lest someone take away this life-giving substance.

"You play?" he asks.

I'm even more confounded by his seeming desire to play a game of chess, especially when he's yet to take a sip of his coffee. That feels important, so I point out, "Are you going to drink that? Or are you one of those undercover investigators here to review how well you were served?"

I'm being flippant, but as soon as the words come out of my mouth, I realize he just may be one of those undercover reviewers, and the last thing we need is a family member making us look bad to the press. Especially since I'm the family member in charge of public relations.

That's right, if there's spin control to be done, it's my job. So I shouldn't create problems I'll need to fix later.

The corner of his mouth tips up, but it's not a smile. I haven't seen anything resembling a smile from him, so maybe this is as good as it gets. He nods. "Yeah, that's me." I can tell nothing from his deadpan delivery.

He takes a sip and seems to consider the mouthful before swallowing it. Then he nods. "It's good. You're off the hook. No bad review."

"You're not really a reviewer," I confirm, feeling gullible.

"I'm not." He takes another sip. It seems to satisfy him. Now

I'm the one staring with curiosity, trying to glean something from his movements to tell me who he is and why he's here drinking coffee for the first time in his life.

He studies me studying him. "You seem relieved. Are you anticipating a restaurant reviewer? And is this the way you'd welcome him?" He points at the counter where we had our exchange a moment ago.

"Well, yes to the first. No, to the others. And yes, I'd be the one dealing with the fallout of a bad review. I'm kind of a fixer around here."

No idea why I'm telling him that. I'm sure he doesn't care.

His partial smile is back, but this time it looks more like a smirk. He's one of those men who can make any facial expression —a grimace, a sneer, a smirk—seem like it belongs on a magazine cover. I find it vaguely irritating and impossible to ignore, which is also annoying.

"Is that how you impress reviewers?" Again, he points at where Meagan loads pastries into the glass case. Rows of croissants and blueberry scones. I inhale the buttery scent but find it mingling with something else—his damn rosemary mint shampoo. Did he use the body wash too?

"Wh-what?"

"Berating customers? I mean, why not come right out and throat punch them for good measure?" His delivery is so serious, his eyes barely hinting at amusement, that I'm not sure if he's deeply offended by me or giving me a hard time.

I don't feel like justifying my pre-coffee mood to him.

"I only do that when I know they can take it. Didn't want to mess up the mousse in your hair, so I went easy." Equally deadpan.

His eyes flash with challenge, and he nods slowly before a faint tick at the corner of his mouth lets me know he approves of my humor. "Fair enough."

He looks back at the chess board.

"But you like the coffee." I'm telling him, rather than asking, my hand still quivering in my lap because I really want to open a chess game with the French Defense. It's a beginner move, but I have some tricks up my sleeve, and it's one of my favorites.

Before I can control myself, my hand darts out and I move the first pawn. He glances down at it and up at me. Without looking, he moves his black pawn to the expected square.

We face off for a few minutes, each moving pieces quickly because we've both clearly played this game enough to know the standard moves. He captures my rook. I take his knight. More pawns sacrificed. Both queens protected.

It doesn't get interesting for me until halfway through a game, at least when I'm up against someone who knows how to play.

My heart ratchets up a few notches because I see an opening, a way I can lure his queen into a perilous position, and I don't think he sees it. I'm used to this. I've played online a lot, mostly because the people I know don't play, and the online opponents are programmed to make no mistakes.

He may have just made one. Granted, his moves have surprised me. Each time I thought I had him cornered into doing what I expected, he found a way out and forced me to think on my feet. That rarely happens when I'm up against casual chess players. But now, I think I have him sandwiched between my rook and my king with no way out.

The gentle tinkle of the bell over the door to the café catches my attention for a moment, but that's not why I take my eye off the board for a second too long.

"Colin, hey man." My eldest brother Archer's voice rumbles from the doorway. I feel his sudden presence in the pristine space like a gray cloud moving in front of the sun.

Of course, there had to be a reason the man across from me is here. I've been so wrapped up in our silent game of chess that I didn't bother to introduce myself or wonder more about who he is. Once the game of chess takes over, I find it hard to focus on anything else.

"Arch." Colin pushes his chair back from the table and leans forward to shake my brother's hand and clap him on the back in a half hug.

That momentary distraction is all it takes. I move my castle—something I've done countless times before—but somehow, I don't see what this guy sees. The next sound I hear is his deep voice declaring, "Check."

A jolt of panic hits my chest, and my eyes snap to the board, where he does, in fact, have my king in check. Worse than that, I've cooked my own goose by moving my castle, and now there's no way for me to win this game.

"I see you've met my little sister." I've never minded him referring to me this way before because it always felt like an endearment. But right now, it feels demeaning when I'm about to get my ass handed to me by his friend in the one game I know how to play well. Sure doesn't look that way right now.

"Checkmate," he says by way of answer. Then he extends his hand. "Colin Hathaway. Visiting chess nut."

"And astrophysicist," my brother adds helpfully. My gut hollows and I blink hard. Seriously, I can't catch a break. Ever.

"Arch, unnecessary info," Colin grunts.

I shake his hand, keeping my grip firm because I don't want him to see how much it costs me to bear this defeat. My cheeks heat, and I will the temperature in the room to drop to arctic levels and cool me down. Meeting his eyes, I tell him my name. "PJ. Resident coffee addict."

"And fixer," Colin adds. Still no smile.

"Right," I say. "When there's something that needs fixing." Like this whole situation.

And I'm at a loss.

"Pleasure playing with you." The politeness feels like a kick in the shins. Something to placate a beginner who gave it her best try.

I nod. Then I push my chair back from the table and offer it to my brother. The last three moves play over and over in my head—

where I went wrong, where he took an opening I practically handed him. I still can't believe I didn't see it.

That never happens.

But given that Colin Hathaway is just visiting my brother today, I doubt it will happen again. Even though a part of me really wants a rematch.

CHAPTER

Two

COLIN

"I don't think I ever met that sister," I say casually, as though my brain hasn't spent the last five minutes at war with itself. *How* can she be his sister?

For one thing, the woman who challenged my indecision about a coffee order and managed to be funny through her exasperation doesn't bear any resemblance to him. He's a big guy, muscled from spending an hour easy at the gym each day after he runs. Never a hair out of place. Granite expression that puts fear into the minds of lesser mortals. Or even an unfortunate delivery person.

PJ, for all her irritated sass, exudes light. I couldn't help noticing the blue steel in her eyes as she fought against her indecision about the French chess opening. How her rosebud mouth turned down into a scowl when she realized she couldn't win. How her blond hair fell in waves, and she didn't even seem to notice the wild tangle framing her face like it was art.

I've known Archer for years, and his whole vibe is different— not playful, that's for sure. Not quick-witted.

Not that Archer isn't smart. He is. But he's more bookish, and his intelligence is hard-won. It's a different kind of smart from his sister, evidenced by her sass and the quick calculations each time I made a move she didn't expect. I liked watching the wheels turn, her eyes darting across the board, hands steady until she decided on the best move. Been a while since I played against someone with real skill.

"PJ? Yeah, we're ten years apart, so she was never around back in the day."

The day he's referring to is college, when we were both at Stanford, freshman-year roommates who believed we were God's gift to the modern world.

Being at a place where everyone had so much untapped potential made me restless. Which, in turn, made me creative.

I'd started two businesses and invented three apps by the time I graduated, mainly because it seemed like everyone else was doing it, and I always wanted to be better. Second place was never an option for me. My parents, both academics and researchers, drilled that idea into me as a kid. I was an only child without an older sibling to chase around, so I tried to compete with my parents. An elementary school kid trying to design a science fair experiment worthy of two adults with PhDs.

Destined to Fail, party of one.

I suppose my "Type A+ or Bust" personality put me on an Autobahn highway to my current predicament. But I'm getting ahead of myself.

"Ten years, that's a lot." I put my crack math skills to work and calculate that ten years puts PJ at twenty-six years old to my thirty-six. When Arch and I were in college, PJ would have been all of eight years old. Not exactly old enough to visit us on campus and beg us to take her to a party, like her sister Beatrix did during her senior year of high school.

He rubs a hand over his face and nods. "Yeah. It's like a different generation. She's all about having fun, living in the moment, and being a wiseass, generally. Keep your distance, and you'll have a pleasant two weeks." His eyes go hard. "Seriously."

In other words, she's off-limits. Doesn't take an advanced degree to know when a guy's cock blocking his best friend and his sister. Even if hanging out with a pretty, fun wiseass was the reason I'm holing up at Archer's family winery. Which it isn't.

"Anyway, I really appreciate you doing this for me," I tell my closest friend.

He waves a hand like it's nothing and goes to the counter for coffee, leaving me to stare at the chessboard once more. I replay the last few moves in my head, noting where PJ made the mistake that cost her.

Obviously, I don't know her, but she doesn't strike me as someone who makes mistakes. Maybe that's what makes her a good "fixer," whatever that is.

Archer returns with a steaming cup of something and drops into the chair where his sister sat a few moments ago. The view of him is nowhere near as good, and it annoys me. Everything annoys me lately.

"You go out for a run or something?" I ask, gesturing to his long-sleeved, moisture-wicking tee and recalling all the mornings in college when he woke up, ran six miles, and showered before I'd even gotten out of bed. Pretty much most mornings.

"Yeah. Stayed on the property, did a few laps."

"You'll have to show me around." I should be more enthusiastic about spending two weeks holed up at a vineyard. From what I saw on the drive in this morning, there are acres of vines, trees, and open space. Just what I need.

Then again, leaving my house at the crack of dawn and speeding along the highway didn't exactly make for a relaxing chance to take in the scenery.

"Done," Archer says. "Let's do it." He pops up from the table as abruptly as he sat down and signals me out the door of the café.

"Thanks," I call out to the barista on my way out the door. She nods while polishing a large espresso machine that already looks spit-shined. I wonder if Archer keeps the employees around here on a tight leash. Maybe the moment we're out the door, she'll throw down the rag and pull out her phone.

Pretty sure that's what my employees do when I'm not around.

At the thought of my company, where I will *not* be spending the next two weeks, I feel an uncomfortable surge of disappointment. If not downright unease.

Archer leads me down a gravel path I barely noticed when I sleep-walked from my car to the café. He gave me directions and said he'd meet me here. "Get a bite to eat if you want, and I'll be there by seven," he'd said.

A forest-green golf cart sits parked in a small area shaded by live oaks. Archer slides onto the white seat and gestures for me to join him. I've barely pulled my legs in before he whips the thing into reverse and turns it out of the driveway. He points vaguely with his left hand while his right hangs over the top of the steering wheel, spinning it easily when we need to turn.

"Down that way is all sauvignon blanc grapes. They'll be ready for harvest first." I follow his hand motion to row upon row of staked grapes, their star-shaped leaves shading the fruit beneath. Mostly, it looks like neat rows of greenery, and I marvel at how different it is from my life at work.

"I can't believe you're a farmer now," I say without thinking. I know Archer is positioned to take over Buttercup Hill from his father, but in all the years he's talked about his job running a billion-dollar business, I've never come up here and seen it. Now, looking around, it's abundantly clear that he's in charge of something that looks a lot more like gardening on a mammoth scale than sitting in board rooms, which I do all too often. I can't help feeling a little bit envious.

"Pretty much," Archer says. "Except for the part where I don't actually pick the grapes or graft them onto new plants to make this whole thing happen." He swings an arm wide to demonstrate the expanse of it.

"Still, you can be out here, looking at these vineyards every day. That must be nice."

He casts me a side-eye while swinging the golf cart down another smaller lane. He points at a lake we're approaching. "It is nice. I'm still in my office way too much, but that's changing as I take on more of the primary winemaking job."

"So your dad isn't doing any better?" A while back, he told me about his dad's dementia, making it clear I was the only one he trusted with the information. I haven't told a soul, and I recall hearing Archer's voice break when he told me how painful it is to watch his father's memory begin to fail.

Looking down, Archer shakes his head. "It's advanced to Alzheimer's. We had to file a legal thing to take control of the company. He doesn't even understand what we tell him half the time. That's how much he's already slipped away." He clears his throat when he chokes up.

I look at his profile, but he's already swallowing down the moment and inhaling a deep breath. Archer is as stoic as his father.

I remember Kingston Corbett visiting Archer, and the man terrified me. Even when he was ordering wine for a couple of underaged kids and treating us like adults, I still feared he just might pound a fist through the table if the server forgot our breadsticks.

It's hard to imagine such a man crippled by a disease that eats away at his mind.

"Jesus. That's a lot."

Archer hits the brakes, and the cart pulls to an abrupt stop beneath a stand of olive trees. Tipping his head, he gestures for me to follow as he hops out of the cart. We walk to the edge of a small lake, about a hundred yards across, where ducks float lazily on the surface of clean, dark water dappled with water lilies. I hear the croak of frogs on lily pads, but I can't see them.

"It's a lot. And I'm a winemaker, suddenly."

I have no idea where he's taking me, but I follow him down a grassy path that wraps around the lake. He hasn't bothered pointing out any landmarks so far, which gives me the sense this tour is more for him than for me.

"Is that gonna be okay for you?" Based on what I know of Archer, he's never wanted to follow in his dad's footsteps. Back in school, we both had big dreams of starting companies, running them according to new principles no one had thought of, and retiring young and wealthy. None of that spelled working for his dad or inheriting a business where he didn't have a say.

Archer shrugs, and his shoulders don't fall fully. He walks, hunched as though protecting himself from a nonexistent force of wind. "Eventually."

Tipping his head, he indicates a bench on the far side of the lake. We head there in silence. I decide not to press for more details. Mainly because I'm not really in the mood for sharing details about my own business disaster.

Archer has other ideas. We sit, and he swivels to face me. "So what happened? I read the stuff online, obviously, but it doesn't sound like you. Did you have some kind of breakdown or what?"

I feel glad I grabbed my half-full cup of coffee before leaving the café because it gives me something to do while I stall. After a long sip, I shrug. Maybe it qualifies as enough of an answer in bro-speak.

"Tell me," he says.

I close my eyes and can hear myself ranting when someone caught me in a moment of irritation after a meeting I hated. Our investors were goading me to lobby for lower standards on carbon emissions so AstroTech could be a polluter and still make ungodly profits. I always left these meetings feeling a little dirty after the wining and dining and pressure to put profits above everything.

My pent-up frustration turned to recklessness when someone

stuck a phone in my face outside the restaurant after lunch. "When are we going to Mars?"

It was an innocent enough question, one I've been asked a hundred times, but something in me snapped.

"We have no business trying to explore other planets if we can't take care of our own. I'll shut down the whole space program at AstroTech if it means being part of the solution instead of the problem. I'd do it in a heartbeat." They were the right words, even if I've suffered the gut-punch of people's reactions every day since.

"I lost my cool."

Archer elbows me in the ribs. "Sounds unlike you. So you just fucked up like the rest of us?"

Not liking the way those words sound, I whip my head around and shoot him a stony look. If I leveled that death stare at the people who work for me, the conversation would be over. Not with Archer. Which is probably why he was the one I called when my company's publicist told me to get out of town and lay low.

I needed someone who'd understand but not judge. From his question, however, I'm thinking I may have picked the wrong guy.

"I didn't fuck up."

I may have fucked up.

My hotheaded remarks went viral, and now I'm getting canceled. People took my rant as stupid predictions about troubles down the road for our company because I was frustrated and felt like stirring up trouble.

We really should be looking out for the planet. I stand by that.

I've said minor shit like this before, and no one's made such a big deal out of it, but this time, for whatever reason, investors got bent out of shape. *Really* bent out of shape.

Exhaling a long breath, I watch the cloud of steam drift into the cold air. It's so sunny today. Cloudless sky. Yet still cold enough to frost the tips of my fingers and snag my breath at the bottom of my lungs.

"Was there a life-or-death reason you needed to take the media bait and spout your mouth about the company's prospects and future losses?" Archer's growl sounds like a hungry bear pissed off about an empty trashcan.

"No." I hate people who ask questions when they already know the answers in order to prove a point. Right now, Archer tops that list.

"So you fucked up."

His logic leaves no room for subtle deliberation. "Yeah."

"Lawsuits?"

"Probably. Shareholders are pissed. Stock's in free fall." I haven't said these words to anyone on the chance that not saying them would make them less true. But I can't lie to Archer. He knows me too well, for one thing. He also reads the news.

Without a second thought, Archer offered to put me up at his family's winery for two weeks while I "cool off" and avoid the reporters who'd lined up outside my company headquarters and my home, baiting me into the stupid things I'm just itching to say.

"You getting good counsel?" he asks.

I nod.

"Great. I'll make you a little deal. While you're here, we're just old friends with a few weeks at our disposal to drink wine and talk about old times. You don't ask me about my problems, and I'll leave you alone about yours."

He presents his hand to shake, even though neither one of us needs such formality. This is why he was my first phone call. He cares enough to leave me the hell alone when I don't feel like recounting my wrong moves for the eighty-seventh time.

We sit by the lake for so long that the sun finally rises high enough to offer a little heat. It's still crisp and chilly—an unusual mid-summer snap of cool weather—but I don't mind it one bit.

The way the media's had my feet to the fire for the past two days, I'd be happy in a cave made of ice.

CHAPTER

Three

Staring at a host of splashy news items about Colin Hathaway on my office computer, I berate myself a little for not paying more attention to science, if only because the astrophysicist is very nice to look at. Then again, despite his recent troubles, the man himself is famously aloof and media-shy.

From a spin control perspective, it's a smart strategy. The less time the head of a company spends talking to the media, the less likely there is to be trouble. Colin should have just kept his head down and continued in that vein.

But like the dummy most people are, he eventually said the wrong thing at the wrong time in the wrong place.

And *kaboom*.

I feel a little sorry for him, but only a little. Guys like him need to learn to keep their dicks in their pants and their thoughts to themselves. Not necessarily in that order.

I have no evidence about what Colin does with his dick, other than what I read in the tabloids while I'm waiting to buy Greek yogurt and cheddar cheese at the market. I'm savvy enough to know very little of that breathless blather is true. Or all of it is true, depending on who you ask.

"Billionaire heartbreaker," according to one breathless exposé. "Tech's most eligible bachelor," declares another. "Mogul seeks heiress"—I don't even know what to think about that one.

A quick media search tells me he made some bold statements that have investors believing AstroTech won't be able to send a human to the red planet anytime soon. And somehow, through the public relations mess, someone gave him the advice to get out of Dodge and hide.

Wouldn't be my advice, but he didn't ask me.

Archer isn't exactly the chatty type, and my work rarely requires me to know what scientists are doing. Colin Hathaway has never been on my radar, which explains why I didn't recognize him.

It also explains his aloof smugness and, I suppose, his ability to play chess.

Astrophysicist, for heaven's sake.

He could have cut me a break when I made the comment about his coffee order not being astrophysics. But no, Colin Hathaway is apparently just the kind of smug, hot billionaire who plays his cards—and his chess pieces—close to the vest.

No harm, no foul. It's not like I'll need to cross paths with him again. He's my brother's problem now, and I have enough to do without giving him another thought.

I spend most of my day on the phone with reporters from local and national media outlets, making sure they'll all attend our next industry event. It's a big fundraiser in two weeks, and all the who's who of Napa Valley will be in attendance. That includes small vintners and the largest estate owners who've been making wine here for generations. The donations will go toward building a new theater at the high school. A *lot* of money will be raised.

It's not until the end of the day that I get a phone call that changes my mood from average to pure crap.

"Hey, it's Trevor Stagwood," he says when I stab at the speakerphone button on my cell. I'm expecting Molly Stratton, the style editor for the Times, who always calls from a blocked number. I assume she's calling about our upcoming event.

With the way my dad's health has deteriorated, my siblings could use some good news, and I intend to provide it. A little love and good press will lead to better brand awareness for Buttercup Hill, and the wine sales will follow. I'm good at my job, even if my siblings call me the "social media maven," as though all I do is post selfies.

"Oh. Hey there," I say, half thinking he'll tell me he misdialed and meant to call someone else. We've known each other for half our lives, ever since his family moved to Napa Valley and took over Botticelli Vineyards, which was in bankruptcy. People accused his family of being vultures, but as a seventh grader, all I knew was that Trevor had soft brown eyes and cute dimples when he smiled. Financial details didn't matter to me at all.

He was a flirt, and for several years, we were friends. He sought my advice about whichever cheerleader caught his interest while I did my best to get him interested in me.

He never was until the day I turned my attention to someone else in our class. Then he pursued me like a leopard on the hunt. We dated for two months during our senior year until he cheated on me with, yes, a freshman cheerleader.

We've been frenemies ever since. Friendly because our families work in the same industry in a small town. Enemies because I'll never trust him.

You know what they say about leopards.

Trevor Stagwood doesn't ever call me unless he's upset that Botticelli Vineyards didn't get enough press attention at one of our events. And I always tell him that I don't control which photos the media features in their splashy montages and who they choose to photograph in the first place.

But I do.

In reality, I control every last camera angle and list of who's who and the people Molly Stratton sends to our industry tastings.

It's no accident that our profits go up each time someone from the Times comes to an event at Buttercup Hill. And it's no accident that Botticelli somehow always ends up left in the dust.

I don't hold our high school past against Trevor—that would be petty.

I hold our present against him, one in which he's proven to be even more of a vulture than his father, always looking for an angle. Loyal to no one but himself.

Trevor's voice makes me exhale a sigh of relief, certain now that he's only calling to gripe about something. I'll feign apologies, tell him once again that I don't control the media, and get on with my day. He likes to blow smoke, and I'm betting he'll feel better once he rips me a new one.

"What's new?"

"Oh, the usual. So listen, I'm hearing some things about Buttercup, and I wanted to go to the source." He's all business, and for the first time, I start to worry that he *isn't* calling to tear into me even though I hate when he does. My heart starts thudding in my chest, and a wave of nausea hits me.

"Okay…happy to help." Politeness and a light, even tone will set the stage here. No panic.

"Yeah. I heard that Buttercup Hill is in financial trouble. Big debts on next quarter's balance sheet, big losses. True, PJ?"

"Really? Who said that?" I know he won't tell me, but it buys me a second to gather my wits.

What he's referring to is not public knowledge—but he isn't wrong. We recently discovered that our dad spent half a billion dollars, and Jackson can't account for where the money went. He's been following breadcrumbs to figure out who received it, but all he knows is that there's some link to a tiny winery down the road called Duck Feather.

Our dad made a vague reference to Hayden Lanes, and Jackson searched everywhere for a business or a person with that name, only to find that Hayden Lanes is painted on a street sign at

Duck Feather. We've been trying to get a meeting with the owner, but he never returns our calls.

Meanwhile, to keep our investors from noticing the big hole in our balance sheet, my siblings and I borrowed money against our share of the vineyard to shore it up. It's only a temporary solution because if we can't repay the loans with real money from Buttercup Hill, we'll lose the vineyard.

We don't want this out in the open before we get our ducks in a row. The last thing we need is word spreading to our investors. My siblings are the only ones who know about any of this, or so I thought…

"I have it from someone close to Buttercup Hill. More than one person, actually." His clipped mimics a bored reporter with a hot story, and he just needs a "no comment" in order to go to press. I know how this works.

Or rather, I know anecdotally. In the years since I took the reins on Buttercup's publicity, my job has mostly entailed courting reporters to write splashy stories in wine magazines or style sections featuring our events. I pepper our social media accounts with images of the vineyards and fun photos of people enjoying our wine. In other words, mostly fluff that makes us look fun and trendy so we sell more wine.

There's been no tea to spill; therefore, there are no messes to clean up.

Jackson and Archer handle all the investors who ask questions and levy threats about pulling the plug if we're not profitable enough. They have thick skins and big dicks to swing around.

I've made friends who do my job at wineries where there have been scandals—husbands cheating, ex-wives starting wineries to compete with former husbands, business partners falling out and suing for ownership of vineyards. It happens all the time, and in a small town like Napa, news doesn't stay hidden for long.

I've spent evenings listening to how my friends spin these scandals into less important news once a media outlet grabs hold. It takes a professional stance and a magic touch. But I've never had to manage another winery owner—let alone a former high school flame—who found out something we didn't want known.

Until now.

"I have no idea what you're talking about." I know it's the right thing to say, but it won't hold back the freight train of truth if word has gotten out about our finances. I just can't understand how it has. No one knows except my siblings.

Right?

I feel the crawl of nervousness across my skin. I don't want to speak out of turn and jeopardize our winery with a careless remark.

"Sure, right." Trevor sounds smug and sarcastic, as though now we're adversaries.

"Anyway, it was good of you to call and check in."

"Yeah. Of course. And not for nothing, if you ever *are* looking for an investor, Botticelli's always interested."

It irks me that the vineyard he had no part in founding always seems to be flush with cash to buy up land. I wouldn't give him the satisfaction of investing in Buttercup if we were down to our last dime.

Just hope my siblings feel the same way. I'm the one with the history with Trevor, but no one in my family likes the Stagwoods very much. Something about how they swept into town and acted like they owned the place.

"I'll keep it in mind. Say hi to your family."

The line clicks without a goodbye.

Still sweating, I get up from my desk, walk down the hall in a daze, and hold the wood banister as I make my way downstairs. Our offices are in the main house, set back at the end of a commanding wide driveway that takes visitors from the main road to the reception area. From there, they can take tours of the wine cave, catch a golf cart to one of the restaurants or the inn, or walk to the big brown barn for wine tasting.

It's late in the day, so no guests linger downstairs in the reception area, which has tall bookshelves filled with memorabilia from the early days of Buttercup Hill. Photographs of the winery perch atop shelves lined with older bottles that have the original label design.

It's an unguided tour from the shelves displaying framed wine reviews to every wine award under the sun. We display magnum bottles, glass vases with sprigs of olive leaves arranged perfectly, and a replica of the original brown barn.

Each shelf is lit by tiny spotlights. And right now, I don't care about any of it. Plopping into one of the worn leather chairs that flank the stone fireplace, I drop my head into my hands and try to reason through how my day went from bad coffee mojo to an all-out fail.

Then I close my eyes and coax my brain to think quickly. I need to call a meeting and let my siblings know there might be local gossip about our finances. It will hopefully die just as quickly as Trevor Stagwood lit his little fire.

Rumors fly all the time in our small community, and most people are smart enough to know there's nothing to them. Just because Trevor happened to take a lucky guess at what's really happening at Buttercup Hill doesn't mean he knows anything. Doesn't mean anyone else does either.

At least, I hope so.

Otherwise, we're looking at the tip of an iceberg that could torpedo the whole Titanic.

"We meet again."

From bad to fail to...what's worse than an all-out fail? Certainly, it's the presence of a smug billionaire to kick me when I'm down. And stressed. And not in the mood.

I don't bother lifting my head. "We don't have to meet again. I can't actually see you, so we can pretend it never happened."

That's when I hear it. An unfamiliar sound, at least when it comes to this man I barely know. Is he...laughing?

It's surprising enough that I raise my head. Still not smiling, he does appear to be making a sound similar to what I think of as amusement.

Great, a smug billionaire who finds my suffering funny.

"What's wrong?" He crosses his arms and tilts his head to the side. He looks slightly more animated than he did this morning, if only because his five o'clock shadow softens the hard line of his jaw. He also looks as tired as I feel.

"Nothing." At least, it's nothing I plan on discussing with him. I look away, indicating that I'm done with the discussion. I don't mean to be rude, but he's not here to visit me, and this isn't exactly a great moment for me to shoot the breeze.

Entitled billionaire asshole.

He doesn't move even though I've basically dismissed him.

"What does PJ stand for? I assume it's not your given name." I wish the deep tenor of his voice didn't sound like it's rumbling from the engine of a vintage Mustang. I want to jump in that car and drive away. It's distracting.

"Didn't anyone teach you never to assume?" I can't help firing back at his question with a challenge. It's the "little sister" in me.

He rubs a hand over his chin and taps his lip with one long finger. "Okay, let me rephrase. Did your parents really name you after cute bedtime onesies with feet?"

I fight the urge to smile because damn him, he's really great to look at, and right now, his face is a balm to my frazzled nerves. He looks like he came from a vacation on some European riviera, with crinkles around his eyes from squinting at the vacation sun and hair rakishly ruffled from exiting his helicopter. Or yacht.

My mother was the only person who ever called me by my full name. *Penelope June, come give me a hug.* I can still almost hear the lilt of her soft voice, wrapping around my middle name like a snuggly, warm blanket and bathing my name in a subtle Southern lilt. As a New York City native, she had no such accent, but I guess she liked the way it sounded.

That was a long time ago. It's been years since I've seen her. She travels quite a bit and does a lot of volunteer work in Central America, so she's hard to pin down.

"It's Penelope June. No pajamas were harmed in the making of my nickname. It's just easier."

"Anyone ever call you Junebug?"

"Nope." I pop the "p" at the end to make sure he knows that "nobody" includes him.

I'm rewarded with another deep chuckle. It's oddly soothing, and right now, I'll take that.

"Okay then. Arch and I are grabbing dinner, so I'll be out of your hair. Nice seeing you again…Junebug."

I don't bother to respond. He can call me whatever name he pleases. Once again, it's the last I plan to see him. Nothing will change that fact.

CHAPTER

Four

COLIN

"What's your sister's deal, anyway?" I ask the question that's been on my mind all evening, ever since I ran into her in the main house before dinner.

Over oysters and yellowtail crudo appetizers, I think about how new lines had creased her forehead in the hours since I beat her at chess, something that caused the first faint lines. I hated being the one to mar the delicate features of her face, but I'm a competitive son of a bitch, and she left me an opening.

I've never learned how to do what's good for me, especially nudging an able chess opponent to see her mistake. Even if she is the prettiest goddamn chess opponent I've ever faced.

I suppose I could have gone easy to be polite, but it's not in my nature. And judging from her reaction to losing, I doubt she'd have wanted that.

"What do you mean?" Archer asks as we're joined at the table by his younger brother, Jackson. I didn't mean to ask my question in front of more Corbett siblings, but it's too late to reel it in.

"Hey guys." Jackson slides into the red leather booth next to Archer. "Which sister?"

"Never mind." I was willing to talk about PJ with Archer, but I don't really feel like dragging another brother into the mix. He'll make too much of my question. And my interest.

I wave a hand and reach for another oyster, but Jax acts like a puppy who sees I'm hiding a liver snack. His eyes brighten, and he might as well be wagging his tail.

"PJ." Archer grabs a breadstick from a basket on the table and bites off an end.

"Oh." Jackson rolls his eyes. "What'd she do now?"

I pick up the bottle of wine from the table, knowing it's probably a faux pas not to let our server do the pouring, but I'm determined to steer the conversation in another direction.

"Nothing. She seems like a bit of a spitfire, is all. Practically told me to take a hike the two times I've seen her. It was…interesting."

"Yeah, that's PJ," Jackson says, picking up his wineglass and taking a sip of the cabernet. "She has big opinions, and she's pretty loud about them. Not her fault. When you're the youngest, you have to shout louder, or you get ignored."

"She wasn't shouting," I tell him, wondering why I feel the need to defend her. As an only child, I was the eldest and the youngest, and even though there was only one of me, it was still hard to get my parents' attention. Both scientists, they were devoted to their labs, and I spent a lot of time with babysitters.

I can't help feeling weirdly protective of PJ, as if she experienced anything like that while her older siblings took the lion's share of their parents' attention.

"You like her," Archer observes, scooping the last piece of yellowtail onto his fork.

I shrug. "Sure. I don't come across many people that into chess. As I said, she's interesting."

Archer leans back and crosses his arms. If it were possible to shoot missiles from a person's eyeballs, Archer would have killed me eleven times in under a minute. I meet his stare with a stony look that conveys nothing. It's not the first time we've faced off. In fact, it reminds me of all the times he and I disagreed back in college—about everything from what class to take to which girl to date.

Archer always had opinions then, and clearly he still has them now.

"What?" Jackson asks, looking back and forth between us.

Archer continues to glare, and I shrug.

"Tell me what I'm missing," Jackson says, peering at Archer with a lopsided grin that says he knows what's bugging Archer but enjoys any chance to bait his older brother. "Did something happen between you and Peej?"

Before I can answer, Archer bites out, "She's not 'interesting.' She's normal. And often a pain in the ass." Archer takes a sip of his wine. From the distasteful look on his face, you'd think someone substituted paint thinner for cabernet.

Jackson laughs, enjoying his brother's discomfort way too much. Knowing Archer as well as I do, there's about a fifty percent chance of him losing his shit if Jackson goads him. And as long as I'm not the one baiting him, it might be fun to observe. "Dude, you're being way too protective. I didn't hear Colin say he's trying to bang PJ."

I think actual smoke spirals from the top of Archer's head. His face gets red, and he bites his words out with such intensity that he risks chipping a tooth. "Don't even fucking say those words."

I nod slowly, understanding now that Archer's sudden mood shift is all about guarding his younger sister. From me—the guy whose marriage imploded and who hasn't dated anyone seriously in five years. Work is my priority one hundred percent of the time. There's no point in trying to wedge a relationship where it couldn't possibly fit.

I'd find Archer's reaction comical if I wasn't forced to admit that I found his sister a bit more than interesting. But I've been warned now, so interesting is where I'll leave it.

"Understood." I put up a hand as a sort of peace offering in a fight I didn't know I was having. "I wasn't even considering going there. But...understood."

Archer lets out a long exhale. "Sorry. Just...Jax, you're such an asshole. Why do you need to bait me all the time?"

Jackson's guilty grin says exactly why. It's what younger brothers do. "Let Colin date her if he wants to."

Archer's shoulders creep up again, his voice tense. "Just...stop it. Colin is here to escape stress, not create more of it. Why do you fucking persist, Jax?"

"Because it's really fucking fun, dude. That's why." His grin widens, and Archer matches his look with a scowl. Turning to me, he takes one last swing. "You have my permission to date PJ if you want to."

I play it straight, hoping to defuse Archer's brain grenade before it explodes. "Thanks, but Arch is right. Work's a bear these days. I don't need more drama in my life."

Archer points a finger at Jackson's chest. "A year ago, this guy'd be agreeing his ass off. But he falls in love and all the attitude disappears. I dunno who you even are anymore, Jax," Archer mutters. He's probably just jealous. I haven't met his girlfriend, Ruby, but I can see that Jackson's new relationship looks good on him.

Even before he fell in love, Jackson never had anywhere near his brother's intensity. For that matter, neither do I. Looking back, it's hard to imagine how Archer and I ever became friends. The first time I met him in the dorm cafeteria, he stood in the food line, glaring at the salad bar. I remember wondering if he saw a bug crawling among the lettuce leaves or something equally horrifying, so I waited and gave him space.

When he didn't move for a minute straight, I cleared my throat. "You good?" I asked, having no real desire to get into a conversation about bugs or lettuce. I'd seen this guy around a little bit. He was tall, muscular, and lean, like he spent several hours a day at the gym. I figured he was probably an athlete, and I'd lay money on football being his sport of choice.

And it didn't take a research professor to observe that the women of Stanford found him easy on the eyes. I'd never observed a hush fall across a room when a person entered until I saw Archer. The sea of people practically parted for this guy.

All that is to say that I concluded he was probably a dick, used to having people fawn over him, and unlikely to have anything in common with a guy more interested in staring through a telescope than staring at porn. At age eighteen, that made me a major outlier, and I was used to it.

In the years up until college, I'd kept my head down, excelling in the STEM classes and science fairs that were the only way to get any attention. I hit puberty so late that I thought it had skipped me entirely.

It wasn't until my senior year that I grew eight inches, and once I'd gained early admission to college, I had newfound time on my hands. I started rowing, which meant that I bulked up in a hurry. By the time I graduated, I looked like a different person and had a promising college future ahead of me. Girls took notice, but before I could take advantage of their interest, we were all shipping off to college, where I showed up as a grade-A virgin with no game.

I got to campus as a freshman, ready for...everything. Ready to be more than a science fair nerd, even though inside I was very much still a science fair nerd. I just hoped maybe I could distract a few women long enough with my newfound muscles that I could lose the V-card and have some fun.

Enter Archer Corbett.

We had very little in common financially—I was at Stanford on a scholarship, and he was a second-generation legacy—and he was studying business to my hard sciences.

I'd been right. Archer was a walk-on running back on the football team, where he was all but guaranteed to warm the bench. He didn't care. Neither did the female population on campus.

He ate his meals late after evening practices, which coincided with when I had a break from working in a physics lab. I gave him shit about how many glasses of milk he lined up on his tray—at least eight—and he ribbed me for being "an actual astrophysicist."

"I'm only an aspiring astrophysicist." That only proved to Archer that I was "the guy I never would have been friends with in high school."

We ended up being roommates for the next three years, one of which Archer made it off the bench for some playing time. Fifteen years later, here we are.

"Anyhow, message received. If I see PJ again, I'll ignore her." I speak into my glass, drowning out the words with a sip of red wine.

"It's good, right?" Archer points at the wine, the other topic apparently forgiven and forgotten.

I don't want to make him feel bad by telling him the wine vintage doesn't make a difference to me. "Yup."

I go to way too many fancy dinners where expensive wine and trendy food are thrown around like loose change. It's part of how business gets done in the rarefied world where venture capitalists and investment bankers are all jockeying for the best places to make money grow.

And for the past five years, that place has been my company. Everyone wants in, whether it's venture capitalists dying to put up money for what's been a guaranteed return or friends and friends of friends wanting…something.

The longer I've been in the business of making other people money through my company's space missions and future exploration, the more I've begun to question what the hell I'm doing. Am I keeping a good enough eye on the environmental impact of our missions? Are we a green enough company? Do investors care as long as we're making money? Do I care if they care?

No wonder I couldn't keep my shit together anymore. No

wonder I ran my mouth and got myself into trouble. It was that or make myself crazy.

"We ordered steaks," Archer tells his brother. "You staying for dinner?"

"Nah. I'm eating with the girls." The girls are Ruby and his seven-year-old daughter. Archer explained earlier that Jax is so smitten that he rarely sees his brother outside of work anymore. I try to imagine being that enamored of another person, but it doesn't square with any relationship I've ever had.

Different strokes, I guess.

Which brings my thoughts back to PJ. Not that I see her as anyone I'd presume to be in a relationship with or even date. But she's the first woman—hell, the first person—I've met in a long time who didn't try to kiss up to me, either because they wanted me for my money or for some strategic position at work.

That makes her interesting.

"Hey, are we still on to see Dad in the morning to talk about the financial stuff? He's been having a rough week, and when I went a couple days ago, it was pretty grim," Jackson says. I notice Archer flinch and realize how hard it is for him to be around his dad.

"No, I think PJ and Trix are going. I don't want to overwhelm him," Archer says. He sometimes abbreviates his sister Beatrix's name into that of a breakfast cereal. What's with this family and their nicknames?

"Oh, okay," Jackson continues, seemingly oblivious to his brother's scowl. Maybe because Archer has been scowling since he got here.

"Yeah," Archer grunts. I shoot him a look. Even for him, he's unusually prickly. He doesn't meet my gaze. I opt to ignore his mood until Jackson leaves and I can ask him about it.

"Heard you're staying here for a bit. We need to catch up for real one of these nights," Jackson says. He used to hang around with Archer and me back when we were all in college, but it's been a while.

"Sounds good, Jax. You tell me when."

He takes another sip of his wine and shrugs. "We'll figure it out." His attention turns to our server, who appears with two large takeout bags. "Thanks."

Jackson takes the bags and moves between the tables, saying hello to a couple more people he recognizes before walking out the door.

Archer smooths the white tablecloth, which doesn't need smoothing. I've known him long enough to spot this tell. "What's bothering you?" I ask.

His head jerks up, surprised at first that I've nailed it. Then he nods. "Financial fuck-ups. My dad's health. Worrying about the future of the business. You know, basic shit."

"Guess I picked a bad time to come." I realize that I've only been thinking of my own problems, and it can't be easy for Archer to see his dad's memory deteriorating.

I'm at a loss. "Wow. I really wish you didn't have to go through that. Anything I can do?" I know there isn't, and Archer confirms it with a shake of his head. "I probably wouldn't have said anything if Jax hadn't opened his big mouth.

"Well…I'm here if you feel like getting into it," I tell him. After sipping a bit more of his wine and popping another bite of breadstick into his mouth, Archer shakes his head. "It'll be fine. Just… complicated financial shit. I don't need to tell you, right?"

He doesn't. And that's the beauty of this age-old friendship. There's no need for pleasantries or wasted words. If he feels like talking about whatever's going on at the winery, he will. Otherwise, I won't press. The less conversation, the better.

For now, I'll eat some steak, walk the pretty winery grounds, and try to clear my head. The real world will intrude soon enough.

And by the time we've finished our steaks and topped the meal off with more wine and a slice of chocolate cheesecake, I'm convinced that for once I'll be able to sleep through the night.

CHAPTER
Five

"What the hell is that sound?"

I have no problem talking to myself, and I don't think it's weird. If anything, I think it's strange that people don't do it more often.

After all, I can be both a keen observer and a good audience, so why wouldn't I voice both of those out loud?

Unfortunately, my audience of one has no idea of the source of the metal cracking against metal sound that seems to be coming from outside my front door.

Looking down at my plaid flannel pajama shorts and tank top, I debate throwing on a sweatshirt. But this is Buttercup Hill. It's gated at night with high walls around the property and security cameras. No one is here other than my family and a few seasonal workers who live on-site for a few months a year.

Hence, nothing to be afraid of at ten at night when I fling my front door wide open.

And now I wish I'd just put in earplugs.

It's Colin. Of course it is. I just can't seem to lose that guy.

Struggling with the deadbolt on the cottage directly across the pathway from my front door. The small one-bedroom cottage was supposed to be a detached garage, but I had the bright idea of turning it into an extra living space several years ago. At the time, I'd just finished college and thought it would be great fun to have a revolving series of friends pass through and stay on the property.

It *was* great fun when the first few came to visit. Less fun when all they wanted to do was drink wine all day and invite other friends from the Bay Area to do the same. Eventually, I nixed the open door to my college friends. Since then, the cottage has hosted newlyweds, friends of the family, employees—whoever needed a place for a night or two.

I check the time even though I already know it's late. He's probably drunk. Maybe he's been out at a bar and hustled up a hookup for tonight.

The thought turns my stomach because it's just so perfect—the fancy-ass dude rolling in from Silicon Valley for a night of small-town fun. Then he'll go back to being fancy-ass and keeping a low profile, or whatever the heck he does with molecules and telescopes.

Only now, it appears he's spending the night. Or trying to. Man can't even work a simple lock.

Leave it to my brother to invite his friend to crash here without bothering to mention it to me, his immediate neighbor.

"Are you kidding me with this?" I don't even try to stifle my annoyance.

Colin looks over his shoulder as though he's not sure he heard me correctly. At least the damn key in the deadbolt goes silent for a minute. He turns around slowly like a suspicious chipmunk caught with half a sandwich in his mouth.

I wish the sight of him didn't turn my insides to what feels like flaming maple syrup, flooding my senses and telling me they want more. Much more. Of him. Up close.

Maybe this is the universe's way of telling me it's been too long since I've had any fun with a man. Well, the universe would be correct, but that's because I'm tired of lame hookups that don't lead to anything. Well, anything except a reputation as someone who flirts but doesn't follow through with a relationship.

Sounds about right for my high school and college years. Even I've started to believe that's all I'll ever have with a man.

Flirting is like slipping into an old, worn pair of sweatpants. Comfortable and familiar. Easy.

And heck, if he's going to disrupt my peace in my own house, I'm going to appreciate the sight of his broad shoulders. They push the limits of his Henley and force my eyes to trace the shape of his pecs and abs, which I can see right through his damn shirt. With very little effort. In the near-darkness.

"PJ?"

"Um, yeah. Good memory." I don't hide my sarcasm, but I do yank my eyes away from where they're roaming downward. It's been so long since I've been with a man that I find myself taking in his belt buckle and wondering how many seconds it would take me to unbuckle it. I'm betting less than three.

Stop it, stop it.

I force my eyes back to his face, which looks ten times sexier than it did this morning, and I wonder how he manages that. Must be some Schrodinger's cat physics trick that lets him be hot and not hot at the same time.

But really just hot.

As I'm taking in the vision of him, I notice his wild eyes roaming over me—all of me—because I opened my front door wearing a sheer tank top. My perky nipples have jumped to attention from the cool air. And the hot guy.

Not to mention that my flannel shorts are frayed enough to be very comfortable and good for sleeping. Less good for covering much of my legs.

I start to cross my arms over my chest, but then I think better of it. This is my house, and I'll wear what I want. He can just deal with it.

And again, the urge to flirt rears up.

"What are you doing here?" He looks a little rumpled, which softens his starched appearance. It's a much better look. His eyes are less focused and a little hazy. The genuine confusion on his face would be comical if he weren't standing outside my front door making a hellish racket.

"I live here. What are *you* doing?" I'm hoping he'll tell me he got lost between Archer's house and the road south, taking him back where he came from. And I'm really hoping he doesn't answer with the words I can already see forming on his lips.

"I'm crashing here for a couple weeks."

"A couple *weeks*? Ugh, of course you are," I mutter. Because this is my life. Can't get away from the kind of men who work my last nerve with their insistent, broad shoulders, financial gossip, and chess moves. Colin Hathaway standing four feet away is the last thing I need right now.

"I'm sorry." He holds up his hands like I've pulled a gun on him. "I didn't mean to wake you. I just—I think the lock is jammed."

Letting out a long exhale, I pad toward him on bare feet, holding out my hand for the key. "It's just stubborn. Been a while since anyone used the place, and the tree over there has big roots." I point at a live oak that's been here longer than the Corbett family has.

"Big roots?" He squints at me, confused. Maybe he's never spent time around plants *or* coffee.

"Yes. Roots. The things that provide nutrients to plants? They tend to grow when they're watered," I huff, sticking out my chest a little. Maybe I'm being confident. Maybe I'm just making a point —or specifically, two very sharp points grazing the thin fabric of my top.

"You don't say," he deadpans. He doesn't attempt to hide his focus on my nipples.

Good. He tortured me with his noise. I'll torture him with what I've got.

"I do say."

"Great."

"It's the biggest problem with the way the property was built. All the homes and buildings here were supposed to take advantage of the environment. All the porches and balconies face east and west, with trees all around for shade." I point, but in the dark night, not much is visible beyond the small garden between my house and the cottage.

Colin nods. "But no one realized how big the roots would get."

"Basically, so they push up on the foundation under the houses, and sometimes the doors and windows stick."

I jiggle the key in the lock, which is one of those European bolts that turns over three times before it unlocks. Half the time, I forget which direction to turn the key. I spend a minute or so making the same clanging noise as Colin before the bolt chugs into place and the door swings open.

"Oh!" A peculiar odor wafts from the cottage—a cross between overripe potatoes and moldy coffee grounds. I take a step back in reaction to the smell and step on a metal garden ornament shaped like a smiling snail. As I topple to the side, I reach out for anything to steady myself so I don't faceplant, only to feel a strong arm wrap around my shoulders and a warm hand reach for my hip.

"Careful," Colin says, righting me and making sure I'm steady. His hand has pushed my shirt up a couple inches and stays wrapped around my waist, his hand cool against my hot skin. A sheen of sweat coats my forehead as my face warms with embarrassment.

"Didn't see that." I look accusingly down at the snail, which continues grinning like a maniac. Colin removes his hand from my waist as if testing to see if I'm really steady. Then he takes his arm from my shoulders. "Thanks. Wasn't expecting that smell. What the heck is it?"

Colin sniffs the air and seems to agree there's something amiss, waving a hand in front of his face.

"Is that…normal?"

"Normal for rotting garbage, maybe. Could be the last person here left some trash?"

The lights are off in the cottage, so I reach just inside the front door to turn them on, only to have a rather large squirrel scurry out the door right over Colin's foot. He jerks his foot upward just as the animal makes a beeline for a bush. We stare as the sound of rustling leaves proves it's long gone.

"Um…is that just a perk that comes with staying at Buttercup Hill? Squirrel as roommate?" Colin asks, holding the side of his face with one hand. I'm surprised he hasn't run for the hills by now, except that it's the direction the squirrel went.

I'm about to close the door to the cottage when I hear a squeak, and two smaller squirrels waddle out the door. When they reach the lighted patio, their eyes squint, and they too head for the underside of the bush.

There's more squeaking and scurrying and rustling in the bushes. Then, from beside me, I hear it again—a low chuckle of laughter.

"You're…laughing?" It's not what I expect from a captain of industry who's probably never seen a wild animal before, let alone had one jump over his foot. I'm not sure why he hasn't launched into a diatribe about cleanliness or orderliness or whatever else most powerful people say when they find a family of squirrels in their fancy winery digs.

"You better believe I am."

"But…why?" I wish I didn't sound so completely baffled, but I am completely baffled by him. "You can't stay here."

He shrugs. "Probably not, but let's check out the place anyway." He nudges open the door and takes a step into the entryway, then another step farther. Turning around, he cocks his head. "Coming?"

"Hell no," I say. "This make-your-own-adventure is all yours."

He extends a hand to me. "Come on, Junebug. What's the worst that can happen?"

And there it is—for the first time in our several interactions today, Colin gives me a smile. It's magnificent, all straight teeth, plump lips with just a hint of a sexy smirk, and even a dimple in one cheek. Holy crap, Colin Hathaway can smile.

You know…if the astrophysics ever falls through, you could make good money just smiling at people all day. Or just do it as a public service. These are my inside thoughts, and I'm oh-so glad he can't hear them.

"I'll keep it in mind." His smile dims as he regards me like I'm slightly strange and interesting. And I realize I said the words out loud.

Well, it doesn't matter because, yet again, I'm convinced this is the last I will see of him. If making a dumb chess mistake, berating him, and exposing him to large rodents wasn't enough, my lack of filter should seal the deal.

Buh-bye, Colin Hathaway. Nice not really knowing you.

"Come," he insists, still extending his hand.

I stand there, mouth agape, trying to piece together the logic of what I see in front of me. There's none. This man is poised to put the first human on Mars and revolutionize space travel. And now he seems downright giddy over the prospect of entering a squirrel den and searching for rotten potatoes or vermin or, for all I know, crocodiles.

When I make no move to come closer, Colin walks back toward me, wraps his hand around mine, and gently tugs me inside the cottage. My legs move, but I don't feel anything besides the warmth of his hand, which is like a silken security blanket, the kind I'd want to keep in my grasp all night long.

I am not expecting it, but maybe it's good that I'm distracted because the cottage is a downright mess.

The kitchen looks tidy enough, with its butcher block island sitting beneath a pot rack with copper pans and spotless granite counters. But the living room is a mess. One of the couches is missing all its cushions, which are scattered on the floor, some ripped in places with stuffing hanging out.

"I think we know where our squirrel family slept," Colin says, voice calm, walking me through the room.

Then there's the trash—orange rinds, Styrofoam takeout containers with the dregs of noodles stuck to them, plastic salsa cups. Foil burrito wrappers are strewn everywhere, ripped to shreds, along with a paper bag from one of my favorite takeout places. At least the squirrels ate well before they trashed the place.

We head toward the bedroom, where the bed is unmade beneath a casement window that has been left wide open. "And I think this is how they got in," Colin says.

"You think so, Sherlock?" I don't mean to be salty. "Sorry. I just can't believe no one came to make up this room after the last guests were here."

"Arch said it doesn't get used much."

"Not by humans, anyway. Why are you so understanding and not more…freaked out?"

He's still holding my hand, and I'm still enjoying how his touch sends a calming flood over my skin and along my arm. I should let go because it's obviously not necessary for him to lead me around, but I don't.

Colin blows out a breath and shakes his head. "Guess it takes a lot more than this to freak me out these days."

For the first time, I remember the media shitstorm and feel a little sorry for him. So wrapped up in my own stresses with Trevor Stagwood, I completely forgot that Colin might not be so happy.

And now I'm curious.

"Why are you holing up here?"

"Because I needed to get away." He drops my hand and crosses his arms. I feel ten degrees colder.

"I know you're hiding out from bad press. I mean, why are you staying *here*? Is your mansion being fumigated for opossums?"

He rolls his eyes and goes over to the window, which he slams shut. He slides the bolt into the latch. Then he looks around the room, taking in the messy sheets on the bed and the yellow-striped pillows strewn on an overstuffed beige chair.

He picks one of them up and squeezes it, testing its heft and softness before tossing it back onto the chair. Then he walks to a closet and opens the door, revealing twin terrycloth bathrobes tied at the waist like a proper hotel.

I feel a momentary surge of relief that at least one part of the place looks semi-inviting.

"Cozy. I like this."

"You didn't answer my question."

"No, I didn't."

He's still on the move, walking into the bathroom and fluffing the towels as though he's actually thinking about spending the night in the squirrel den. I follow him like a sheep into the second bedroom, where the bed is made, but it's a twin bunk bed. He sits down on the bottom bunk and bounces, his large frame comical in a room he outgrew three decades ago.

"You're not sleeping in here." I'm stating the obvious because of course a fancy Silicon Valley business dude isn't sleeping in this crap hole. I can't even imagine why Archer planned on having him stay here when he has plenty of room at his own house on the Buttercup Hill property.

"I'm not?" I can't tell if his blank stare is supposed to be ironic or if he's legitimately confused. "I don't have a lot of other options."

"You can do better than this."

My mind churns through possible scenarios. I should just call Archer and tell him to come get his friend. He really should have escorted him here in the first place. Then *he'd* have been the one getting run down by a squirrel family.

"Did Archer just send you here with a map and a key?" I shake my head at the incompetence of my thirty-six-year-old brother, who still has a long way to go if he ever hopes to land a girlfriend or, heaven forbid, a wife.

"He offered to drive me here, but I wanted the walk. It was nice, actually, after dinner."

Standing in the doorway of the bathroom, he looks too big for the cottage. Like the width of his shoulders barely fits through the door. He did manage to walk into the bathroom without getting stuck, but as I size him up now, I notice he's well over six feet tall. With his sleeves rolled up, I see the roped muscles of his forearms, and my eyes go to what looks like the ink of a tattoo on the swell of his muscle.

As though this wealthy, attractive man needed any additional ways to make him hotter.

And yet…he also looks like a lost kitten in need of a warm blanket and a few drops of milk. Maybe I can give him the human version of that before I send him back into the wild.

Shaking my head at my brother's hosting ineptitude, I wave a hand for him to follow me. "Come with me."

"Where?" He shouldn't sound this wary when I'm trying to lead him away from a place that just got tossed by animals.

"Just…come." I don't know why he frustrates me so much. Maybe it's because he's so slow-moving—from the coffee line this morning to his meandering through the cottage where I'd have bolted as soon as I saw a squirrel tail.

I turn and head back to my own house, unsure if he's following me, until I hear the key rattling in the deadbolt of the cottage once again. "You don't need to lock it. No one else is going to fight you for squatter's rights, trust me."

"And the squirrels have keys, apparently."

"Yes, about that…it's not normally the way we welcome guests around here. I have no idea why the place wasn't cleaned after the last person used it. I'll call housekeeping and get it fumigated or whatever."

Reaching a hand to touch my shoulder, he stops me. I turn, aware again of the warmth of his fingers against my skin. I must really be overdue for a casual hookup if the mere presence of a handsome man is sending electricity from my shoulder down to my core.

Must find hookup. Must put that on my to-do list.

"Please don't worry about it. I don't see it as a reflection on you. Shit happens."

"I don't know what world you live in where squirrel takeovers just 'happen,' but okay." I keep walking, and his hand drops from my shoulder. My skin shivers in the night air in the spot where his hand was, but at least I'm no longer in danger of melting into a puddle.

He follows me through my front door, and I cast a glance around my entryway, clocking all of what he must see. Scarves hanging on a hat tree with no hats. A half-dead fern I should have watered more. A jar of pennies I've had on a console table for years. It may never be full, but I can't pass up a penny I find on the ground, so I designated a spot for them in my house.

I keep moving, hoping he's hot on my heels and not noticing any of that. But because Colin seems never to do what I want or expect him to do, he's missing by the time I get to my living room and turn around.

Retracing my steps, I find that he's taken a side journey to a small bookshelf on one wall of the dining room. "Did I lose you along the way?"

He shakes his head, eyes darting from one title to the next. I suddenly feel exposed, like having him know what books I've shelved there reveals too much about me. "You're a Shakespeare fan?" He points at a large volume containing every Shakespearean tragedy.

"I took some in college."

"Some?" He points at several other paperbacks of Shakespearean plays. "This is more than some."

I move in the direction of my kitchen, where I was sitting at the table nursing a glass of wine before he started in with the lock earlier. He doesn't take the hint and follow me.

"I liked Shakespeare. Especially the tragedies."

"Yeah, me too. Those are my favorites." His voice sounds muffled, as though he's bent over, looking at the books in the corner. That means he's found his way to my non-fiction collection. I wait for his commentary on that, but he says nothing.

He also doesn't come into the kitchen, and I give up on trying to hurry him along. I'm starting to get used to the idea that Colin Hathaway moves at his own inexplicable pace. I take a second wineglass from the cabinet and place it next to mine on my table, a gray and white slab of marble sitting on a metal base.

Colin finally appears in the kitchen doorway, bracing his arms against the door-jamb and watching me. I open the fridge and retrieve the bottle of wine and a bowl of grapes. "Grapes, huh? Guess that's expected at a winery."

"You are pure comedy, Colin. Did anyone ever tell you that?"

"Nope, you're the first."

I sit back down at the table and uncork the wine bottle. He abruptly moves closer and puts his hand out. "Here, allow me." Taking the bottle from me, he refills my glass and hands it to me.

I gesture to the empty glass on the table. "That's for you, if you'd like some."

He tilts his head to the side. "I already had a glass and a half with your brother at dinner."

"Okay. Water instead?" I offer.

He stands in front of my table. Hovers over it, really. His eyes take me in again like they did this morning. I feel like he's assessing me, but like earlier, I have no idea what observation he makes. Expression stoic and inscrutable, he regards my flimsy tank top, which I really should cover up now that I have the chance. But it's warm in my house, and…it's my house. I don't really feel like changing my actions for a man.

"Coffee? Easy foam, half-caf caramel macchiato, extra hot?"

He watches my mouth as I say the words. I'd normally find it unnerving to be scrutinized, judged, and probably found to be too sarcastic, too sassy, too…much. Wouldn't be the first—or the tenth

—time someone thought that about me. I have siblings to remind me on the daily.

But I don't feel like that's what he sees, even if I can't explain why.

"No, thank you," he says, gaze moving away from me to my kitchen, lit by two overhead pendant globes that hang over a small island. Again, I see my house through the eyes of someone who's never been here before, and that makes me notice things that don't normally snag my attention.

The electric mixer gathering dust because I never bake. The oversized farm sink with brass hardware matching a second sink in the island. A massive stove where I cook dinners for one almost every night.

The pile of newspapers on a corner of the counter because I'm one of those 21st century weirdos who read an actual paper each day. Two of them, actually. Got that habit from my dad. He leans against the island, feet crossed at the ankles, and points at the stack. "Occupational hazard? Gotta read what people are writing about Buttercup Hill?"

"Ha. Something like that." I could pretend he's right. With most people, I'd do that because it's easier to let them think what they want. Especially in a situation like this one, where Colin is only here briefly. It's not worth revealing a piece of myself.

"But...not that?" His eyes flash. Blue like the Adriatic Sea. Almost playful, crinkling at the corners even though I've yet to earn another smile. Apparently, he only smiles at squirrels.

"I like the feel of paper. It's the ritual, spreading it out on the counter." I spit out the words as though he's dragged a confession out of me after ten minutes of water boarding. But his slow nod and the dimple that pops feel like anything but a punishment.

His eyes move to the counter as though imagining me reading there each day. Arms crossed. The more time I spend in his presence, the less I feel like I know him. Which is odd.

"I think I'll take that glass of wine now," he says, slowly

pulling out the chair opposite me and sitting down. Here we are again, a replay of this morning.

"You sure?" I don't want him to feel pressured to drink wine just because I'm having a glass.

He picks up the bottle and studies the label, which shows our Buttercup logo, and pours a second glass. He returns the bottle to the refrigerator. "Sure. When in Rome…"

Seated opposite me again, he drums his fingers gently on the table and picks up his wine with the other hand. "Like I said, I don't usually drink much, but my life doesn't feel like usual right now, so I guess I'll branch out."

It's the first time he's alluded to why he commandeered a helicopter onto the property at the crack of dawn, and I can't resist the opening. Like he's moving the first pawn into place and challenging me to meet him. "Let's talk about that."

He blinks longer than necessary, but when his eyes return to mine, they're focused and fierce. "Fine."

"I have a chess set. If you feel like playing," I offer casually, starting to sweat from the effort it requires to act nonchalant. I don't want this day to end without kicking his ass at chess.

My hands tense under the table with the idea of all the openings I could use. Adrenaline floods my brain at the thought of beating him.

And that's the only reason I'm the least bit excited to be sitting across the table from Colin Hathaway. I swear.

CHAPTER
Six

COLIN

It's probably safest that we stick to chess.

Otherwise, my mind could wander to what else I could do with PJ Corbett in her house while she's dressed like that. It's a foreign thought, an indulgence I can't afford, which is why it surprises me how easily my mind betrays me. Now, I can't think about anything else.

It's the fact that she's Archer's sister, and he's saving my ass by putting me up for the next two weeks, that has me quickly talking myself down.

I do my best to keep my eyes focused on her face. "Eyes up here," I can hear her saying in that slightly irritated voice that *does* something to me when I hear it. Every time PJ seems annoyed with me, it makes me want to spend more time getting a reaction.

Fortunately, I have endless questions I want to ask her, so there's probably no shortage of ways I can irritate her.

For one thing, it's quite hot in here, and unless we're playing strip chess, I'm going to have to open a window. "Do you… always keep your house this warm?"

I prepare for her response, something about how little I must know about thermodynamics, even for a physicist.

"Oh." She looks down at her tank top and up at my denim jacket over a button-up shirt over a tee. "Yeah, it is hot in here, isn't it? I was cold when I came in, so I cranked the heat and forgot about it. Lemme turn it off."

She leaves the kitchen and returns a few minutes later wearing a long-sleeved shirt over the tank top. My brain struggles to come up with a reason she shouldn't be wearing it, but even a PhD doesn't get me there. Just as well. Now I don't have to try too hard to keep my eyes from wandering south of her face. I'm acting like a teenager who just discovered a tube of lube and a porn channel.

Seriously, man, what the hell is your problem?

It's a legitimate question, given that I haven't had this reaction —or any reaction—to a woman in years. Staying focused on my job has allowed my company to grow like an over-fertilized weed. Investors are happy, and so am I.

At least, I thought I was.

Maybe I was just kidding myself. Maybe all my stupid decisions of late are because I'm unhappy. Or just bored.

PJ swipes across a few screens on her phone, tapping as she goes until music starts playing from unseen speakers in the walls. "Hope you like Taylor," she says, not seeming overly concerned whether I'm a Swiftie.

"So this is why you lured me to your house," I say, leaning back as she sets up her chess board. I'd offer to do it for her, but I can already tell that PJ doesn't like people patronizing her. I watched how her face reddened this morning when Archer called her his "little sister." It annoyed PJ almost as much as it bothered her to lose at chess.

"Don't flatter yourself."

Something about how the flush crawls over her cheeks makes me think I've hit a nerve.

Was she trying to lure me here out of anything other than good old hospitality?

I tell myself to stop that line of thinking before I take it any further, but I already feel my dick getting different ideas about the situation. Need to shut that down before it starts.

"Kidding," I amend.

"Right. I know." She blinks those long lashes over the pale blue of her eyes that I'm dying to stare at, despite my better instincts. So I change my tack.

"Need help with anything?"

Her eyes leave the chess pieces only long enough to shift upward and glare at me. "Nope. I'm good." Her terse reply has nothing on the pink blooming over her face. She may think she's glaring at me, but there's no fire behind her eyes. Just sultry smoke.

It surprises me that I'm reacting this way to her. Maybe it was the stern warning earlier from Archer. I don't exactly like being told what to do—or what not to do. He and Jackson described her in unflattering terms, but I think they were just saying, "Keep your damn hands off our sister." I guess I should go talk with their brother Dashiell and see if I can make it three for three.

Up until thirty minutes ago, I had no plans of putting my hands on her. But once my fingers grazed the soft skin of her shoulders and waist when I caught her, all bets were off.

And now…I'm talking myself down because the last thing I need right now is to look at Archer's very *young* sister as anything more than a somewhat irritating chess opponent.

She finishes setting up the pieces, white on my side, and extends her hand so I can open.

I move a pawn. She does the same. I move a rook. She counters.

The first few moves are rote for anyone who plays a lot of chess, and she already knows where I'm headed.

She castles and looks up at me, gauging whether I expected the move. I have nothing, if not a good poker face, so I meet her gaze and try to keep my face a mask of indifference. It's hard because I'm very *not* indifferent to how she looks. The pretty pout of her lips, the curve of her cheek, the fresh-scrubbed skin free of makeup—my kryptonite.

But the second I put my hand on my knight and move it to the square I'm considering, she levels me with a question, almost like it's part of her game. Who am I kidding? Of course it is. She's playing to win.

"So how is hiding out here going to help your company's stock? Or the media shitstorm you stirred up, for that matter?" she asks. Direct. I like it.

She's the first person to ask me this question—well, the first other than me. It was the primary question I had for our company publicist when he told me to lay low and let the weight of my ill-timed statements blow over.

I can't help it. I let out a chuckle.

Her quizzical stare is so unexpected that I laugh some more. "You want the real answer?"

"Yes, please."

"I don't fucking know. My public relations person told me to disappear for a bit. I'm not sure I agree."

"Do you always follow advice you don't agree with? Is that your strategy for running a billion-dollar company?"

"That seems like a rhetorical question."

"Only if you agree."

Maybe it's the stress I've been under for the past couple days. Or the burrito-fest had by a family of squirrels. Or just the fact that she doesn't even know me, yet she knows exactly what questions to ask.

Maybe I just like looking at her. But the sum total of it results in a new peal of laughter, and this time, I can't stop.

I still have my hand on top of the knight because I'll have to commit to the move if I remove my hand, and I haven't fully thought it through. I have no doubt that the timing of her question was a ploy to distract me, but the fact that I can't stop laughing is a bigger problem.

Lifting my hand away, I tip back in my chair as tears begin flowing down my face. I can't stop. It's the combination of the stress I've been under and maybe the wine and the goddamn squirrels, but I'm a goner.

PJ watches me for a moment like I'm insane, and I see the corners of her mouth turn up in amusement. Before she can stop herself, she erupts into her own fit of giggles.

We sit across from each other in inexplicable hysterics, and each time I feel myself starting to calm down, her laughter ratches up a notch and I start in anew. The same thing keeps happening to her.

Finally, the waves of laughter subside, and each of us wipes down tears and regains composure. I take a long sip of wine and try to come up with a way to explain what just happened.

"Sorry. I think it's just the stress." I shrug.

"Don't apologize. That's the first time I've laughed like that in ages. Even if I have no idea what I was laughing about."

She looks back at the board, her forehead creasing when she sees where I've left my knight. I blink hard because I've just lost the game unless she makes a colossal mistake.

Her knowing smile tells me she has no intention of making a mistake.

"Check and checkmate," she says.

I throw my hands up. She won't really have me in check for three more moves, but we both know where this is headed. I can't win, so I lay down my king. "You got me. You're not only good at your job, you're also good at chess."

Her head jerks up as though I've startled her.

"You okay?" I ask.

She gawks at me with wide eyes. "What makes you think I'm good at my job?"

"Instinct. And you just gave me better advice than I've ever gotten in a week." I start setting up the pieces again. "One win apiece. Looks like we need a tie breaker."

When I look up, I find her regarding me warily, like maybe she doesn't know whether to believe me. It gives me the sense that people don't compliment her often enough. Even if I'm only here a couple weeks, I plan to change that.

Finally, she nods slowly and leans back in her chair. She picks up her wineglass. "Not tonight. I'm wiped out from my day."

I remember how dazed she looked when I ran into her earlier, and I feel like an asshole for not asking her about it.

"Anything particularly tiring about today, or is it always a lot, being a fixer?"

She huffs a laugh. "The fixer thing was kind of a joke since I do PR, but today, something came along that might actually need fixing."

I wait to see if she feels like elaborating. It's none of my business, but I find myself wanting to know more about her, whether it's her job or something else. "You want to talk about it?"

Her jaw goes slack, and she blinks as though the concept is foreign. "Wow, um, I'm not sure. I normally just work stuff out on my own."

I take a sip from the glass of wine and shrug. "No pressure. It was an offer."

Nodding slowly, she considers it. I wait, taking her cues on whether she wants to talk. She stares off and says nothing.

"I like this wine." When I lift the glass, the overhead light cuts through the pale yellow of the chardonnay like the sun. "I don't know a lot about wine, the making of it, anyway," I admit. Might as well be honest.

She snaps back to focus and looks at the wine. A couple strands of hair sweep across her forehead, and she tucks them behind her ear. "That's easily remedied here. Do you drink a lot of wine?"

"Only when I have to."

Her eyes go wide. I really need to work on not blurting out my thoughts. It's going to get me in serious hot water. "Well, you made an unfortunate choice of where to hang out for two weeks."

"Sorry. Does that offend you as a winemaker?" I'm out of my depth when I leave the world of astrophysics and business, and I know better than to sling bullshit and try to make someone believe I know what I don't.

She shakes her head slowly, a corner of her mouth tipping up. "No, because I didn't build Buttercup. I don't consider myself a winemaker. That's Archer's purview, at least it is now. I just do the publicity."

I pick up one of the pawns from the board, feeling its cool weight in my hand, and harken back to the couple hours of conversation with Archer over dinner. I feel my forehead crease with the disconnect.

"He told me about your dad's diagnosis. I'm sorry."

It feels like the right thing to say under the circumstances, so I'm not expecting PJ to react as though I've brought her a bunny and tucked it against her chest. She…sucks in a jagged breath that sounds both surprised and maybe a little bit horrified.

"Oh. Um, thanks." Her eyes have turned large and round, making her look a bit like a frightened deer. Her face turns a light shade of pink, and she pushes back from the table. Moving over to the sink, she turns on the faucet and splashes water onto her face before reaching for a paper towel.

And now I feel awful because it seems like I've upset her. "I didn't mean to open up something—"

She cuts me off. "No, you didn't. It's just…I guess I'm naïve if I think information stays within my family. Makes me think the guy who called earlier might have real intel. Maybe it wasn't just a fishing expedition."

She doesn't elaborate, but I start to get the picture. I also sense that she'll tell me more when she's ready.

I inhale a long breath and let it out slowly. "Ah, well, I'm not sure about other people, but I'm very discreet when it comes to things my friends tell me." I want her to trust me, though it shouldn't matter. Especially now that Archer has warned me away from her—twice. And yet, I do want her to trust me.

"Okay… Well, thanks…" The way she says it with a distasteful frown makes it seem anything but okay. "I know you're just being nice. I don't mean to be weird about it…It's really…it's fine." But I can tell it's not okay and it's not fine.

I get up from the table and go over to where she's standing by the sink, wadding up the paper towel and straightening it out again. I'm not sure she realizes she's doing it, so I gently take it from her hands. Then I realize I don't know my way around her kitchen, so I open a couple of cupboards until she points me to the one with a trashcan inside.

Once I deposit the paper towel, I return to where she's leaning a hip against the sink and watching me. I'm at a loss. I barely know her, but I don't want to keep my distance.

I want to sit down and get comfortable, but she hasn't invited me outside of the kitchen. So I go back to the chair and lower myself into it. It has a stiff back, and it's not particularly comfortable, which makes me wonder about who designs chairs.

My kitchen table chairs at home are equally awful, though I can't take responsibility for picking them. I was so busy with work when I bought my house that one of my VPs sent her designer over. Before I knew what had happened, I had a fully furnished house with things like sconces and valances and other details I'd never have included if left to my own devices.

I'm still idly fascinated by the design choices people make when they know about these things. So I find myself smoothing a crease in a single flowered placemat in the middle of PJ's table and wondering about her thought process.

"Did you have the option of a tablecloth?"

"What?" Her answer is sharp, like she's snapping a fortune cookie in half.

I point at the placemat. "Doesn't protect much of the table. Just wondering."

"I have no idea. I think I just liked the design."

I don't know why, but I find it a relief that she didn't reason through a long process to arrive at the single placemat. It makes me feel like I'm not so far outside of normal.

On her way back to the table, PJ opens a long cupboard and takes out a box of Wheat Thins. Scraping a finger under the flap, she opens the box and digs in for a handful before offering it to me.

"I'm good." I shake my head, and she deposits the box between us on the table.

"How much did Archer tell you?" Her wary tone makes me sorry I brought up her dad, which is obviously a sore subject.

"Not much. Just that his dementia had advanced to an Alzheimer's diagnosis, and he's no longer in charge of the company."

Slapping a hand over her forehead, she lets it drop down over her eyes. "Were there people near enough to you in the restaurant to have overheard the conversation?"

I think back, picturing our table in a booth in the corner of the busy restaurant. It was so loud in there with its hardwood floors and nothing to absorb sound that we could barely hear each other, let alone conversations one table over. I assure her that no one could have overheard, which seems to put her slightly more at ease.

"What's going on, PJ?"

She shoots me a look and presses her lips together as though there's not a snowball's chance in hell she'll tell me anything.

"Remember, I'm a guy hiding out here because I made my own mistakes talking out of school."

"Exactly. You're a talker."

"PJ, I swear, everything you and your family tell me is in the vault. I'm very discreet. I have to be. I only say stupid things in public forums about my own company, and that's only when I'm fed up with what's going on around me—at my own company. Trust me."

That at least gets a small laugh out of her, and I see her shoulders relax an inch. This woman is an interesting combination of spitfire and vulnerability, and it intrigues me to follow where the line between the two leads.

She tells me a little more about the old friend who seemed to be sniffing around an opportunity to invest in Buttercup Hill if the winery is in financial trouble. "The last thing I'm going to do is confirm his bullshit info."

"Is it bullshit?"

"It is until I say it's not."

I like her confidence.

"What does your family say about it?" It seems like the logical question to ask.

"Ha. I haven't told them. There's no reason to get everyone all upset about something that he *might* pursue when I told him to take a hike."

I nod and look away, afraid that making eye contact will convey what I think.

"You think that's the wrong decision."

"Didn't say that."

"Didn't have to."

I turn the chess board around so the white pieces are in front of her and dig into the box of crackers. A peace offering. "One more game?"

"Agree to disagree about the other thing, then sure."

We set it up, and she makes her opening. I follow with a standard counter.

A few moves later, we're locked into another battle, and neither of us has an advantage. I've only captured five of her pawns, and she has one rook, a knight, and two of my pawns. Statistically, we're about even.

"So why are you taking bad advice and running away from your company right when you should be there doing damage control?" she asks. It's the same strategy she used on me earlier, interrupting my thought process with a question and taking control of the board. But this time, I see it coming and try to ignore the words.

It's hard because I want to know why she thinks the advice is bad, but I also want to win the game.

Now that she's turned the tables to my problems, I feel a lot less like talking.

So I drink more of the wine from my glass and look around the kitchen for some other task to occupy me. I find nothing. "I have a person who said I should let things blow over and wait until people find the next thing to obsess about."

"Who is this person?"

"He does what you do, I guess."

"Yeah. Not very well." I'm grateful she seems to have found her feisty energy, but I'm not looking to trade talking about her problems for talking about mine right now. But she seems smart and capable, so I'm also curious about her observations.

"What would you do differently?"

She looks me straight in the eye, and there's no hesitation, no minced words. "I'd quit hiding and get out in public. Showing people that you're human—showing them that the handsome, brilliant billionaire is imperfect sometimes—will make you relatable. Maybe the way you said it wasn't smart, but you obviously had something you wanted to say. Be contrite and honest, and people will love you for it. That's what I'd do."

As soon as she says the words, she leans back in her chair, seeming unburdened by telling me the truth.

Mirroring her movements, I lean back in my own chair and try convincing myself she's got it all wrong.

But I can't. She may be the first person in my life who sees me clearly.

CHAPTER
Seven

PJ

"You did *what*?" Archer's voice isn't quiet. Each word booms from his chest like he swallowed a subwoofer.

I don't really think he expects me to repeat what he's just heard, but I do it anyway. "I had him sleep on my couch." And he slept all right, like a felled tree. Even with the noise of my smoothie in the blender, he didn't budge. I had to shake him awake, pull up a map of Napa on his phone, and escort him out the door on my way to work.

I felt rude for not inviting him to lounge around for as long as he'd like, but I barely slept after all his racket and four games of chess, so my mood this morning is not exactly bright.

I glare at my brother. "If you'd been reachable, I'd have sent him to your house. Do you turn off your phone at night?"

"Um, yeah. It's the only way I get any peace."

"Okay, well, this is what happens when your friend disrupts *my* peace." I tap my pencil on the table. It's an old habit that drives my family crazy, but I can't help it. Archer's glare shifts from my face to the pencil, but I don't stop tapping it.

"You could have driven him to my place."

"You could've left your phone on. And I have a perfectly good couch where he didn't seem to mind sleeping all night. When I last saw him, he was pulling on hiking boots and heading up toward the peak."

"You told him how to get there?" Archer sounds slightly less perturbed, but it still annoys me. I don't like being questioned, especially by Archer, who thinks he knows more than everyone in the room just because he's the eldest.

"No, I blindfolded him, spun him around, and wished him luck."

For the life of me, I don't understand why he's so bent out of shape about me doing his friend a favor. He should be thanking me, but once again, I'm just the little sister. Here to make mistakes and be reprimanded by my brother, who thinks he knows better.

"Just...don't pull any of your usual shit with him," Archer warns.

"You're such a jerk," I mutter. It's barely worth correcting him and reminding him that I haven't "pulled my usual shit" in years. I know he remembers the times when I practically threw myself at Beatrix's friends—Jackson's too. And Dashiell's, if I'm being honest—but I was just a boy-crazy teenager trying to get some attention and mostly failing. At least with my siblings' friends.

I probably didn't do myself any favors by making it public knowledge when I did get a date or two, despite their insistence that I was too young. Their attitude only fueled me.

Archer took a stern tone with me when I was a college freshman, warning me about the reputation I'd get if I kept hooking up with guys indiscriminately. He tried to put the fear of God into me, but he didn't seem to realize that I was just having fun.

There was an endpoint in my mind, and by my sophomore year at Berkeley, I'd settled in with a heavy academic load and a steady boyfriend.

Unfortunately, I couldn't undo the way my brothers saw me. Even though Dash hooks up on the regular, I'm still the one they point to as a ballsy boy chaser. Seriously, it's time for a new song. It would be nice if they saw me differently, but I don't have high hopes.

"I'll make sure we get someone from housekeeping to clean up the cottage so he won't be in your hair later. You won't see him for the rest of the time he's here, I promise."

"He's pretty easy on the eyes. Don't know if I'd agree to that," my sister, Beatrix, says, sweeping into the room with a paper cup of coffee balanced on top of a folder.

We're sitting in the industrial kitchen that functions as an employee lunchroom and catering area where our team preps snacks for people on wine-tasting tours. A large walk-in fridge sits in contrast to a knotty wood table and chairs that give the space a rustic appeal.

My siblings and I meet here once a week to make sure we're all on the same page about the winery business, so the staff sets up trays of sandwiches and an urn of lemonade. Sometimes, it's the only time each week that we're all in the same place, even though we all live here.

"I'll gladly agree to it," I gripe, feeling oddly wistful at the idea. Not that I need some vacationing billionaire in my business, but Beatrix is right that he's nice to look at. And I haven't found a worthy chess opponent in ages.

Once Dashiell sweeps in looking like he just woke up, it's a full house. I grab an eggplant parm panini and roll my chair up to the big table in the center of the room.

Beatrix and Archer are still talking about Colin and how little Archer cares that he's the "hottest thing to hit Napa since last year's drought."

I can't recall him ever being so protective of a friend before, but then again, Colin is not your average friend. He's one of the world's wealthiest men and a visionary. He's famously private, and given the public thirst for information about the wealthy, it surprises me how successfully he's stayed out of the spotlight. It makes me think twice about the advice I gave him last night.

I still stand by my opinion that he should get out in front of whatever gossip will unroll, but I'm impressed by the spin control his publicist has managed so far. He's practically a ghost, other than what the company has stated publicly, and that's no easy feat.

"Okay, let's get rolling," Jackson says, passing out a sheaf of papers to each of us. He has a computer connected to a monitor at one end of the table, and I roll my eyes when I see him pulling up a PowerPoint presentation.

"Really, Jax? Do we need a slideshow?"

"Really, PJ?" he mocks in a high voice. "Do we need an eye roll? You're worse than Fiona." It doesn't offend me to be compared to his seven-year-old daughter because she's more awesome than all my siblings combined.

Everyone grumbles their own feelings about the slides. "Just get to the point, Jax. How bad is it?"

He warned us a month ago that our dad had lost a lot of the company's money, and in his confused mental state, he hasn't been able to explain a lot of it. That's sent Jackson and Archer down a series of blind hairpin turns as they've tried to figure out where the money went and why.

"The slides are just so you don't have to read through all the numbers," Jackson says, pointing at the piles of pages he's distributed.

"Oh, in that case, bring it on," Dash says, never one to take much of an interest in numbers. Good thing he handles the hiring and firing at the winery because he's a people person.

We spend a half hour going through scenarios in which we can keep the business afloat for another quarter, namely by bringing in an investor or extending our bank loans even longer. In both cases, we lose control to an outsider, especially if we don't come up with the funds to repay everyone.

"Isn't it possible that Dad invested in another winery? Maybe he didn't just piss away the money. Maybe he has something to show for it." Dash says.

"Sure. Has he mentioned it to you? Told you what winery we own?" Jackson's tone is as dry as toast. Dash's shoulders go up and he looks ready for a fistfight.

Archer waves a hand, silencing them. "I've been trying to get a meeting with Duck Feather since he specifically mentioned Hayden Lanes. No one's returning my calls, so I'm tempted to just show up there, if anyone feels like a field trip..."

"I'll go."

Four heads turn to look at me because I never volunteer for such things. But I know that if I want my siblings to take me seriously, I need to show them my capabilities.

"It will give me a chance to gather some intel because we may have another issue on our hands. I'm not worried yet, but I think we need to stay ahead of it."

The room goes silent, and all eyes turn toward me. I have a flashback to my childhood when we'd all sit at the dinner table fighting for our parents' attention. The biggest laughs went to whoever could tell stories the loudest, and Archer and Jackson, with their booming older brother voices, always won that contest.

Beatrix was quieter like me, but being the middle child, she was our dad's favorite. If someone who only loved work is capable of having a favorite kid. Beatrix had some health issues when she was younger, which meant she had to miss school sometimes. Our dad always took her to work with him on those days instead of leaving her at home with one of our several nannies.

If anything qualified as favoritism, it was bringing one of us to the vaunted vineyards for the day. He held it out like a prize, and Beatrix won more than the rest of us.

That left Dash and me, and being the youngest boy and a bit of a rascal, Dashiell had no problem getting attention, even if most of it was negative. He skipped school, broke curfew, ate all the Halloween candy, and developed a playboy reputation by the end of middle school.

If I wanted anyone to hear me above all the noise, I had to be the loudest or the most daring. I opted for both. I shouted for whatever I needed and resorted to jokes and bold outfits if the volume didn't attract enough attention.

All these years later, a lot of those behaviors have fallen away, but my siblings still see what they see.

"Stay ahead of what?" Jackson asks.

I tell them about the call from Trevor Stagwood. "If word is starting to get out about our financial issues, we need to know who's talking, who's listening, and who has money to spend. And something tells me it's connected to Duck Feather and Dad and everything else. I want to be proactive, so I'm not chasing rumors around and putting out fires."

It's probably the most I've said at a family meeting outside of discussing social media opportunities. My siblings look at me, then at each other, then back at me.

I'm sure they're all thinking that I can't possibly know what I'm talking about. They probably don't trust me to take the lead, but that's too damn bad. "This all affects my ability to handle PR for the winery, so I want to be part of it."

Jackson flips a chair around and straddles the seat. Archer leans against the table and sips his lemonade. They don't seem overly concerned.

"And what if you poke at a pile of sand and find an anthill?" Archer asks, arms crossed.

"Better that we know about it rather than letting it sneak up on us. What if we have a leak here at the winery? What if our financial problems get worse? What if we have to sell the family business?" I ask the questions I haven't wanted to consider, but we need to look at all angles when there's even more we're trying to keep under wraps. A lot of money is at stake.

Four pairs of eyes stare back at me as though they'd prefer I answer the question myself.

"I guess some of us are taking a field trip to Duck Feather and not leaving until we talk to the owner. I'm in." All eyes turn to Dashiell, who hasn't moved from his spot at the table. In fact, he's helped himself to a second tuna sandwich like he just might stay a while.

"Okay, then. Dash and I are taking a field trip to Duck Feather," I say, trying the thought on for size. I'm not sure how I feel about it. And judging from the ambivalent expressions on my siblings' faces, they're not sure either.

CHAPTER
Eight

COLIN

After spending an entire day outside, I've come to two conclusions—the world contains a lot of beautiful places, and I don't spend nearly enough time away from my office to enjoy any of them.

The thought strikes me as particularly profound as I descend the last set of switchbacks of Buttercup Hill, the second hike I've taken today. It shouldn't take a scandal of my own making to get me out of the lab and into the fresh air, but apparently, it does.

All the fresh air I've been breathing has given me clarity on how to tackle my image problem when I get back, and I've already penned a few versions of contrite apologies in my head. The issues seem smaller now. More manageable.

I'm also considering what PJ said and wondering if I need two weeks away. I could apologize now and get back to working on the upcoming spacecraft launch.

"Oh good, you're back?" The words would be friendly if not for their tone and the scowl on PJ's face telling me she isn't glad to see me as I park Archer's car next to hers.

Her scowl should be yet another reason to leave, but it has the opposite effect on me. She's the prettiest woman I think I've ever seen, even if that mouth and her attitude should make me dislike her. She's downright rude. But call me a glutton for punishment because I only want to get an even bigger rise out of her. I want to see how far she'll go to be the last one standing.

"Yes. I am."

"You look…relaxed." Despite the tone of annoyance, PJ's voice hits me like honey pouring over a stack of perfect pancakes, and it surprises me how much I like hearing it.

I want to take PJ at face value, but something about the way she hesitated before saying the word "relaxed" makes me think she was fighting back a different word.

"Is that another way of saying I'm dressed like a slob?" I look down at my rumpled khaki shorts, gray tee, and unbuttoned chambray shirt.

"If slob is another way of saying you could have stepped out of a Patagonia ad, then yes, definitely. How about if we both agree to say what we mean and not mince words?" she proposes. Once again, her candor surprises me.

It must show on my face because she lobs back, "What?"

"Just…very few people are interested in saying what they mean when it comes to me. I…let's just say I work around a lot of people who tell me what they think I want to hear."

She laughs. "And how often are they right?"

I shake my head. "Rarely."

"Fuck those people."

I choke out a laugh, surprised that she doesn't self-censor, especially given that her world at one of the country's biggest wineries can't be that different from mine. "Don't you have to deal with a lot of those people too?"

She shrugs and pulls her keys from her bag. "I learned a long time ago not to worry about what those people think. It's the only way I can do my job. Then again, I'm not the public face of the company, and I didn't build it from the ground up. I'm sure you have a whole different set of issues to deal with."

"Maybe so."

Tipping my head toward the cottage, which I haven't yet set foot in, I make an offer I'm not sure I can support. "Assuming this place doesn't have any new tenants, you want to check out my patio? I'm told it's a nice place to sit and have a drink."

She flinches at the words, and I immediately wish I could take them back. Of course, she doesn't want to babysit me again tonight. It's not her job just because she lives next door to where I'm staying.

"I'm sorry. I'm sure you have your own plans and stuff to do —" I can't let her off the hook fast enough, but she holds up a hand before I've rambled through the apologies I have teed up.

"No. It's good. I have no plans."

I wait for a "but," and then I wait some more. She doesn't say anything, and it finally dawns on me that she's agreeing to hang out with me.

I don't know why, but it feels like a victory. Same rush of adrenaline as the day I took my company public. Different circumstances, obviously. Different stakes, I guess. But maybe not.

Who's to say that the stakes of connecting with another person are any less important than the largest financial transaction I'll ever make in my life?

Standing in front of PJ Corbett, it feels like no contest. If anything, maybe being here is the more important decision.

That both thrills me and scares the hell out of me.

I open the door to the fresh scent of candles burning and see PJ's face relax. "So glad they cleaned."

She peeks inside past me before taking a bold step through the door. I wait for her approval before following her inside. Not because I'm afraid of what I might find, but because she seems to have more at stake in this place being clean since it belongs to her family.

"Looks good," she says after scanning the various rooms. "You'd never know what took place here last night."

"Hey, it could be a lot worse. A family of humans having a party could do a lot more damage." I carry my overnight bag into the cottage and toss it on the bed.

Taking a fresh look around the place, I nod my approval. "This is exactly what I need. Simple digs, no fancy turndown service or people changing my towels. No people in my face." I'm more talking to myself than to her, confirming why I needed to get away in the first place.

When I turn to look at her, I catch her squinting at me. She either needs glasses or I'm confusing her. And I know she won't hesitate to tell me which it is.

But she doesn't. She just stares at me.

"What?" I ask, finally.

"You just…" She shakes her head. "I guess…you're not the way the media portrays you."

I huff a laugh at the irony. "Imagine that. I assume you're aware that what the media prints isn't always true."

She's walking through the cottage, checking the rooms to make sure they're okay, which takes about a minute. When she returns, she looks no less confused. "I mean, of course, I know that. But have you seen Archer's house? He's got three guest rooms and a home gym. Why wouldn't you want to stay there?"

I drop onto the beige sofa in the small living room and pick up one of the throw pillows. Navy striped with thinner gray stripes in between. "I like my space. And I don't want to be treated like a guest. I want a break from all the fancy shit in my life."

She walks over and sits on the leather chair next to a small brick fireplace, then pushes a button to turn on the gas flame. "Hmm, you may be the first person to show up at Buttercup Hill who didn't want to be treated like a guest. I'm not sure what to do with that." She taps a finger against her plush bottom lip, and I feel a twinge in my chest at the thought of my finger touching her there. I'll never do it, but I can let my mind wander without getting myself into trouble. No harm, no foul.

"I'm sure you'll figure it out."

If an eye roll had a sound, it would be the huff of dismissive breath and the stomp of PJ's feet out of the cottage and over the gravel outside.

I peer out to see her walk back to her car and return a few moments later, struggling to carry a large box.

"Here, let me help." I walk outside and try to take the box from her, but she holds onto it as though I plan to make off with her most treasured possession.

I cross my arms, withdrawing my offer. "I'm not gonna fight you for it."

Her eyes bore into me as though I might have an ulterior motive in offering to help. Does no one ever give her a hand without wanting something? Guess I'm preaching to the choir on that one.

Finally, she mutters a thank-you, and we carry the box together to her front door. It's fucking heavy, and I can barely fathom how she was managing it herself. Sheer force of will, apparently. Her stubbornness should be off-putting. I've fired people for being less mule-headed than her—it doesn't work in a collaborative scientific environment. Yet, on her, it's appealing. Goddamn sexy, if I'm honest.

"What the heck is this?" I ask. She shoots me a guarded look, eyes narrowed, bottom lip jutting out. I prepare for her to tell me it's none of my business, which it isn't. But I'm the kind of inquisitive bastard who needs to understand everything about the world around me, so I take my chances.

"Shelves."

"What kind of shelves?"

We've made it through her front door, which she managed to open with one hand while still holding her half of the box. She looks up at me, exasperated. "Do you always ask so many questions while holding a sixty-pound box?"

"Which you were trying to carry yourself. You're welcome."

"Thank you," she spits out. When we get to where she seems happy in the living room, she indicates with a nod to put the box down. It's the same room where I slept on the couch last night, and I see that she's straightened the room up, so there are no signs of my presence. Pillows are fluffed. The fuzzy green blanket hangs off the arm of the couch.

Heaving a breath and wiping a bead of sweat from her forehead, PJ looks flushed. Pretty. And a little tired. Her chest heaves gently, and she bites her bottom lip as she surveys the box. My dick twitches in my pants at the thought of what else I could do to bring out the same rumpled look in her.

"Bookshelves."

"What?"

She points at the box. I've almost forgotten I asked her about the shelves.

"Cool. Do you have a lot more books besides the Shakespeare I saw?"

Her teeth clamp down on her bottom lip as though she's trying to tame the string of curses she has planned for me. I want to hear them all, though, so I prod. "Ooh, books you don't want anyone to know about? Lemme guess, bodice rippers?"

That does it.

"What the hell is wrong with you? You just assume because I'm female that I only read steamy novels?"

"I didn't say they were steamy."

"They're not." She bites her lip. "Mostly."

"So tell me about them."

"They're mostly…" She pops her lips shut, and I see the hint of a smile. "I'll make you a deal. If you feel like putting your physics knowledge to use building bookshelves with an Allen wrench, I'll let you see all the books when we put them on the shelves."

Peering at me skeptically with her hands on her hips, she probably expects me to be repelled by her suggestion.

"Sure, let's do it." I watch her mouth hang open.

She shakes her head. "You *want* to build bookshelves?"

"I do. I never get to do normal stuff like that, and I miss it."

"What do you mean, you never get to do this kind of stuff?"

"I'm always working. If I need a bookshelf, some designer orders it, and it shows up."

"Yeah, that's called awesomeness." She stomps to the kitchen and comes back with two bottles of water because, again, she has the heat turned way up. "Should I feel sorry for you that you don't get to do menial labor?"

"Not at all. But you should let me help you build this shelf. C'mon."

Grabbing a pair of kitchen shears, PJ starts cutting the tape on the box until it falls open, revealing a lot of pale wood shelves and larger pieces. She picks out a single sheet of paper and turns it back to front and back again.

"Oh, great. No words. Just pictures."

"I doubt it's that hard."

Squinting at me again, she shakes her head. "Do you understand what you just agreed to?"

"Yeah. It sounds fun."

She steps over the box and rests the back of her hand against my forehead. "You don't feel feverish. So you really want to do this?"

"Yes."

She shrugs and hands me the piece of paper. "Suit yourself."

———

Twenty minutes later, we're not much closer to a completed pair of shelves, but we've finally figured out what the pictures mean.

PJ holds the two vertical pieces while I use the wrench to fasten the upper piece between them. It forces me to stand directly in front of her. Even though I'm a good foot taller, I'm still close enough that I smell the lemony shampoo she uses.

"Got it. Let me do that bottom one, and it should stand in

place. We're nearly there," I say, grabbing a large chunk of wood with cutouts for two drawers we've yet to build.

She looks at the floor behind me. "I don't want to burst your bubble, but there's a second one still in the box."

"I know." I twist the wrench until the screw is tight and the shelf stands on its own. Then, I step back to admire our work. She's right—we still have a ways to go. "You're good at this. Are you some kind of DIY queen disguised as a pretty publicist?" She flinches at the compliment, but like hell am I taking it back. Seeing her cheeks blaze pink is worth my own discomfort at revealing how attractive I find her.

"Um, you know. I do some little projects."

"I like a woman who isn't afraid to follow instructions." Her cheeks heat to a fiercer shade of pink as my brain trips over itself, trying to figure out how I managed to turn bookshelves into a sexual invitation. "How about we take a dinner break?"

I should not be asking her to have dinner with me, but Archer already told me he's busy entertaining some investors tonight, so my evening is free. I reason that we both just need sustenance if we're going to keep working on the bookshelves, but my real motive is to spend more time with her.

"Sure. I can order something. What do you feel like?"

"Can we drive somewhere? I never get to drive."

Her head whips around so fast that her features are a blur. "What do you mean? Oh, 'cause you have a chauffeur?" She rolls her eyes.

I feel like the asshole I apparently am. "Well, mostly because I ride an electric bike to work. But then, yes, when I go to a function, I usually have a car service so I can work in the car on the drive."

"Oh." Her expression softens. "You really work a lot, don't you?"

I nod. "Pretty much all my waking hours."

She grabs my hand and leads me to the kitchen, shaking her

head while muttering something that sounds like, "You need more than two weeks off."

In the kitchen, she points me to a chair at her kitchen table, then changes her mind and leads me to the living room couch. "Sit here. Don't move."

She leaves me there and returns a moment later with a full, uncorked bottle of cabernet and two glasses. "Let's start with this. You're at a winery for two weeks. You need to be sweating wine by the time you leave this place. Or at least knowledgeable of every vintage we have."

Apparently, we're having wine for dinner.

Her bright blue eyes sparkle, and a few loose tendrils of her gold waves fall from the topknot where she's piled her hair. She looks angelic and fierce at the same time, and it takes everything I have not to pull her onto my lap.

Stop.

She just barely seems to find me tolerable, and I'm grateful for the company. The last thing I need is to jeopardize that by making a pass at her. Reining in my inappropriate thoughts, I do exactly as I've been told. I stay on the couch and don't move, except to sip my wine.

Eventually, we both move, albeit more slowly after the first glass of wine, and begin building the bookshelves again. It goes much faster now that we've gotten the hang of following the ridiculous drawings that don't look like the parts and pieces that came in the box.

A half hour later, both bookshelves are finished and we stand side by side, gazing at them like proud parents. "They're so beautiful," she says, dramatically placing a hand on her chest and pretending to tear up.

"All grown up." I give her a playful bump with my shoulder. "Don't forget, you promised me a look at your smutty books if I helped."

She grins. "Later. Come in here first."

I follow PJ into the kitchen when she beckons me with our empty glasses and the half-full bottle. She puts them on the table and fills two water glasses for us.

"You know, I thought about what you said, how I should apologize and move on with things. It makes sense."

She perks up at that. "Yeah? You told your publicist to jump in a lake?"

"Not exactly. I'm still going to take the time off because of something else you said, which is when you pointed out that I… possibly…work too much. But when I get back, I plan to do the contrite apologizing."

Shaking her head like she's not sure she heard me correctly, PJ stares at me. "You really listened to what I said."

"Um, yeah. It was good advice."

She stands there, blinking at me like she's stunned. "I just… people around here don't always see it that way."

I assume she means her family. I pour more wine into her glass. "Maybe you should also be sweating wine by the time my two weeks here are up."

She laughs. "Maybe."

Holding her glass up to the light, she examines the way the overhead kitchen lamp filters through the burgundy wine. "I rarely take time off either, if I'm being honest. I'm always too worried my siblings will think I'm a flake if I have too much fun. It used to be kind of a thing."

"I don't even understand those words, 'having too much fun.' How does a person have too much fun?"

Her eyebrows bounce. "Oh, there are all kinds of ways," she says with a smirk. Is she flirting? It's not that I don't know what flirting looks like—there are always women at my business lunches making it clear I can have whatever I want from them, but I don't want anything.

Since my marriage flamed out, it's always felt safest to keep my head down and work. I had no use for women flirting with me. But now…if that's what's happening, I'm interested.

"Maybe you can show me while I'm here."

She takes the last sip of her wine, draining the glass. I pour each of us a refill and realize we're almost done with the bottle. PJ goes to her refrigerator and takes out a glass container with a green lid. Opening it, she offers me some sliced cheese, prosciutto, and tiny pickles.

When I take a slice of cheese, she holds up a finger and puts the glass container on the kitchen table. She goes to a tall cupboard and grabs a box of water crackers and a plate. By the time she's back at the table, we have the makings of a charcuterie tray.

She grabs one more bottle of wine and two more glasses. "This one's a cabernet blend from a few different growing areas. In case we want to try something else," she says, sitting at the table.

"I like it. I also like our dinner." I spill the crackers onto the plate and pile one with prosciutto and cheese. I offer it to her and make a second one for myself.

"Ha. This is my single girl dinner about half the time."

"I'll take it over a pretentious omakase sushi dinner any day."

She smiles and tucks a loose strand of hair behind her ear. "You're not gonna get me to feel sorry for you, Billionaire Boy. At least, not because of that."

"I don't want you to feel sorry for me."

"Good. So what do you want to do while you're hiding out?"

"Honestly? I want to do the normal things I never have time to do—build a bookshelf, watch hummingbirds flock to a feeder for an hour, hike in the middle of the day, take a nap. You know, normal things. I'm open to ideas."

"I can help you there. I can absolutely help you."

"If that's an offer to do normal things with me, I accept."

I'm on precarious ground, and I know it. I shouldn't be asking to spend more time with her, but I can't help it. And fuck it if I haven't gotten pretty far in my life by doing the opposite of what people tell me to do.

"Great. When?"

"Saturday's my day off."

"Saturday. Looking forward to it."

I toast my first Saturday off in ten years with cheese on a cracker. And sneak another look at the woman I already like more than I should.

CHAPTER

Nine

PJ

What Archer doesn't know won't hurt him, which is why I didn't bother to tell him about my offer to spend Saturday with his best friend doing "normal things." Once I figure out what those things are.

As the evening light streams through my kitchen window and I stare at how the sun seems to warm every leaf on the grapevines, I wonder if walking through miles of vineyards qualifies as "normal." When Colin said he hasn't taken a day off in ten years, I had a hard time wrapping my brain around it.

It means he's been working around the clock since I was sixteen years old. And that makes our age gap feel like a chasm.

It also gives me a little perspective and takes my raging libido down a few notches. I'm not the sexy, brainy woman Colin Hathaway has been waiting for all his life. I'm his friend's younger sister and temporary neighbor. End of story.

The fact that I haven't seen him in two days since he helped build my bookshelves tells me he hasn't thought about me nearly as much as I've thought about him. Or he'd find reasons to run into me. He does have entire days to figure out how to do that, after all, and he's been MIA.

I've heard him leave the cottage at dawn for the past two days, presumably to go hiking, but that's about it. I need to come up with a couple of activities for Saturday and get over thinking he's interested in me as anything more than a tour guide.

That's my prevailing thought as I stir a pan of lemon butter sauce in my kitchen. A few minutes later, there is a knock on my door, and I open it to find Colin standing there like he has a homing device for sauce. "What? Is? That?"

At first, I'm not sure what he's referring to, but after he inhales a long breath through his nose, I realize the browned garlic must have wafted over.

"Oh. Barefoot Contessa."

"Sorry?"

"I'm using her recipe. It's a good one."

He leans forward to inhale another whiff. "Smells amazing."

"It's a big recipe. You want to join me?" I expect him to say no. He's probably eating with Archer. "Or do you have a low-key meal of instant ramen noodles all teed up?" Hard to tell. He's a mystery to me, but I'd be lying if I pretended I haven't had my eyes peeled, trying to observe him for the past couple of days.

I've never met anyone like him. Interesting that he likes to duck the limelight and the fancy trappings of his world. A reluctant billionaire. Nope, never met one.

He offers me one of his rare smiles. "I'd love to, if it's no imposition."

Standing there in a dark green apron with a wooden spoon in my hand, I can't help but laugh. "It's already made. I can't see a way you could be imposing."

His expression goes serious. "If you're expecting a guest, I suppose."

"I'm not."

Does he look…relieved? Like he was worried I was cooking for a date?

No, it's my imagination running wild. Why would Colin Hathaway possibly care if I had a date? I suppose he might be really invested in the garlic and lemon butter he's hoping to eat, but other than that, he surely couldn't care less.

"Come on in." I signal for him to follow, leaving the door open.

"One sec. I need to grab a couple things," he calls, his voice retreating in the distance. I vaguely wonder what things he's referring to, but maybe he needs a personal electric fan because my kitchen is pretty warm from cooking.

I go back to stirring my sauce, and Colin shows up a couple minutes later with a bottle of wine from a neighboring vineyard. "Is this sacrilege, bringing something from another winery onto the property?" He asks the question, but if he really cared about the answer, he wouldn't be holding a bottle from Caymus.

"Did you do some wine tasting today?" The one morning I ran into Colin at the café, he told me he didn't plan to leave the property, other than to go hiking. "Venturing back into the public eye?"

His eyes go wide, realizing what he's unintentionally done. "Oh shit. I was driving back after my hike and stopped at Caymus because my assistant likes it. I bought her a case. I didn't do any tasting. I was there for like five minutes. Did I just fuck up my publicist's whole strategy for laying low?"

I hand him a breadstick, take out a corkscrew, and go over to my cabinet for some glasses. "Doubtful. Did anyone take photos?"

He looks around my kitchen as though paparazzi may be lurking in the corners. Then he takes the corkscrew from me and opens the wine. "I don't think so."

"So don't worry about it. Besides, you know I don't really agree with this PR strategy anyway."

He pours a bit of the rich cabernet and hands me the glass for a taste. I swirl the burgundy liquid and let it roll over my tongue. "They make a good cab," I admit. "Not as good as ours, but good."

He fills my glass and pours wine into his own. Holding his glass up, he proposes a toast, "To good cabs and bad publicists."

I laugh and take a sip before returning to the stove to dump my pasta into the strainer and add it to the sauce.

Colin pulls out a chair and sits at my table. "Someday, you'll have to tell me what you'd do if you were mine."

My breath catches as I inhale, but I have my back to Colin so I don't think he notices. *If you were mine…* My reaction to his words surprises me. I know he's merely talking about what I'd do if I worked as his publicist, but I can't help the way my skin heats at the suggestion of being *his* in other ways.

"This kitchen gets so warm when I cook," I grumble, reaching for the latch to pry open the window above the sink. It sticks, so I give it a shove to no avail.

I flinch when Colin's large form approaches behind me. He braces a hand on the sink and reaches around me to give the window a sharp push, his bicep grazing my arm as his body leans into mine.

The sharp intake of air into my lungs startles me. It's a direct reaction to having Colin so close to me, and every fiber of my being wills him to stay right where he is. I have to work to stop myself from leaning into him, feeling his chest more fully against my back. I fight against my reaction to his smell, something like fresh pine needles underfoot after it rains.

Once the window cracks open, a welcome ribbon of crisp air cools my heated cheeks, but I don't dare turn around, lest Colin see exactly how much his proximity affects me.

I edge around the kitchen with my back to him, puttering uselessly over my dinner until it's ready. By then, I've regained some composure, even though I haven't actually spoken in five minutes.

When I turn around, Colin is sitting at the table again, sipping his wine and observing me whirl around the kitchen. A hint of amusement creases the corners of his eyes, and I press my lips together.

"You okay?" he asks, unable to keep the smile from his voice.

"Yeah. Um, so, it's ready."

"Awesome. What can I do?" He stands, but I quickly point him back to his seat, not wanting to risk him coming closer.

"Stay." I realize I sound like I'm taming a dog. "I mean, you're good there. I'll bring you a plate." Colin sits at the table watching me, and it occurs to me that he does this a lot. Quietly files away information.

Maybe that's part of his brilliance. He watches the world around him without feeling the need to talk it through. I tell myself not to make anything more of his eyes on me than that. He's a scientist. He observes.

But it feels different now.

Because now I'm observing him.

I'm curious about how I could sit across the table from him and play chess three days in a row without feeling the heat, and now he almost has me breaking out in a sweat tonight. I'm not sure what to do because he's sitting next to the chair where I have my glass of wine.

Sitting that close to him seems dangerous, but the chair opposite him is wedged between the table and the wall, making it awkward to sit there. I'd have to move the table, which makes no sense.

I'm thinking about all this while I dole out the pasta I normally love onto two plates and try to game out how to eat it as quickly as possible and send Colin on his way.

I notice he's taken two placemats from the stack on the counter, placed them on my table, and refilled our wineglasses. All we need are some candles and dim lighting, and this will look like a date.

Going to the switch on the wall, I turn the dimmer to make sure it's as bright as possible in the kitchen. It's for my benefit, not his. Maybe if the room is lit like an operating room, my body will get the message that this is just a transaction. Food into the mouths of two people. Instead, my body hums like I'm a windup toy and he's turned my dial. Hard.

I toss some sliced bread into a random basket and throw it on the table. Then I put the two plates of pasta down.

"Hang on, are you forgetting something?" Colin asks, sliding his chair back and going to the sink, where he must have noticed the washed lettuce in a colander when he was helping with the window. "Why don't you relax and I'll finish the salad? It's the least I can do."

"I—" No words follow because it's so surprising that he's pointing me to a chair in my own kitchen and offering to do the work. I haven't dated much over the past few years because, let's face it, I mainly only meet Napa locals. I've either already dated them or figured out why I don't want to date them. And at age twenty-six, it doesn't bother me much that I spend most of my time at work. Maybe it should, but it doesn't.

So this man standing at my sink, patting lettuce leaves with a paper towel to dry them, is anything but normal.

I'm still standing in frozen surprise next to the table when he turns around and waves at me to take a seat. "I've got this. Do you have dressing mixed already?"

"Mixed?" I finally find my voice when I can focus on something other than the sight of his broad shoulders flexing as he tears the lettuce. "If you call buying a bottle of vinaigrette from the store mixing it, then, sure."

He dries his hands and goes to the fridge. "That'll work."

"You probably have a chef working for you who makes dressing from scratch or something," I mutter, thinking he'll return my sarcasm with an appreciative eye roll. But his face falls instead.

"Oh my god. You *do* have a chef who mixes your dressing. Of course you do. You could hire a team of shepherds to tend to an olive farm, press fresh oil every day, and bottle it with the blessing of monks."

I'm just making it worse. He'll probably be so bored by my

lack of billionaire knowledge that he'll take his pasta dish to go and eat in the cottage. Which is why I don't expect his low chuckle.

"Why is that funny?"

He shrugs. "It's a hell of a good image. I think I'll hire a few monks and have them start blessing things."

"Now I feel like you're making fun of me. Or monks." I still feel chastened for having such a poor idea of what his life must be like.

He pours some dressing on the lettuce, puts the cap on the bottle, and looks around for other ingredients. Spotting a hunk of parmesan cheese on a cutting board next to a grater, he picks it up and dusts the top of the salad with cheese before tossing it.

I make room on our plates for the salad, pushing aside the heap of pasta while he sits.

"This looks amazing," he says, surveying our plates. At least, I think that's what's happening. I'm doing my best not to look directly at him lest he see that I'm sweating. I'm still trying to get a grip, so the last thing I want is for him to know.

His index finger sweeps under my chin, tipping my face to look at him. "Hey, you okay?" Forced to meet his gaze, I see concern in his warm eyes. His mouth turns down, and worry streaks across his forehead in faint lines. It's the way he seemed the first day I met him, before he beat me at chess.

I don't like the look of it, so I make my best effort at a half-smile. "Yes. All good."

He nods, eyes not leaving mine, like he's assessing whether he believes me. I need him to take his finger away from my face so I can breathe again. At the same time, I want him to touch me in more places.

Shaking some sense back into my head, I pull away from his hand and pick up my fork. "Bon appétit."

The pasta is perfect, and I let the delicious carbs cure the shitstorm in my head. He's just a guy. And after tonight, I'll do my best to avoid him again. Easier that way.

Spearing a couple of noodles, Colin digs into his plate of food. "Mmm, oh my god, this is delicious," he says before he even swallows the bite. I know I'm a good cook, so hearing praise about the meal shouldn't feel like such a victory, but his approval warms my skin again.

"Thanks. Does that chef of yours cook Italian food?" I wonder if he eats seven-course meals every night.

He shakes his head. "She cooks whatever she feels like. I'm at work so late most nights, I'm just reheating stuff in a daze and barely tasting it. It's just sustenance, you know?"

I don't know. "Do you love your job?"

He looks at the ceiling and considers the question while chewing another large mouthful of pasta. His plate is half-empty, and I've only taken two bites. "I used to…It's complicated. I've given everything to it, and I've certainly reaped the rewards, but just being here for a few days has shown me how much I've sacrificed—my free time, my relationships…"

"Can I ask…what happened with your last relationship? Or do you not want to talk about it?"

"No, I'll talk about it." He blinks a few times as if recalling the details. "Bottom line was I didn't know how to love her." Exhaling after he says the words, Colin looks unburdened from a secret he's been carrying.

I want to know more, but I feel so grateful for this nugget and I don't want to take it for granted. "You were young."

"You don't have to defend me."

"I'm not. I'm stating the obvious. Most of us are bad at relationships until we figure out what we want. Maybe you weren't ready for love. Maybe you just wanted a girlfriend. And then a wife."

He gives me a closed-lipped smile that feels hard-earned. "You didn't even know me then, and you basically just hit it on the nose. You're probably eighty percent correct."

"So what happened?"

He shrugs and presses his lips together again. If I didn't see evidence of that dimple trying to peek through, I'd worry that he really hates discussing this. Then again, he's the one who brought it up.

"I thought I wanted a girlfriend. All through high school, when I was this tall, skinny nerd waiting for puberty to hit, all I wanted was for a girl to notice me. I know that's kind of pathetic, but that's how I felt."

"It's not pathetic. It's what most of us want, especially in high school. First love and all that."

"Yeah, except high school passed me by. No girlfriend. Not even a date. I was the lanky kid with acne and braces on my teeth until senior year. I told myself it was fine because I'd won a ten-thousand-dollar science fair grant and spent my prom night building a robot that could shoot baskets into my trash can."

"That's actually kind of adorable." I reach for his hand and brush a finger across his knuckles.

He rolls his eyes. "Not the kind of adorable I wanted to be."

"Understood." I want to tell him he's kind of adorable now recounting this story, but I'm afraid he might not finish if I keep interrupting him.

"By the time puberty really hit me my senior year, I'd given up on dating in high school, but I was ready to give it a go again in college. Your brother can tell you. I was kind of out of control as a freshman. Slept with anyone who'd have me, and surprisingly, there were many. Turned out that being a brainy kid who'd finally grown into his body appealed to the women of Stanford."

Pressing my lips together to suppress a smile, I nod. I can imagine the women of Stanford lining up for Colin, who makes it sound like he was so wide-eyed and dumbfounded by his new hot face and body that he couldn't understand his own appeal. I grip his hand a little tighter. I feel possessive, not wanting him to suddenly realize that any woman in the room would probably die if he asked her out. I want him for myself.

"Anyway, by the end of college, I'd met someone I liked, and not knowing any better, I proposed to her at the end of senior year. We got married at twenty-two, and it was pretty much a disaster from the get-go. I was getting my PhD and working all the time, trying to build my company, and I had venture capitalists who'd funded me to answer to. I owed them every waking hour, and I gave it to them. Big surprise, the marriage fell apart after five years. Frankly, I'm surprised we lasted as long as we did."

I nod. I've read what little information exists about Colin Hathaway's personal life, and he's just told me twice as much as any Wikipedia article.

"Like I said, you were young."

"Young and dumb. And then I learned my lesson. The demands of my company were too great. Two thousand people depend on me to write their paychecks every month, and billions of dollars in shareholder equity are on the line all the time. I have to satisfy them too. So I work my tail off." He gets a faraway look on his face before inhaling a deep breath and shaking his head. "I do still love my job. I have to remind myself why I started this company and what we have the capacity to do."

I wait for him to elaborate, but he doesn't. "Well, hopefully, you can get back to that mindset. Everyone feels burnout sometimes."

He nods. "Being here is helping. Just doing a lot of nothing. Normal things. I really appreciate your offer to show me around," he says, and—oh shit—I promised to spend a day with him doing all the lowbrow, normal things he wants. How will I do that now when I can't even look at him without breaking out in a sweat?

"You still want to do that?" I ask, half hoping he'll change his mind and say he's happy with his daily hikes.

"Even more than I did when we first talked about it. The past few days here showed me how much I need to chill the fuck out."

Yeah, okay. That makes two of us.

CHAPTER

Ten

PJ

In the week since Colin arrived at Buttercup Hill, he's chilled the fuck out.

It probably wouldn't be obvious to the casual observer because he gets up each day at the crack of dawn and goes out for a grueling three-hour hike, followed by an egg white omelet at the café. Not exactly decadent living.

For the past couple of days, his breakfast has coincided with my latte, and we've gotten in a game of chess before I head to my office. I don't want to admit how much I look forward to seeing him sitting at the table by the window each morning.

He no longer grits his teeth when he's planning his next chess move. He's settled into a "my usual" coffee order, a flat white with two percent milk.

"Not high maintenance yet, but you're headed in that direction," I tell him as he sets up the chess board on the table by the window on Saturday. I still don't have a plan for doing "normal" things because he's already hiked all of the local hills, and I like to spend my free time doing that.

"One game?" he asks when he's finished setting up the pieces, holding out his hands like a magician. I hear the espresso machine whir to life, a satisfying noise that gets my adrenaline going in anticipation of my coffee. Or maybe it's him. Maybe it's being in the same room as him *and* coffee that gets my adrenaline going.

Not like the feeling is mutual. He clearly doesn't know the effect he has on me.

"No, we should head out. I have a lot of ideas for today." In other words, we need to keep moving. Sitting across the table from Colin will only make me yearn for him to reach out and touch him. And that's not going to help me stop thinking about him in inappropriate ways.

In fact, I have no ideas.

I can't imagine what kinds of things would be fun for a guy who works sixteen-hour days but who also carries an Amex Black card and can use it anywhere he pleases. Colin Hathaway is a romance novel wrapped in a whodunnit.

We leave the café with coffees to go, and I find it fitting that after a few days of experimenting at Sweet Butter, Colin's coffee drink of choice has turned out to be a flat white—not too austere, not too high maintenance. Like him.

"My brother's fond of the golf cart, but I like to walk when I have time." I don't bother to add that I rarely have time to walk the Buttercup Hill property, especially right now when everyone's nerves are raw, worrying about the future of the company and our financial situation.

If we don't figure out how to infuse half a billion dollars into the company's coffers, my siblings and I will lose our entire savings. Or we'll have to take on investors and might lose control of the winery.

But I can't think about that now because I've promised to entertain this man for the day.

"Walking works for me. My main walking at work is pacing the halls between my lab and various meeting rooms."

I squint out at the early morning sun, which is bright, yellow, and shining across the vineyards and into my eyes. "You're really not making a very good case for being a CEO." I lead us down one of the footpaths that winds past my house down to the small lake.

He runs a hand through freshly-showered hair and nods. "Yeah, I don't imagine I am. And look, I don't want to sound like a whiny asshole who isn't grateful for the life I have. I know I'm lucky—"

Holding up a hand, I stop him. "This is all between friends. I don't think you're a whiny asshole, and you're allowed to complain."

"I still shouldn't complain."

I study him for a moment as we walk, feeling a little more relaxed now that we're moving. "You're pretty hard on yourself."

He stares at the ground as we walk. "Yeah. It works for me most of the time. Long days, long weeks. My parents are grinders. Both academics. Publish or perish, so they work really hard to stay relevant in their fields."

"I get that. My dad wasn't exactly trotting out to Little League games during the week. Though he managed to come to some of mine. By the time I came along, he'd already grown the vineyard to pretty much what it is now, so he took the occasional break. It annoyed my siblings, but half of them were in college by then, and Dash doesn't let much get to him."

"I remember your dad. He didn't suffer fools." I like the way his eyes soften the same way mine do when I think about my dad.

"Nope. It's why I still can't figure out how he funneled half a billion dollars out of the company without a good reason. Even with dementia, I feel like he's hardwired to make good financial decisions."

"Maybe he thought it was a good decision, whatever it was."

"Probably. Just wish he could tell us. He's always speaking in tongues."

"You'll figure it out. And until then, tell the potential investors to talk to the hand."

I laugh. "Hard when I'm the one who's used to smoothing things over."

"But not impossible. Take it from someone who may have just ruined his company by talking about climate change."

Without thinking, I reach for his hand. Heat races through my veins, and my brain instantly scolds me for my recklessness, but I try to ignore it. I sense that this man needs someone to be kind to him more than I need to protect my feelings.

He casts a glance my way and tightens his grip around my fingers. His large, warm hand engulfs mine, and somehow, I end up feeling like the one who's being comforted.

We walk like that until we get to the lake. I'm fully aware that if Archer sees us together like this, he'll probably blow a gasket, but I don't care. I'm just being a good host. I can make myself believe that lie for a little longer.

"As promised…" I point at a family of ducks, the mallard dad sailing across the water by himself, green head feathers glinting in the sun. The brown mother duck drifts behind him with a trail of ducklings. In truth, I got lucky. The small lake usually has ducks, but there's no guarantee.

We take the path that loops around the lake, eventually stopping at a bench in front of where the ducklings fan out their tail feathers and play in the water. "They have a good life here," Colin observes.

"They do."

I sit on one end of the bench, leaving ample space for Colin, but he sits right in the middle, closer than I'd like. Clueless. Here, I'm trying my best to be a tour guide and gal pal, and he's thwarting me at every turn. I can't even remember what we were talking about two minutes ago.

"So what's it like living in Napa?" he asks, dropping my hand and stretching his arms overhead like he's settling into relaxing. My hand feels cold, and I briefly leave it on the bench between us, hoping he'll pick it up again, but he doesn't. He's oblivious to what I'm feeling because he's feeling none of it. Clearly.

It's good, I tell myself. It helps me reinforce that I should not and do not have feelings for Colin Hathaway. However, he is proving to me that I may need a man in my life. My body obviously craves being touched by someone—anyone—and I need to remedy that before I jump all over my brother's best friend like the horny kid sister Archer portrays me to be.

"Napa is a small town. Everyone knows everyone else's business."

"Sounds like Silicon Valley, only with wine instead of tech." He unscrews the cap on a metal water bottle he's been carrying.

"So you get it. It's why I mostly hang out here and work. If I'm going to make plans, I usually drive down to visit friends in Berkeley just to get away a little bit."

He nods. "Anonymity is nice."

"It is. But no one's taking pictures of me on their phone and posting them every time I go to Starbucks."

His gaze snaps to mine. "I haven't been photographed at Starbucks…" he denies. "But that's only because I never go."

"Because you work sixteen-hour days."

"Yeah."

"Okay. In your wildest fantasies about taking a day off, what do you imagine yourself doing?" If he says something that requires us to fly in a private jet to an island, I won't be able to pull it off, but maybe I could arrange a private tour of an exclusive winery or something. People are always trying to get a spot for a tasting at Oakville Farms winery, and they have a six month wait list.

"I know it probably sounds weird, but what I'd really like to do is just walk around a grocery store."

My snort laugh betrays the absurdity of his request, but I quickly recover. "Sure. I can do my shopping. Win-win."

"Ah, see? Your brother would never do this with me. He'd say he did enough grocery shopping during our college years to last a lifetime." The comment brings me back to earth. This is not a date.

I'm only filling in for my brother, who has better things to do than look at produce.

"Shopped for a lot of ramen back then, huh?"

"Yeah. And green apples. One per day."

"Just to be clear, you're in a region with world-class wines, and you want to wander the cereal aisle?" I use the excuse to stand from the bench and face him. Instantly, I can breathe a bit easier now that he's not so close.

"Yes."

"Okay, but we should go late at night or something, so no one catches you buying Kit Kats and blasts our snack choice on social media."

"I'm more a fan of popcorn and Junior Mints."

"Spoken like a man who spends a lot of time in movie theaters."

His face falls into a blank expression.

"What? Don't tell me you've never been to a movie theater?"

He offers a sheepish half smile. "Not never. But it's been…years."

"Oh my gosh. What do you do for fun?"

He forms his hands into a triangle, tapping his fingers together like he's scheming. "This. This is fun. And I'd love to see a movie. Is there a theater nearby?"

The question surprises me because I know he doesn't want to get caught in public, but this is a small town, so it shouldn't be a problem.

"There's one a few miles away in St. Helena. Has some cute shops, restaurants, and a movie theater. Mostly locals, and we get a lot of tourists in the summer, so it's not exactly a good place to lay low. People would probably recognize you."

"I'm willing to take the risk. I'll wear a mustache and glasses or something. I haven't been to a movie theater in years."

"Years?" I'm not sure I heard him right, and I'm half-laughing at the idea of him in a fake mustache. "Like, what was the last movie you saw in a theater?"

He blinks a couple of times and taps his finger against his lip. It's crazy how such a throwaway gesture has me squirming like he's lit a fire inside me. I want to bite his finger. "I dunno. E.T.?"

I laugh, and he grins at me. It's getting easier to elicit a smile from him, but each one still feels like a gift.

I find myself wanting to be deserving of them. So I pull up an app on my phone and look at movie times.

"We're in luck. There's a classic movie thing going on this weekend. We can find one even older than E.T."

"Perfect. I'm in."

I shouldn't feel the warm thrill race through my chest at the thought of sitting in the dark next to Colin Hathaway. I shouldn't feel a lot of things I've felt when I'm close enough to Colin for my body to quiver in anticipation of contact—the accidental brush of a finger, the weight of his hand against the small of my back when he escorts me in front of him, and the sexy rumble of his deep voice.

But I feel all of them. And I can't make it stop.

CHAPTER
Eleven

COLIN

According to PJ, the area has only one big grocery store, so there's a good chance it will be crowded on a Saturday morning. As a preventative measure, she outfits me in a baseball hat and sunglasses. No mustache.

"Don't you think this makes me look like more of a pretentious asshole?" It was one thing to wear a hat and glasses on my hikes, but wearing shades inside a store seems like overkill.

"Fine, take the glasses off if you want, but keep your head down if you don't want someone snapping a selfie with you picking out Oreos and tweeting that you're ruining the planet by supporting Big Snacking," PJ says, making me laugh. She pulls her electric car into a spot far away from any other cars.

I appreciate the lengths to which she's going to help me do lowbrow everyday things without the risk of running into people who might recognize me. Even though I keep telling her I'm not that recognizable, she insists it doesn't matter. "All it takes is one. Then your whole attempt to lay low is blown."

She's not wrong, but I feel a little guilty taking up so much of her time. Especially because I'm enjoying it far more than I think I should.

Walking down the produce aisle, I follow slightly behind her, noticing the curve of her hips, how her waist nips in, and the way her hair trails down her back in ribbons. As if she can feel the heat of my stare, she casts a look over her shoulder, and I try to hide my wolfish admiration. "Do you like Rainier cherries or red ones?"

I barely hear the question, so consumed with watching her lips move. They're the color of ripe cherries themselves, and I'd so much rather take a bite from them than any fruit in this aisle.

"Come with me." I extend my hand, knowing that the moment she puts her hand in mine, I'll be crossing a line I promised myself I wouldn't cross. Just like that moment by the lake when her palm grazed my skin, I won't want to let go.

Her soft skin slips against mine as I surround her hand with my palm. She looks away, but I see the creep of blush across her cheeks.

I've been feeling her gravitational pull, along with my closest friend's warnings to stay away. Well, fuck him. Except that he's not wrong. She's ten years younger than me, and our lives are complicated by work and expectations that we follow a course that's already been set for each of us.

But he is wrong in thinking I need a warning. I can make my own messes just fine, thank you very much. And I really like this woman. It's the carefree way she goes about any activity without a glimmer of self-consciousness. It's the way she nailed exactly what my publicist did wrong without a second thought.

I'd have turned tail and told him to follow her strategy because she's smart and right, but a selfish part of me wants to have these two weeks with her at Buttercup Hill. I never let my emotions guide me, but around her, I can't help it.

And right now, this is harmless fun, the two of us spending a casual day doing normal things. No one would accuse us of going on a date to a grocery store.

Except that all I want to do is push her against the paper towel display and kiss her.

Pretty sure that's not a normal response to grocery shopping, but that's the magic of PJ Corbett. She makes a mundane stroll past canned peaches feel like a hot date.

"Where are we going?" she asks as I lead her away from the produce and toward a snack food aisle. The fluorescent overhead lighting paints everything in an otherworldly glow, but I only notice her.

And…the chips.

"I haven't been in a store like this in years. I wanted to see all the kinds of chips there are," I tell her, knowing I sound like an astronaut who's just returned to Planet Earth.

"They've changed quite a bit," she deadpans, mischief in her voice. "Now potato chips are no longer made from potatoes."

"I've seen potato chips, and I've eaten potato chips. I just haven't shopped for them."

PJ shakes her head. "I really don't think you're missing anything. The only difference between this and grocery delivery is getting to push a cart around."

With that, I change direction and drag her to the front of the store to get a cart. "Now you're talking," I say, sweeping her into my arms and depositing her in the basket of the cart. She squeals and hangs onto my shoulders, and for a moment, I'm tempted not to let her go.

As I lean over her curled-up body in the cart, she turns her face toward mine. The air between us stills, and it feels like the most logical thing in the world to hover there, immobile because I don't want to back away.

I want to close the gap between us, and I watch her tongue slip out and lick her bottom lip. Does she want me to kiss her? I find myself wishing I haven't been in a self-imposed solitude for so long. I've fucking forgotten what to do when a beautiful woman is this near to me—when I want her to be even closer.

Her large eyes blink and stare at me, and under the bright lights of Sunshine Foods market, my iron resolve clamps back down. I reluctantly back away and release her from my grip, noticing the corners of her mouth turn down as I do it.

She's disappointed in the lost opportunity, or maybe I'm reading into the situation and manufacturing what I want to be there. Either way, the moment has passed.

Standing up, I hop on the ledge of the cart and let it carry us down the aisle. I feel like a preteen boy who's about to get yelled at by an older supermarket employee, but no one is around at this hour to bother us. I pedal my foot and push us around the store, loading up the front of the cart with the kind of boxed food my organic chef never has in the house—Cheetos, Oreo cookies, and Little Debbie snack cakes.

"You're kidding with all this, right?" PJ asks, observing my high cholesterol bounty. "When do you plan on eating it?"

"I don't know. Later. Tomorrow…maybe I'll bring it back to Palo Alto."

"You do know they have grocery stores there, right? Cheetos are not a Napa Valley thing."

"I do know. This is much more fun."

She swivels around to sit cross-legged in the cart and watches me browse the snack aisle. My brow furrows as I study the variety of chips. "Do you have a favorite?" I ask.

"I like a classic chip. No salt and vinegar or barbecue. Plain Lays are good. Maybe Ruffles for a little more crunch."

I grab two bags of plain Lays chips, and she looks at me quizzically. "Don't buy what I like. Buy whatever you've been craving while your fancy chef cooked your free-range organic egg whites."

I won't be deterred by her resistance. As we move through the aisles, I do pick out some basic cheese, ordinary sliced bread, and a jar of peanut butter. Yet each time I choose something, I subtly ask for advice or her opinion and either grab something she likes or file the information away for a later time and place.

I have no idea if I'll ever be in a position to eat snack food with her after this week, but a part of me is hopeful.

CHAPTER
Twelve

PJ

"I'm pretty sure we can watch this back at my house," I tell Colin, gesturing to the marquee above the movie theater entrance, which announces a summer rom-com festival of classics. Today's film is *Bringing Up Baby* with Katherine Hepburn and Cary Grant.

He shakes his head. "I want to sit in a theater, eat popcorn and Junior Mints, and watch it on the big screen."

I can't argue with a man who knows what he wants.

Even if I've already seen the movie. Twice.

We get our tickets and walk into the small lobby. Colin holds the door open and guides me inside with a hand on the small of my back.

My pulse quickens, and I take in a sharp gulp of air. His light touch on my back has all my senses firing. It's like his hand is the centerpiece of a chemical reaction, radiating electricity in all directions from the point of contact.

OMG, after one day with him, I'm a pseudoscientist.

I walk toward the concession stand, joints stiff and a frozen smile plastered on my face because inside, I'm losing my shit. How can a man's hand feel so freaking good?

And if it feels that good on my back, I don't want to think about how it would feel in other places. Well, I do. Of course I do. But it's a bad idea when the guy has shown zero interest in me despite my occasional attempts to flirt.

I do a quick scan of the lobby, as I've been doing all day, just to make sure no one pretends to snap a selfie across the room while really taking a picture of Colin. The last thing he needs is unwanted publicity when he's trying to escape the limelight.

I'm also vaguely aware of my other motive—to make sure my brother doesn't see us together. It's ridiculous because I have every right to spend time with anyone I want. Especially if my brother has seen fit to house that "anyone" right outside my door. But I'll always secretly want my family's approval. Annoying.

Colin is wearing the baseball cap he's had on all day. Coupled with a pair of sunglasses, he was unrecognizable to the few people we passed when we stopped in Calistoga for lunch. It also makes him look younger and hotter, and I've been practically salivating over him all day long.

What is it about this guy? Half the men I know wear baseball caps on the weekends, and I don't look twice. They look…normal. Not Colin. He looks like a film star trying to avoid being recognized and somehow appearing even more like a film star.

He turns the hat backward, and the hot meter ticks up another thousand notches.

Now I can see his face more clearly. The sharpness of his features meshed with the softness of a few days of beard growth are an intoxicating combination. His eyes flash with that Adriatic blue that makes me want to leave the safe haven of shore behind and dive in.

His brow furrows as he stares at the list of snacks and drinks posted over the concession counter, and my brain goes mushy as I stare at him. When he turns to ask me a question, the concentration melts into laughter. "You okay?"

I nod, shaking myself back into sensibility after the momentary lapse.

Must not stare at hot guy. Must focus on snack food.

"Yes. Sure. Spaced out for a sec." My cheeks feel hot, and I look away. Let's face it, I have the snack menu memorized. That's what happens when you've been to the one theater in town a hundred times.

"What do you want?"

"Oh. I guess a chardonnay and popcorn," I say without thinking. It's my usual when I come here.

"They have wine at the movie theater?" He looks again at the snack sign, where he must have missed that option.

"It's Napa." I shrug. "Would be sacrilege if you couldn't get wine."

He digests this piece of information, nodding. "Two glasses of chardonnay. Actually, scratch that. Can we get a bottle?" he asks the lanky, bored-looking cashier slouching in a tight black tee.

"How many glasses?" The cashier scratches the back of his neck and adjusts a pair of hipster glasses.

Colin points at me. "Two. And an extra-large popcorn, a box of M&Ms, and some Junior Mints." I can't remember the last time a man took charge and ordered without asking my opinion, and I like it.

There's something about Colin that's different from the guys I casually dated through the first half of my twenties. They were more like teenage boys in adult bodies with nice-enough-looking faces. They had swagger, but they didn't command a room.

Colin Hathaway commands any space he enters without even looking up from the floor. Standing at the concession counter in a worn tee and vintage San Francisco Giants cap, he looks every bit the chill Silicon Valley tech employee, and I know they're a dime a dozen down where he lives. And here in Napa, guys come up all the time casually dressed like him.

None of those men do what Colin does when he walks into a room. He owns it. His presence magnetically charges the air around him. People don't know why, but they know something is different when he's entered their immediate space.

His tone when he speaks is velvet. His movements graceful. His intellect hotter than the midday sun.

I should know. I've been listening to him talk about satellites all day long and haven't understood half of it. And yet, I'd listen to him talk for another day because he's so invested in the potential for technology that he makes me feel invested.

Colin tucks the bottle of wine under one arm and accepts the cardboard takeout carton containing plastic stemless wineglasses and our snacks in one hand.

He gestures at the popcorn for me to carry, and I have to laugh at the size of the extra-large bucket I'm handed. "This is enough popcorn to feed half the population of Napa." I half-expect him to reconsider his choice and tell the concession guy to downsize the order.

Instead, Colin nods. "So, perfect amount."

The theater isn't jam-packed, but people sit in pairs and groups throughout the place, and we scan the rows. "Front or back?" he asks.

"Back."

We find seats a few rows down from the last row and work our way to the empty pair in the center.

"PJ? Heeeey!" I recognize the voice. Mallory Rutherford is a friend of the family, though if you ask my brother Jackson, she's more of a frenemy. The two of them had a fling for a hot minute after his wife left him, and he avoids her now like the plague.

I like her enough, but I don't know her all that well. I just know that half the time I eat dinner in one of Napa's fancier restaurants, I run into her. Not in the movie theater, however. I'm surprised to see her here in the afternoon, but her focus immediately jumps to Colin, and I watch her give him the once-over. Slowly. She looks back at me. Her eyebrows bounce in approval and she smiles.

"How's it going, Mallory?"

"So good. I can't believe you're here. I've been meaning to call you."

"Taking a break. Doesn't happen too often." Colin mumbles something about how it should happen more often, and Mallory's eyes return to him. I need to introduce him, or it will be rude.

"Mallory, this is Colin."

Her eyes brighten with recognition. "Oh, of course. I know who you are. I thought you looked familiar, but totally, you're Colin Hathaway." She looks at me with a sneaky smile.

He nods and stands, extending his hand. "Nice to meet you."

"Oh please, don't stand. But since you're up, do you mind if I get a selfie? This is just too fun." She has her phone out and is backing her way in front of Colin and me without waiting for an answer. I start to protest, but she's already clicked several photos.

"Anyway…" I figure Mallory will take that universal cue and hurry along, but she takes a step closer to us as soon as Colin sits back down, so now she's basically standing in front of our seats. I debate banging my knees into her to dislodge her, but I'm not convinced it'll work. So she persists.

"How do you two know each other? Are you two dating? Are you buying a place in Napa?" Everything comes out in a delighted squeal. So many questions, and I don't have answers for any of them.

"We're just seeing a movie. Colin went to college with my brother," I say, regretting giving her any information at all.

"Ohhhh. So you go way back. Friends." She looks back and forth between us as though that's the only possible reason he'd be here with me.

A few heads turn at her enthusiasm. And her volume, which I don't think she knows how to mute.

Fortunately, the movie theater gods smile on me, and the lights begin to dim. "Time for the movie. Nice seeing you." I make a move to look past her as though the movie has already begun playing on the screen.

Mallory takes the hint and scurries off to her seat a few rows away, waving and making me promise to get lunch with her soon.

I turn to Colin apologetically. "I really thought no one would be here during the day."

He shrugs. "No worries. You don't come here during the day, normally. How could you know?" The dim light from the movie screen paints his face with a pretty glow

Colin fits our glasses into the cupholders at the end of each armrest and holds up the two kinds of candy.

"Are you the type who mixes candy into the popcorn?" he asks, opening the yellow cardboard box of peanut M&Ms and offering a handful to me.

"Is there another type of person?" I pop two of the candies into my mouth and bite down hard. "Mmm, I forgot how much I like these."

"Right?" He tosses a couple into his mouth and pours the remainder of the box into the giant trough of popcorn. Then he holds up the Junior Mints box. "These too?"

"Please."

I skim a few handfuls of popcorn off the top to make room to mix the candy, and it's not pretty—me shoving popcorn into my mouth indelicately and shaking the tub to mix in the candy. Several more handfuls bounce out and land on my lap, the floor, and Colin's shoes.

I do a semi-decent job of kicking the popcorn on the floor under the seat in front of me and picking up some of the kernels from my lap while Colin busies himself pouring us wine. I'm hoping he didn't see the cascade of popped kernels fly every-where when I tried once more to shake the mixture together.

He doesn't seem bothered by my lack of grace. Turning toward me, Colin hands me a full glass of wine, holding it up for a toast. "To a perfect day. Thank you for showing me around."

He's leaning close, much closer to me than he's been all day. I tell myself it's because we're confined in the intimate theater space. People around us are chatting loudly, so he has to lean close in order to be heard.

I force myself to breathe normally even though his proximity is making it hard. I think about adding my own toast to his, something lame about neighbors, but thank goodness I just limit it to "cheers."

Sanity prevails. For once.

We clink plastic glasses and each take a sip. I use the moment to try to calm my nerves. If I'm going to sit this close to him for two hours, I need to steady my breathing, or I'll sound like a steam train huffing along beside him.

I expect Colin to lean back into his seat and get comfortable. That will allow me to surreptitiously fan the heat from my face and dab what I'm certain is sweat on my temple. Instead, he surprises me by reaching a gentle hand toward my shoulder, where he plucks a stray kernel of popcorn off my shirt.

He offers it to me to eat, and I open my mouth so he can drop it onto my tongue.

Placing it into my mouth with two fingers, he's being cute and friendly. I should leave it at that. But crazy instinct takes over, and I close my lips on his thumb. I watch the surprise take over his face. His jaw goes slack. His eyes heat and darken.

It fuels me, and I lick his thumb slowly, drawing circles around it with my tongue. I can't take my gaze from his face, and his eyes watch me as though I have a plan. When I part my lips, he leaves his thumb for a moment, and I suck it between my lips once more before letting him go.

He inhales a shaky breath, and it's all I need to feel calm.

Because I just needed to know he isn't made of stone. And that sharp inhale and how his face looked tells me everything. He's not immune to me.

The way he leans a little closer, eyes tracing my face and landing on my lips, drives that point home even more. His face is inches away. I could close the gap and fuse our lips together, but I've already made my move. The next one belongs to him.

Under the dim house lights, it feels like we're sealed inside a bubble of privacy.

Dangerous thought. It's that kind of thinking that causes people to get sloppy and make mistakes with their hearts and minds that will come back to haunt them later. I know this. I earn my living because of this.

But I can't back away. We're in Napa. It's a small town. No one has paid a bit of attention to Colin all day, and we're in the last few rows of the theater. All of these thoughts and none of them play through my mind in a discordant, unhelpful maze.

"Junebug…" Colin breathes my name like it's the answer to a confounding riddle.

"Yes." His face is a little blurred at this proximity. I can feel his breath when he speaks.

He shakes his head. "This is not a good idea."

"I disagree."

His eyes drop closed for a beat. When he opens them, the blue is a different, fiercer color than I've seen before. "I—I can't do what you're asking."

"I don't know the difference between can't and won't. If you're not feeling it, just say so."

He leans his head back and takes another long breath. Shaking his head slowly, he finally returns his gaze to mine. "If you only knew how much I fucking wanted you, you'd run."

"Why would I run?" My voice comes out in a whisper because he's sucked all the remaining air from my lungs. I feel dizzy. He can't have just said what he did. He can't mean it, even if he did say it.

"Because if I thought I could have you the way I want to, I wouldn't be able to stop."

"Who says I'd want you to stop?"

"You'd be wise to be careful around me. I don't do relationships, and you deserve better."

"Who says I want a relationship?" I don't want one, or at least I never did. Now I don't know what I want.

He lingers, face so close to mine for so long that I stop breathing. He has to kiss me or I just might suffocate. And yet, I should be listening to what he's telling me. I should be hearing him.

"Why no relationships, just out of curiosity?" I try to keep my tone light, but the weight of my question falls like a boulder on my ears. I gauge his reaction to see if he feels it too, but he doesn't flinch.

"I'm married to my work. The one time I tried being married to a person at the same time, it did not end well."

He snaps his lips shut after the brief explanation as though he didn't just open a trove of new questions. At the same time, I have my own set of responses that I wasn't expecting. For the first time in my life, I'm not sure I want another fling, even though he's hotter than sin and he's right here. Maybe I do want a relationship.

And I know better than to try to create one where it can't ever exist. I've made that mistake before, and I won't repeat it.

So I do the unthinkable, given how goddamn much I want to kiss him. I do the right thing, even though I want to know how his lips taste just one time.

I back away. I lean back in my movie theater seat. And when the lights go down, I slowly wipe the cool cup of wine against my forehead and watch the hot nerd played by Cary Grant try to wrangle a leopard.

He's way too smart for the job he's doing, and Katherine Hepburn's character knows it. But she plays along, each of them hitting the comedy notes perfectly until they can't stay away from each other any longer. Then they fall in love.

The tight tether between them pulls like a heavy rubber band until it snaps with such a satisfying explosion of desire that it makes the audience fall in love with them too.

It's a perfect movie.

And if life imitated art, I'd be falling in love with the hot nerdy scientist sitting next to me. Because he's even hotter and nerdier than Cary Grant. But he doesn't do relationships. Apparently, that's a deal breaker for doing anything else. An immovable rock. A friend, just like Mallory, labeled him.

It's why I'm not expecting it when he reaches over and clasps my hand in his. I'm so surprised that I forget to breathe for nearly a minute. A dribble of sweat makes its way down my neck and into my shirt. I'm aware of my hand trembling in his, and I hope he can't feel it.

I've never been so grateful to have already seen a movie because I'm not paying attention to any of it now. Katherine Hepburn could end up married to the leopard by the end of the movie and I wouldn't know the difference.

How can holding someone's hand make me feel like my entire body has been invaded by twirling butterflies and tiny beams of light? It's such a basic gesture, yet I can't even recall whether the previous men I dated ever did it.

Maybe that's exactly it. We were too casual, too focused on hooking up and having fun to let anything resembling a feeling enter the mix.

And now...I have all the feels. And I like it.

Heaven help me.

———

For the remainder of the movie, it feels like a forcefield exists between us. Pulling us closer and warning us away at the same time.

I walk out of there more exhausted than if I'd climbed Mount Kilimanjaro in a day. I wanted to haul myself into Colin's lap and move to the farthest edge of my seat. I wanted him, and I was afraid of where wanting him would lead.

Because if he felt the same way, it would be explosive. There's no question in my mind.

"We should get back," I mumble, turning the key in the ignition. I suddenly feel exposed in the late summer light after my near certainty that Colin was about to kiss me in the movie theater. I cast him a side-eye when I can afford to take my gaze off the road and find his eyes on me. Nothing abashed about it. He's staring.

I'm a little hesitant to take Colin to a dinner place in town because now I'm convinced we'll run into more locals. Even if they're not equipped with selfie sticks, gossip will still fly, and neither of us needs that.

"This has been a great day. What are you doing tomorrow?"

"I, um…" Words lodge in my throat because we haven't talked about anything beyond this one favor he's asked me to do. One day of "normal."

"I have a family dinner with my brothers and Beatrix. It's kind of a Sunday tradition thing."

"Sounds nice."

"You should come. The family would love to see you, and you have to eat." I try to sound casual. Anyone would do the same under the circumstances: invite an old family friend to join us for dinner. It's not because being around him *does* things to me.

But it's also that. And I want him to do more of them.

"Yeah?" His expression brightens at the invitation. "Should I check with Arch?"

"No. You should just come. I'll let Dash know to set an extra place."

He should *not* come to dinner.

If there's any hope in hell of me getting over what is surely a raging lady boner crush on this man, having him come to dinner will foil every last bit of that hope.

"I'll mention it to Archer, but he'll be excited to have you. You're practically family." *Family. As in practically a brother. Only a hot one I'd like to fuck.* The words spill from my mouth as though it's sprung a leak. I have no business inviting him to dinner. That's Archer's domain since they're besties and all. But I have gone batshit crazy, and all I can think about is how to concoct a way to see him tomorrow.

I don't want to leave my fate to chance and hope he happens to walk by my front door when I happen to be leaving for work.

But really, he shouldn't come to dinner. It will take all my wherewithal to sit across a table from him and not openly stare. I already know it's going to be a problem.

CHAPTER
Thirteen

COLIN

I should get a fucking medal. Right up there with the Purple Heart for bravery or the Nobel Prize for Not Fucking a Guy's Best Friend's Much Younger Sister in a Movie Theater. Pretty sure that award exists. It should be a nationally sanctioned prize telling everyone I am a man of spectacular self-restraint.

When she closed those gorgeous, plump lips around my thumb, I nearly lost my goddamn mind.

But then she heard me loud and clear. As much as I wanted her—that amount being a vast expanse no astrophysicist has yet been able to quantify—I also felt a sigh of relief when she took my warning at face value.

As she should. A relationship is something I can't give her.

There's no point in starting something with her when we both know that.

Right?

For the first time in my life, I don't have a ready answer. Not one that makes sense, anyway. If I want to do something about it,

I need to do it now. I need to let her know exactly how much I want her with no "but" at the end of that sentence.

For the entirety of the movie, PJ sat about as far away from me as her seat would permit, scrunched against the outer edge, lest I invade her space. She drove us back to the winery, making idle small talk about the movie.

"I love when we find out it's a leopard," PJ says, pulling into the small parking area behind her house.

"Yeah. That was good." I nod and try to remember the movie. It's not like me to have nothing to say about a film, but I couldn't focus on it for even a minute at a time.

She shoots me a glance. "Super specific movie review. Remind me to consult you instead of Rotten Tomatoes next time."

She's returned to the easy banter of the earlier part of our day. Meanwhile, my brain is stuck in a loop. All I can think about was how PJ's tongue felt wrapped around my thumb and about how much I want it wrapped around my dick.

But that's not where her mind is at all. I've made sure of it.

Whatever instinct she may have had in that theater seems to have disappeared with the last dregs of popcorn and chocolate at the bottom of that mammoth bucket. I'm back to being her slightly irritating neighbor, and she's my friend's sister.

I fucking hate it.

Because it's entirely my fault. My fear that getting involved with a woman will derail my focus on work. Hell, I've managed to derail it all by myself. So why am I punishing her? And me?

We reach the midway point between the front door to the cottage and the walkway leading to PJ's house. "Okay, well, this was fun. Have a good evening." She turns, and in seconds, she'll be inside her house, and whatever opportunity I have to turn things around will be gone.

I *need* to turn this around.

"Hey," I venture, reaching for her shoulder. She flinches at the contact. Maybe she feels the same jolt of fire that practically consumes me every time I graze her skin with my hand.

Or maybe I've just startled her. Maybe she feels nothing.

Stop second-guessing.

She looks over her shoulder at me. Eyes wide and expectant, pillowy lips parted. I want to pull her into my arms and taste those lips.

I don't say a word, and she searches my face for clues. Guiding her to turn around, my fingers sink into the flesh of her shoulder. When she's facing me, her eyes search mine.

"Everything okay?" she asks, face softening.

"What did you mean earlier when you said your siblings don't take you seriously?"

A flicker of discomfort sparks in her eyes, but she stands up a little straighter and shakes the moment off.

Then she relents. Her shoulders drop, and her breath releases. "Just exactly that. They think what I do is a job anyone could do. I'll always be the little sister who'll say the wrong thing to the wrong person, and they'll have to clean up my mess." She nods as though validating her own words. "There was a time when I was less responsible. But I'm different than I was, and they just can't see it."

"Families are tough. I get it." I lock eyes with her to make sure she hears me and understands. "But for what it's worth, I see it. I see you."

Her subtle intake of breath is quiet, but it tells me my words landed. Her eyes go a little glassy, and she nods. "Thank you."

I take a step closer to her, watching every minute shift in her expression as I move into her space. Her lips part, and she leans slightly forward.

With my index finger, I trace the shape of her cheekbone, letting the contours guide my hand over the apple of her cheek and down toward her chin. She stands frozen in place, trembling under my touch. Feel her shaky exhale.

Her eyes give me the permission I need to cup her cheek in my hand and feel the soft skin of her face. I want my hands in her hair, pulling through the wild tangle, but I'm getting ahead of myself.

"I'm sorry. I've been thinking about doing this since my missed opportunity in the theater."

She inhales a ragged breath. "Opportunity for what?" Her voice shakes, but I understand why she needs me to be clear about what I want.

"I should've kissed you when I had the chance. Now I'm not sure I can ask for a redo."

"You can ask." Her voice is soft, breathy. It looks like it takes effort to fill her lungs and exhale the air slowly. She slides her hand up my arm, and even through my shirt her fingers heat my skin as they roll over it, massaging each muscle as she goes. When she reaches my bicep, she squeezes.

I tilt her head up to face mine and lean forward. We're only inches apart, just like in the movie theater, only now we don't have the excuse of being seated close to each other. Now, I have her this close because it's where I want her to be.

"Okay, that was a lie, just now."

She flinches but doesn't back up. "What was?"

"When I said I've been thinking about it since the movie theater. The truth is, I've been thinking about kissing you for the past four days. It's…all I can think about, if I'm being completely honest."

"Always be completely honest. Please." She moves an inch closer. Her features blur, and I'm more aware of her scent—all fresh grapefruit and spring grass.

I pause a moment to take her in, just like this, because everything will change in an instant. I'll gladly tear down the brittle threads of friendship and replace them with every gut instinct I've had about her.

"Last chance to tell me you don't want this."

She shakes her head.

My heart thunders in my chest, and I blink hard against the last shreds of doubt. "Fuck, PJ. I want you so goddamn bad it hurts." The low growl of my voice sounds like a lion with a deer in its sights.

I lean an inch closer, savoring the moment before our lips meet.

We're too close to see a damn thing, so I close my eyes and wrap my other hand around her cheek. Cupping her face, I brush my lips softly against hers and hear the small moan of approval.

This…it's everything I've been wanting for days and now…

"There you are!" Archer's voice cuts through the cool air like a scythe, sharp enough to draw blood. Just like the daggers in my eyes when my head whips around to look at him.

Fuck.

I pull my hands from PJ's face in a startled instant and take a step back. In the dim pathway light, it's hard to see, but I try to clock Archer's expression to discern what he may have heard or seen.

The grape arbor with hanging leaves and fruit obscures the area where we're standing from the pathway Archer walked to get here. His reaction to us standing there looking like two frightened deer reveals nothing. He grins like a Halloween pumpkin.

If he suspects anything, he doesn't show it. Smile wide, he surveys the two of us. PJ took a step back the moment my hands fell from her face and is looking at the ground, holding her hand over her cheek where mine was just moments earlier.

What I wouldn't give to have my hand there now. It feels awkward and cold hanging by my side.

"So…what's up, guys?" Archer asks, a twinge of irony in his voice, as though he's caught us in a revealing position, but he knows it's not how it looks.

Not anymore, asshole.

"N-nothing. Just coming back from a movie," PJ says, her voice raspy. She clears her throat, and I watch Archer, waiting for him to put the pieces together. But he seems clueless about walking in on the most obvious scene of his best friend about to make out with his sister.

The guy has a degree from Stanford, and he's dumb as a rock when it comes to noticing shit.

"Oh, you went to St. Helena?"

"Yeah. Rom-com festival," I say. Like he cares.

He nods. "Oh. Okay." He looks from me to PJ and back. "Thanks for entertaining him." He nods at PJ, and it annoys me how he seems to be dismissing her as my babysitter.

She takes another step farther away from me, and it hurts. "Sure. What's up, Arch?" She crosses her arms, her defenses mounting. Her brother doesn't bring out the softer vulnerability she showed me earlier.

Archer scrubs a hand over his face, his grin reappearing. "Got in touch with Conner and Ethan. They drove up for a night out with you." He pitches a thumb over his shoulder in the direction of his truck.

"College friends of ours," I explain to PJ, not wanting her left out of the conversation. She nods, expressionless.

"Exactly. Not sure you ever met them since you were—what? —eight when I went to college?" It annoys me that Archer keeps feeling the need to remind PJ how much younger she is. Or maybe he's just reminding me.

Point taken, asshole. I like her anyway.

But I see no way around joining them for a night out when he's planned something with our friends. I can't possibly say, "Thanks anyway, but I'd rather fuck your sister, so if you could just give the guys my regards…"

I cast PJ an apologetic look, and she offers me a small smile. It feels like a consolation prize, but I file it away with all the other tiny gems she's given me.

"Anyhow, they're waiting." Archer tilts his head in the direction he came from, and I hear laughter in the distance.

"Sure. Yeah." I turn to PJ. "Thanks for today." I meet her eyes, hoping mine communicate how little I want to leave her.

I kiss her on the cheek, feathering her skin with a breath before backing away. It's a promise. A hope.

Her eyes heat, and she nods almost imperceptibly.

She turns to go, and I follow Archer to his truck.

"Was I disrupting something?" Archer's voice contains more humor than suspicion. As if it's ludicrous that he could have walked in on the most important moment of my life. Even if that's how it feels.

I swallow hard and turn my baseball cap around so the brim blocks the view of my face. "Nah, just making sure she got in the door okay."

He claps me on the back as we reach his SUV, where I can already hear the raucous voices of our college friends chatting in the back seat. "Thanks, man. I appreciate you watching her back."

If he only knew all the parts of her I've been watching all day, he'd disown me. I feel a little guilty at the betrayal, but mostly, I just feel sad about the missed opportunity, one I'm not sure I'll ever get back.

"Hey, it's the elusive billionaire," our friend Ethan yells through the open window as soon as we're in earshot. He works for Google, and even though our offices are near each other, I haven't seen him in years. One more casualty of my lack of work-life balance.

"Yeah, yeah," I grumble, giving him a high five through the window. "Quit that shit, or I'm not getting in the car."

"Aw, you know I'm just giving you a hard time. I'd trade places with you in a heartbeat, you know that."

Would he? Should he?

As I slide onto the passenger seat and Archer fires up the engine, I wonder about the logic in that. Ethan's married with three kids, who he actually sees, and he'd trade places with me for money I have no time to spend?

I feel like an asshole complaining, but if it would give me free time with PJ Corbett, I'd take that trade, no questions asked.

CHAPTER
Fourteen

PJ

I've been waffling all day long.

A long day during which I haven't seen a sign of Colin Hathaway at all. Maybe he turned tail and went back to Silicon Valley. Maybe all the bro time last night was enough to make him man up and face the criticism back home, and he's gone.

I can't decide how I feel about that. Because the other possibility is that he's still here and still coming to dinner tonight.

I did invite him, after all. And I'm not sure how I feel about that either because seeing him in a house full of my siblings spells "awkward" with a capital A.

Then again, I really want to see him. That fact dwarfs all the other concerns.

I felt certain he'd come by my house to finish what he started last night, but maybe I got it wrong. Maybe he was just motivated by the wine we drank in the theater and the moment under the twinkling lights.

In the light of day, maybe he was glad Archer interrupted us.

All these thoughts swirl in my head as I decide what to wear to dinner. Normally, I don't give it a thought. Dinners with my family are slightly more fun than business meetings. In fact, we usually talk business for about half the time, then bicker the other half of the time. Sometimes, we do both at once.

Dash is hosting the dinner at his house, which means we're having tacos. He only makes tacos with the help of a few of the guys who work at the vineyard. They roast chilis we grow in the food garden, and Dash makes a killer salsa. In his mind, the food he cooks is just a vehicle to get salsa into his mouth. Doesn't matter if it's a taco or a quesadilla.

After staring into my closet for ten minutes, I pull on a short black dress with spaghetti straps. It's still warm in the evenings, especially under the heat lamps on Dash's deck, but I grab a rose-colored sweater off the chair in my bedroom and tie it around my waist.

Surveying the look in the full-length mirror, I decide I look too college co-ed and not enough intriguing twenty-something woman. If Colin does show up, I want to err on the side of cute, but not little sister cute.

Instead of the sweater, I opt for a sheer black short-sleeved shirt, which I put on over the dress and leave unbuttoned like a jacket. Cuter, and with a pair of slides with a chunky heel, my legs look longer and I feel good.

I leave my hair down but go easy on the makeup. Nothing to suggest to my siblings that I'm trying too hard.

Then I wander over to the industrial kitchen behind the big brown barn and get to work baking a batch of brownies. Dash asked me to bring dessert, and I knew he meant the brownies I bake in a special S-shaped tin that ensures that every brownie comes out with edges. My family doesn't like the middle pieces.

Mixing the batter, I gaze out the window at the long rows of grapes, all ripening in the late afternoon sun before the fall harvest. It's my favorite time of day here, when the sharp yellow rays cut through the vines in an almost-blinding kaleidoscope.

"I smell brownies." The voice behind me makes me smile, and

I turn to hug Marissa, our head gardener. She takes care of all the crops on the property that aren't grapes, which means she's in charge of several dozen acres of plants.

"You can't smell them when I haven't baked them yet."

"True. I saw you walk in here a few minutes ago when I was checking the soil on the fruit trees."

"Everything look okay?" We had a dry summer, which doesn't always bode well for the stone fruit.

"Yeah. Peaches are ripening early, cherries late. It doesn't make a lot of sense, but I can roll with it." Marissa tucks the purple-dyed ends of her dark ponytail into a bun beneath a lavender bandanna tied over her hair.

Shoving her hands into the pockets of her usual work outfit of denim overalls, she regards the brownie pan and shakes her head. "I don't get you Corbetts. The middle is the best part."

"Next time, I'll bake a regular batch, and you can have all the middles," I promise, putting the tray of brownies into the hot oven.

She pumps a fist. "Cool." Marissa and I have been friends since Dash hired her three years ago. We're close in age, and she's one of the few people who can convince me to go into town for a night out every so often. "Hey, so I heard you were out with some hottie McHotpants at the movie theater."

It shouldn't surprise me that even after my thorough scan of the theater, someone saw me and reported back to Marissa in record time.

"Yeah, that's Archer's friend. He's staying here for a couple weeks. I was being neighborly." I hear the lie in my voice and wonder if Marissa picks up on just how unneighborly I'd like to be.

She crosses her arms and regards me suspiciously. The tiny diamond nose piercing glints in the overhead light, mirroring the sparkles in her dark eyes. She doesn't believe me for one second.

"Archer's friend. Yet, you went out with him."

"I went to a movie with him." I try my denial on for size once more in preparation for any ribbing my family plans to give me later, assuming Colin mentions anything to them

She shakes her head. "You're so full of it. Tell me the truth."

I check my watch. Brownies won't be ready for thirty minutes, so I pull out a chair and gesture for Marissa to sit. "I need help, Mare." My shoulders fall, and I slump over the table, grateful she's here so I can vent. "At first, I couldn't stand the guy, but now..."

I tell her everything. The chess matches. His publicity problems. The late nights and almost kisses. "It's not just that he's hot and conveniently situated outside my front door. He kinda gets me. He sees me as an individual person, not just the youngest of five overachieving siblings."

It feels good to get it off my chest, even if saying the words makes me realize I want Colin much more than I let myself believe.

She nods. "Well, I'm glad *someone* finally gave you a little perspective on yourself. You don't give yourself enough credit." Marissa plays with a salt and pepper set on the table, spinning them and somehow managing not to spill a single granule.

"That's not the point. The point is...I like him, Mare. And that's pretty inconvenient considering I haven't even kissed him, and he's leaving in a week."

But I almost kissed him. And the memory of how much I want that has pushed all other thoughts from my brain.

She waves me away like I'm a silly insect. "Leaving for a town within driving distance. If you're into each other, you'll make something work." Shaking her head, Marissa comes to stand between me and the oven, so I can't avoid her gaze. "But first, you need to kiss him."

As if on cue, the timer dings. My heart starts thumping in my chest, and it has nothing to do with brownies.

———

It takes me twenty minutes to walk from the old barn to Dash's house, but it feels good to be outside rather than driving through the property. Our dad built it so that everything is accessible on foot, but utility roads circle the perimeter so trucks can come and go from the vineyards when it's picking season, and they need to carry grapes back to the fermenting barrels.

Dad bought a half dozen golf carts for employees to use when they need to get quickly from one area of the property to another without having to take their cars. My siblings use them too, so it's not surprising that two are parked outside of Dash's house.

As I approach the house, I hear raucous conversation, which tells me at least half my siblings are present. Slipping through the front door quietly, I head for the kitchen with the warm tin of brownies, which has cooled only slightly on the walk.

I slide the potholder from my hand and put it beneath the tin on the counter. Dash's kitchen smells like cilantro and is a mess of cutting boards with chopped tomatoes and onions. Half the chopped mixture seems to have made it into a bowl on the counter, while the rest sits in piles.

Looking out the window over the sink, I see Beatrix, Archer, and Dash outside. My brothers sit in Adirondack chairs on the deck that wraps around the main floor of the house. A ribbon of smoke wafts from the closed lid of the barbecue, where I know Dash is cooking chicken and steak for the tacos.

Several open bottles of wine sit on the outdoor dining table, along with a smattering of glasses.

"Hey Peej, when's our field trip to Duck Feather?" Dash asks me.

"Next week?" I don't want to tell him that I've been "busy" this week because I've been spending all my free time with Colin. Not that he'd judge.

Meanwhile, I don't see Colin, and I can't decide whether I feel relieved or sad. Maybe some of each.

"Hey, guys." I step through the slider and join them on the deck, which overlooks a cabernet vineyard that stretches toward the horizon. "I come bearing brownies." I gesture toward the kitchen with a nod.

"Nice. All ends?" Dash looks like a schoolkid, with rumpled hair and hopeful expression that almost never leaves his face. The youngest boy has none of the little brother complex that I seem to have. Even though he annoyed Archer and Jackson for years, trailing after them and trying to be like their friends, they always seemed to find him cute like a puppy.

I spread my palms wide. "I'm no amateur." Dash's deck faces the afternoon sun, and it's warm enough that I take off my outer shirt and drape it over the arm of a chair. Summers in Napa are my favorite time of year, even though it gets brutally hot midday. The heat just makes for perfect afternoons where a light breeze sometimes cuts through the stillness of the day and carries through to evening.

"Definitely not. Brownie pro over here." Beatrix points two fingers over my head and leans over to give me a hug. Sisters gotta stick together, and I won the sister lottery. She's my role model for multitasking and having a good attitude at the same time.

My brothers, for as much as they love me and each other, are each a piece of work.

Beatrix walks to the deck rail, staring out over the vines with a glass of sauvignon blanc in her hand. I can tell it's sauv blanc by the color and the fact that it's what she always drinks. Her hair, always perfectly pulled back, hangs in a long ponytail.

Between Archer and Dash is a conspicuously empty chair, where my dad always sits. He liked the middle chair with the most straight-on view. And since he's the one who can take credit for turning Buttercup Hill into the mammoth success it is today, no one would ever begrudge him the seat of his choice.

For a moment, I feel lighter at the idea that maybe he's coming tonight.

I touch the arm of the chair and look at Archer. He shakes his head. "Fifty-fifty. According to the nurse, he was doing well earlier, but he gets more confused in the evenings."

"Well, fingers crossed."

I miss my dad. He hasn't always been the most supportive of me as a career woman, but I never doubted that he had a special place in his heart for his Shiny Penny, as he called me. He's the only one who ever called me anything other than PJ, which is why it's extra odd that Colin has taken to calling me by a nickname.

I let my mind wander once again to last night, and my chest tightens at the memory. My eyes drift shut thinking about the way my skin rippled with goose bumps when he put his hands on my face.

It's why I don't notice him come in. It's why it surprises me when I hear his soft growl near my ear, "Junebug."

I swallow hard and turn around, bumping squarely into his chest because he's that close to me. I look around to see if any of my siblings notice. My brothers are involved in a conversation about the San Francisco 49ers, but Beatrix eyes me from her perch against the rail. She raises an eyebrow before turning back toward the view and sipping her wine.

"Hi." I pant like I just ran up a flight of stairs from the feel of his breath against my cheek when he speaks.

Archer notices Colin and gets up from his chair. On his way over, he grabs a wineglass from the table and hands it to him. "Hey, man. Welcome to the family dinner. Let chaos reign."

"Looks pretty chill to me," Colin observes.

Archer laughs and shuttles Colin over to the table to check out the wine varietals. Colin's gaze sweeps around the deck and lingers on me for a few seconds.

His gaze trails from my face and down to my bare arms, which he warms like the sun. Our eyes lock for a moment, and I feel exposed, my plain lust for him laid out on a platter. I look away before any of my siblings notice.

Or before I drool.

Jackson comes out the kitchen door with a large charcuterie

platter. "No, I didn't make this. I know you're all shocked." He gestures at Ruby and his daughter Fiona, who follow him out the door. "These two get all the credit."

"Wasted words," Dash says. "We know you can barely boil an egg."

Jackson presses his lips together, unable to one-up any of us when it comes to cooking, so he doesn't bother to try.

"Auntie B!" Fiona yells, skipping over to Beatrix, who used to babysit her regularly before Jackson hired Ruby as his nanny and promptly fell in love with the red-headed free spirit.

"C'mere, kiddo. Did you miss your favorite aunt?" Beatrix puts down her drink and opens her arms to Fi, who bounds over for a hug. I wait my turn, knowing she'll get to me. When she does, she whispers, "She's not really my favorite." Even at seven, she's a diplomat.

"I know, Fi. We don't need to tell anyone." I wink at her, and her dimples flash with a smile that's one hundred percent my brother. And for the first time in my life, I'm overtaken with a strange feeling of wondering what my own children might look like. Wondering how much they'll resemble their dad. Wondering who their dad will be.

I quickly shake myself out of that reverie, surprised I went down that road. I'm even more surprised at the small thought I've allowed to creep in—that the future father of my kids could look anything like Colin.

Turning my back on the group, I walk over to the railing where Beatrix stands and look out over the vineyard with her. "You okay?" she asks quietly.

"Of course. Just a family dinner. No big deal."

"Uh-huh, yeah. We'll talk later." She raises an eyebrow and moves to the table where the wine bottles sit. I don't pay attention to her because the acres of greenery are more calming to my senses than the family chaos behind me, so I focus my attention there.

Beatrix reappears a moment later with a cold glass of wine, which she hands me. "Here. This oughtta help."

Fiona continues making the rounds from sibling to sibling, hugging each one and having very involved conversations for a seven-year-old until she reaches Colin, whom she looks at suspiciously. "I don't know you."

He puts on a serious expression and studies her with his arms crossed. "I don't know you either. What are we going to do about that?" To anyone else, he might look intimidating. Tall, muscular, imposing.

But not to Fiona, who has stared down the best of them. "I guess we should introduce ourselves?" She looks at Jackson for permission, well-trained not to talk with strangers, even if they happen to be standing on your uncle's deck. Jackson errs on the side of over-protective, which makes Ruby a welcome balance with her carefree exuberance.

Jackson crosses the deck and stands next to her. "I should've introduced you. Fi, this is Colin. He went to college with Uncle Arch and me."

"Ohhhhh," Fiona says. "Makes sense now. Do you live nearby?"

Colin tilts his head, taking in the sprite in front of him. Her blond hair trails down her back, and she looks up at him with an impish smile. He scans the deck once more, and when his eyes land on me, I catch the barest hint of a smile dusting the corners of his mouth. I will my cheeks not to turn scarlet, but I can feel a rush of heat from head to toe.

Mercifully, Colin looks at Fiona again. "For another week, I do. I'm just visiting your uncle here."

Fiona nods, satisfied enough to move along. She goes over to investigate what Dash has on the barbecue, and I stand frozen, willing Colin to look at me again. And also hoping he won't. I don't think I can take it.

From my side, Beatrix chuckles. "Wow, honey. You've got it bad."

I let out a long breath. There's no point in trying to put one over on my sister. While my brothers can be blissfully oblivious, she doesn't miss a thing. "Yeah. Any suggestions on what to do?"

"Do *him*."

I roll my eyes, but not because the idea hasn't occurred to me a couple thousand times. And in the few minutes since he walked onto the deck, it's occurred a few thousand more. "Why does he have to look like that? It's just…not fair to the rest of the population. Men can't keep up with him, and women can't get over him."

"Oh my," Beatrix says, stealing a look at Colin and nodding. "You're not wrong, and from the way his eyes are undressing you each time he looks your way, the feeling is mutual. Just do it already."

Until she says the words, I realize I've been in denial about the way he's been looking at me, certain that all my feelings are one-sided. Even though he seemed swept away last night, I haven't seen him since. If he felt a fraction of the molten lava coursing through my veins at the barest hint of a kiss, he'd have been breaking my door down the moment he returned from his night out with Archer.

I tossed and turned for hours, listening for the sign of him returning from Wine Town or wherever else Archer took him. The last time I remember looking at the clock, it was after two and I was pretty certain he hadn't come back yet.

Eventually, I drifted off to sleep, and when I woke up to head to yoga this morning, the cottage was silent.

"I…don't know if I want to anymore."

She takes me by the shoulders and turns me to face her. "Why not?"

"It's hard to explain." How can I explain it to her when I haven't thought it through myself?

"Try. Talk it through."

"It's been…a while since I've been with a guy, and it's because it started feeling empty when no emotions were involved. And now I'm feeling all these things, and it scares the hell out of me because what if I'm wrong about him? What if he just has the makings of a fling, and I get attached?"

She smiles at me and strokes my hair. I've never felt more like a little sister. Or a puppy.

"You might get attached. It might end. You might get your heart stomped. Anything could happen. But I can tell you one thing for sure—nothing will happen if you run away and don't at least see what it could be. Don't let your fear keep you from experiencing something great."

We're standing on a rustic wood deck under the shade of an ancient live oak tree, but we could just as easily be sitting in Beatrix's bedroom, where I used to camp out whenever I had a tough choice to make. To her credit, she never chased me out.

She'd pull her drapes closed, and we'd sit on her pink bedspread, and she'd hand me her favorite white fuzzy pillow to hug while I poured out whatever small thing was troubling me— a bad grade, a guy who asked me out and then ignored me for a week straight, a friend who dated the guy who'd asked me out and then ignored me. Trix was there for all of it at a time when my parents weren't.

Our dad was busy building Buttercup Hill into his personal wine empire, and our mother had divorced him and moved to the East Coast. Talking to her on the phone wasn't the same as crawling onto that pink bedspread and pouring out my heart to a sister who always told me she knew exactly how I felt because she'd been there. Whether that was true didn't matter—I secretly suspected that my perfect older sister had never been dumped by a guy or double-crossed by a friend. She'd certainly never gotten a bad grade. But she was always there for me.

Just like today.

"So…what? You think I should gamble on a guy who already told me he doesn't do relationships? How is that going to lead to 'experiencing something great?'"

"Wait, he said that?" Beatrix looks from me to where Colin

stands with Archer and Jax talking about wine. Archer holds a glass of pinot noir up to the light, and I can tell he's saying something about the grapes. He's always talking about grapes now that he's taken over the winemaking part of the business.

I don't look at Archer long, not when my eyes are pulled toward Colin, standing there in a gray Henley that shows off his bicep, which manages to flex just from holding a glass of wine. The sunlight kisses his shoulders like he's an aphrodisiac for light itself.

When I dare sneak a look at his face, cheekbones slicing the air, lips parted the way they were last night, I see darkness in the blue that mirrors exactly the way I feel—the way I wish I didn't feel because it's dangerous for my well-being.

But I can't fight it.

He stares at me unabashedly, and I feel stripped down to my panties. It's a struggle to inhale.

Archer says something that gets Colin's attention, and he's forced to look away. When I do the same, I find Beatrix staring at me.

I smile at her like she's discovered my guilty secret, and she simply nods.

"Yeah. Take the gamble. You have no damn choice."

CHAPTER
Fifteen

PJ

Dash makes a mean street taco. We've eaten three platters of them, slathered with salsa and guacamole and dusted with shredded cheese.

Most of the wine is gone.

I've survived the evening without my insides imploding by sitting as far away from Colin as possible. He sits at one end of the picnic dining table in the middle of the deck. I've planted myself at the other end.

Beatrix gets up and clears away some of the dishes, and Colin follows Dash into the kitchen to help him with dessert while Fiona paints Archer's nails. He grits his teeth and keeps looking around as though he wants to make sure we're the only ones witnessing his makeover.

"No one here to save you," Jackson says, delighted with the pumpkin color Fiona's chosen for Archer. "It's a good look."

Archer grimaces and mouths, "Fuck off," to Jackson, who goes into the kitchen. I'm so immersed in their mini-drama that I don't notice Colin carry the brownie plate out until he drops it on the table and slides onto the bench next to me.

"I heard you made these." His voice is quiet like we're sharing a secret.

"You heard right."

I sit frozen, afraid that if I move a muscle, I'll end up sliding onto his lap and licking his neck.

"What's with the S-shaped tray? It was murder getting them out and onto the plate."

I shoot him a side-eye. "Actual death occurred?"

"Well, not exactly."

"There's a trick. I was going to do it myself, but I got distract-ed." Distracted by not wanting to follow him into the kitchen and lick his neck.

He leans in closer. "What's the trick?" His words are a caress across my cheek. Goose bumps roll over my skin, and I hope his voice drowns out the sound of my sigh. I glance around to see if any of my siblings notice what I feel sure is my pre-orgasm face, but they're all busy doing various dinner prep activities.

Blinking myself back to semi-consciousness, I try to recall the answer to his question. "Um, the pan has a flexion to it. You twist, and they spring free."

"Flexion. Twisting. Got it." He smirks like I've just proposi-tioned him. Maybe to a physicist, I've done it without realizing it.

"Anyway, I hope you like the end pieces. That's the whole point of that pan. My family has kind of a thing for the edges."

He inhales, eyes locking on mine. "Actually, I'm more of a fan of the soft center."

It's not just me, right? Brownies as innuendo?

My skin is so hot that I wish I had on another layer just so I could take it off. While I'm considering that, Colin's hand slides over my thigh and rests there. I almost jump out of my skin, surprised and turned on at the same time. His hand barely moves, and my skin dissolves beneath the fabric of my dress.

"I...um..."

It's pointless to try to form words.

"Yes?" The smirk hasn't left his face. He fully sees how he's affecting me, and instead of removing his hand, he inches it higher up my thigh.

"Is this…are we doing…this? Here?"

He nods. Slowly.

His hand moves down toward my knee, and every part of me wills him not to remove it. Maybe this is a friendly gesture, except the playful glint in his eyes tells me he knows exactly what he's doing. Right here. With my four siblings on all sides.

"I'm doing *this*." His hand drifts higher, and my core clenches. "Unless you don't like it."

I shake my head. Then I nod. I'm like a bobblehead with no sense of direction.

"I like it," I whisper, looking around to see if anyone notices how close Colin is sitting. Beatrix and Dash are still in the kitchen, and Fiona is holding court with the other adults, so they're distracted. Archer glowers at his orange fingernails while he talks on the phone, which keeps him busy for the moment.

Making a mental note to get my niece a dozen new bottles of nail polish, I silently thank her for keeping everyone busy enough so I can have this moment.

That's all it is, right? A stolen moment. A moment of crazy flirtation. A momentary lapse of reason because Colin can't possibly be trying to feel me up on the patio of my brother's house with everyone right here.

Or maybe he can be. And maybe that's exactly what I want.

"Good," he says, his head tipped low so I'm the only one who can hear him. "Because I haven't been able to stop thinking about you for days. And I think I've done a pretty damn good job of resisting you, but I can't do it anymore."

I've stopped breathing. I force in a whiff of air just in order to stay alive.

"Okay." I sound like I'm agreeing to a chess rematch. "So stop resisting."

Feeling emboldened, I move my hand to his thigh, muscular and hard the way I imagined it would feel. His quad muscle flinches, and he inhales a slow breath as though calibrating his response.

And yet…as much as I desperately want him, I don't want just a hookup. A week ago, I felt differently, but now that I've gotten to know Colin, I want something else from him, something he may not be able to give me. But I wouldn't be true to myself if I didn't ask.

"I know this may sound crazy since I've been trying to jump you for a week, but I'd really like to take this slow. I don't just want a hookup," I tell Colin.

I half-expect him to growl in frustration, but he sighs. Maybe that's the same thing.

"I swear, I'm not trying to be a cock tease—"

He stops me with a finger over my lips. "That's not how I see you at all."

I meet his gaze, all molten and dreamy. "You sure?"

Nodding slowly, he winds a loose wave of my wayward hair around his finger and tucks it behind my ear. I don't bother to look around to see if anyone is watching us. I feel like we're safely sealed in a bubble, protected from the world. Even if it isn't true, it feels good to believe it is.

"I see you as gorgeous, smart, and capable of anything. You're so fucking sexy, and I want you any way I can have you, but slow is what I have in mind, Junebug…" He lets the nickname linger on his tongue, and instead of sounding like a teasing name for a friend's little sister, it sounds as hot as sin. I imagine it hissing from his mouth while he comes. And a jolt of fire hits my core.

I nod. "Good."

It seems like he's having trouble pulling air into his lungs.

I like seeing the tiny cracks in the armor of such a strong, brilliant man. I like causing them to break open.

"Can we make an excuse and leave?" he asks, eyes heating at the suggestion.

Oh, how I wish we could. Never have I been more annoyed by the ritual of dinner followed by my brownies followed by game night than I am at this moment.

"I want to…but I don't think we can. Not before game night." I blink and shake my head at the pure unfairness of it.

"Game night? What the hell's that?"

"Game night is when we all play Pictionary or charades. And you need to put a dollar in the swear jar," Fiona says, delighted at catching Colin with his guard down. His hand pulls back from my thigh, and he widens the distance between us. Slowly, reluctantly, I slide my hand from his leg and leave it in the narrow space between us on the bench.

Fiona didn't seem to notice our hands, so I exhale a small breath of relief. "Ruby, did you start hide-and-seek without me?" she yells, running back toward her dad in the vineyard.

Colin puts both hands on the picnic table and blinks himself back to reality. The hungry look leaves his face and is replaced by concern. "Someone should've warned me. I don't really draw."

"You don't?"

"Not unless it requires arrows and launch trajectories."

"Have you been banned from other drawings?"

"Yeah. I'm terrible at it. If I draw a picture of an asteroid, it might look like a potato."

"I like that you're worried you'll be asked to draw an asteroid."

His lips quiver, fighting a smile. "Wise. Ass."

"I really think you can do this. Just give it your best." I watch his expression morph from confident to something else. His mouth pulls down at the corner, and his eyes narrow.

"That might not end well."

"If you don't know you're good at something, you don't like to try it?" It's fun to rib him. It gives me a tiny bit of control while my cheeks have betrayed how much I like having his hand on my leg. I kind of love how he's brilliant in so many ways but uncomfortable about drawing a doodle.

"Maybe. A bit," he admits. His hand crawls higher on my thigh. I swallow hard. He watches me and grins, taking back control in an instant.

I exhale a shaky breath. "I have an idea. Come with me." I extract myself from the picnic bench at the table and tip my head toward the kitchen. Without turning around, I feel Colin behind me like a magnetic force field.

Bursting through the kitchen door, I point a finger at Dash. "Hey, did you all really invite a guest here and not give him a tour of the orchard out back?" My voice is an accusing whine, one I perfected as a kid but rarely use now. It's a particular youngest child pitch that cuts through the noise in a room and demands attention. I got a lot of mileage out of being bratty and loud back when it was the only way to get anyone's attention.

All faces turn toward me. "I didn't think he wanted a tour of the orchard." Dash grumbles like it goes without saying that no one would want to see rows of Pink Lady and Honeycrisp apples.

"He's never been here. He should see it," I gripe, making a big show of rolling my eyes. "You all are terrible hosts."

"Drama queen much?" Dash grumbles.

"Whatever." I'm milking all the old perceptions of me that will make this little charade land.

"Do you *want* to see the orchard?" Jackson asks, skeptical.

"I, um…" Colin looks from Jackson to me, unsure what I'm going on about. "Sure."

I shake my head dramatically. "Seriously, you're terrible. I'll take him out there before Pictionary, just so he can see the fruit before the sun goes down. Back in a few." I indicate Colin should follow me out. "Sheesh," I mutter for one extra dose of realism.

When we get outside, I steer him in the opposite direction of where Ruby and Archer are playing with Fiona.

"Are you going to explain that?" Colin trails behind me because I'm walking faster than usual.

"We've got some nice apples. Thought you should see them," I call back to him.

"I'm looking at some nice apples right here." He catches up, runs a hand down my back, and gives my ass a squeeze. "But that's not what I meant. What was the drama queen bit?"

Does he really want to talk about this now?

"My siblings assume I'm a whiny pain in the butt, so I just worked that angle a little bit to get you alone."

I stop moving and turn around, disinterested in muddling the moment with any more conversation. We're far enough away from the house now to give us some privacy. The hunger in my eyes leaves no room for interpretation. I let my gaze move from the tight pull of his shirt over his pecs to the ripple of his abs, then lower, where I can only imagine the tight V of muscle that leads down, down…

Colin's lips are on mine before I can complete the thought, and any other musings are wiped clean from my brain. All I feel is him.

The closeness of his body.

The deeply masculine scent of him, all woodsy soap and leather.

The feel of his soft lips, which I've been staring at for days. They taste better than I imagined, and all I can think of is *more*. I want so much more than a single kiss.

But that's all I can let myself have right now.

Colin wraps an arm around my waist and pulls me against him. He's already hard and I feel him right at my core, which aches for exactly this.

Our kiss deepens. Tongues meeting and swirling. Breaths growing ragged.

Blurring the line between where I end and he begins.

I want to erase it completely.

Colin slides his hand into my hair and cups the back of my head, holding me against his lips as he trails a line of hungry kisses along my cheek and down to my neck. His tongue circles against my skin there, and I hear myself moan.

It brings me back to reality.

We aren't very far from Dash's house, and I have no idea where Fiona may be hiding. The last thing I want to do is make out in front of a seven-year-old.

"Maybe we should get back." I say the words, silently begging him to disagree with me. To push me up against a tree and show me what else he can do with that magical tongue.

"Is this really happening?" My grumpy brother's voice pulls me back to reality like a jackhammer on concrete.

Ruby and Archer climb the steps from the vineyard to the deck, and from their blank expressions, it's clear they didn't see anything. Jackson comes out to the balcony and grumbles loudly, "Yeah, if we're playing, let's get to it already. This one has a bedtime."

"Oh, Daddy. You can bend the rules. Please?"

My brother is putty in his daughter's hands, and I watch the smile drift over his face as he agrees to her demands.

"Fine. One hour."

I steal a look at Colin, who somehow appears fresh and composed, like he's just been for a nice walk in the orchard. It must help him in business negotiations.

"Sounds like it's on." I hope my flushed face doesn't betray anything.

Beatrix raises her eyebrows when she looks my way, but then she turns toward the kitchen.

"Daddy, I don't need a bedtime. I'm not tired."

"That may be, but if you're in bed before eight, I bet Ruby will read you an extra story."

Fiona turns to Ruby, who nods. "It's a deal."

Beatrix rolls an easel with a large pad of paper onto the deck. She juggles a handful of pens and a box of Pictionary words.

Dash follows her out with another open bottle of white wine and a pitcher of water. "Okay people, be prepared to get trounced."

"Ha. You might want to save your trash-talking since we already know you can't draw." Beatrix, the only one of us with any artistic skill at all, bumps her hip into Dash, sending him off balance.

"I can draw." He sounds less convincing, but my youngest brother hardly lacks for confidence. Ask any woman he's ever dated. And there are many.

Everyone drops onto the picnic table bench or into the chairs that surround a firepit on the deck. Dash turns the gas on, and orange flames dance up through the piled volcanic stones.

Colin takes a seat in one of the Adirondacks with an empty chair next to it, and his eyes dart to mine. I shake my head and take a seat on the bench. His mere proximity sends fire through my veins, and there's no way I can play that off in front of my siblings.

Dash pulls the first card and tells us the rules of the game. He starts drawing something that looks like a baseball bat. The guesses start flying. "Casey at the Bat." "Batman." "Bad News Bears."

"No. You're not looking at it right," Dash grumps, drawing tiny circles around the bat.

"Spaceballs?" Colin guesses.

"Yes! Thank you! This is why we need people outside the damn family at these things."

Jackson rolls his eyes. "I've never even heard of that movie."

"Mel Brooks. It's a classic," Colin says, somehow not sounding like he's bragging that he got it right.

Dash walks over and high-fives Colin. "Damn straight it is." He hands over the blue marker he used to draw it and rips the page from the easel, revealing a clean sheet.

Colin looks down at the marker in his hand as though he's never seen a pen before and has no idea what it does.

"You're next," Dash says helpfully. He holds out the box of cards, but Colin looks like he's glued to his chair.

"C'mon, man. You're up." Archer's encouragement sounds like a dare.

Expression grim, Colin pushes his body from the slanted seat of the chair like a man headed for an execution rather than a friendly game. He really doesn't like to do things if he doesn't know he's good at them. It softens his otherwise brilliant capability in nearly everything and makes me like him even more. I feel a warm twinge of protectiveness over him. But I also want to see what he'll draw.

Colin picks a card from the deck and studies it, his face stoic. He tips his head to Beatrix to start the timer and puts the blue marker against the white sheet. For a second, he does nothing. Then he sweeps a long motion across the page and draws what looks like a wing. Then he draws an arrow pointing on top of it. The guesses start flying. "On Wings of Eagles," Beatrix guesses.

Jackson points at the board. "Wingman."

He doesn't react, just stares calmly at the page, thinking. Then he draws a small image of what looks like a tall triangle divided in two with twigs sticking out at the bottom on opposite sides. The guesses keep coming, and Colin stands there, shaking his head at each one.

"What the hell is that?" Archer grumbles.

"Swear jar!" Fiona's delight at catching grownups makes it worth all the money we put in her jar.

Colin clasps his hands in front of him and waits for us to guess. No attempts to fix the drawing or embellish it. I stare at the tall triangle, which could be anything from an odd skyscraper to a rocket ship. He does spend a lot of time thinking about space, after all, but I can't imagine what movie title relates to a rocket and a wing. "Rocketman?" I suggest weakly. Colin looks at me and shakes his head.

"How could it possibly be that?" Beatrix laughs.

"Hey, she didn't criticize your guesses." My eyes shoot to Colin's, shocked that he just defended me in front of my family. No one else seems to notice.

The timer runs out to a chorus of "What is that?" and "You're kidding me."

Then Fiona points at the tall triangle and says, "It looks like hands. Like the emoji."

Colin's face cracks into a wide grin, and he nods. "That's what it's supposed to be."

We all look again, and I think about which emoji she means, realizing it's the hands clasped in prayer or thankfulness. "On a Wing and a Prayer," I murmur, realizing exactly what he's drawn and how right it looks now that my niece has pointed out the obvious.

"Seems like Fiona should go next," Colin says, holding up the marker in front of Fiona's delighted face.

She grabs the pen and hustles over to the pile of cards.

I watch her stare at the sky as she works out what to draw, all seriousness in her doe eyes. It's why I don't notice Colin slide onto the bench next to me. Instead, I *feel* him.

His presence beside me ignites a firestorm in my veins and takes me right back to where we were earlier. If he kisses me right now in front of my family, I don't think I'll have the wherewithal to pull away.

"I'm sorry we got interrupted." His breath feathers over the shell of my ear with the rough growl of his voice.

"Me too," I say quietly, sneaking my hand closer to his and looking to see if anyone notices. Everyone is focused on Fiona, who drew a curled line she denies is a snail.

"But when I get you back to your house, I'm going to pick up where we left off. I'm going slower than slow, and it's going to last all night," he whispers.

My breath hitches, and a chill races over my skin. "Two more rounds, then let's go."

"Together?"

"Yes. We're going to the same place. You'll look like a stand-up guy if you're walking me home, even if we all know there's nothing dangerous on the way."

"Abso-fucking-lutely."

Two more Pictionary rounds. The longest two of my life.

CHAPTER
Sixteen

COLIN

Archer insists on driving us back to the cottage and PJ's house, even though I insist that we're fine walking.

He holds up a hand. "I haven't had a drop to drink all night. Don't worry." I don't bother to explain that I'm not concerned about him getting behind the wheel. I'm concerned about him delaying my chance to be alone with his sister.

Archer furrows his brow the way he's done since I arrived, and I can tell his mind has already gone back to winery business. It's why we've been friends for so long—we operate the same way. Only my mind is solely on PJ, and I'm grateful that he seems too distracted to notice.

"It'll be faster," PJ says quietly, as though it's all about convenience.

Nodding, I slip her fingers between mine as Archer goes to the driver's side and hops into the SUV. A part of me wants to slide into the back seat and haul her across my lap. To hell with what Archer thinks. It's none of his damn business.

Only out of consideration for how PJ might feel do I let go of her hand when her eyes meet mine, reluctant but resigned to keeping her distance. She gets in the back, and I take the passenger seat. I let my hand hang down next to the door and move it a few inches backward until PJ's soft fingers graze my hand. She wraps her palm around mine as she slumps against the door for the five-minute drive.

Archer rambles on about a wine industry party next weekend where he wants to introduce me to a few locals. "I promise, none of them will give two shits about why you're slumming it here in Napa, and besides, your media ban will be just about over by then."

"Sure. Sounds good." I'm not even sure what I'm agreeing to, so focused on how many more breaths I'll have to take before we arrive at PJ's door.

Archer pauses at a corner, and I remember him telling me there's a long and a short route to the cottage. So help me, if the guy decides to take the scenic route, I might murder him.

He hesitates for a moment, then turns right, which will get us to my door in under two minutes from here. I exhale a sigh of relief, and PJ squeezes my hand.

I've known Archer for half my life, and I've never seen him drive this slowly. It's like he's trying to torture me, even if he doesn't know it. Finally, he makes the turn that takes us to the small parking area behind PJ's house. His car idles while he pops the locks to let us out.

"Okay, guys. Sleep well."

We tell him to do the same, slam the car doors, and walk toward the cottage as Archer's truck pulls out of the gravel lot. Both of us stand frozen, listening for signs he's turning around— God forbid, he forgot to tell us something. But after a few seconds, only silence hangs in the air.

A few crickets chirp in the bushes surrounding PJ's house. They're quaint and bucolic, but they do nothing to settle my nerves. When I turn to look at PJ, her expression mirrors how I feel—hesitant, desperate, a little disbelieving, and dripping with desire.

I only have one thought, and it's consumed by her—how to get closer, how to satisfy this need I have. I want to devour her.

But I promised to go slow, and goddammit, I will go slow if it kills me.

Especially when she looks like every dream I've ever had standing in the sliver of moonlight. Soft beams of pale yellow kiss her face. And now it's my turn.

"If I could go back in time…this is how last night would have gone…" I reach for her cheek and cup it in my hand. I can feel her pulse under the soft skin. It's a steady hammer, while mine is a pounding bass drum.

"If I could go back in time, I'd have a hit taken out on my brother." Her annoyance shows on her face.

I laugh. After a moment, she does too. I love that she doesn't take herself that seriously.

My lips brush against hers, and she sighs into my mouth. I tip her chin up so I can get a better angle and melt into the pillowy soft-ness of her lips. She cups the back of my neck, and I feel her tremble.

It's impossible to slow myself down. Wrapping a hand around her rib cage, I pull her toward me until our bodies are flush against each other. She sighs louder as I deepen the kiss. Her hips press into mine, and it's all I can do not to grind down hard, but I'm trying to be a gentleman here.

It's like trying to control a wild horse that wants to gallop using a string of dental floss. It fights every instinct I have to go slowly when I want to flip her around and take her against her front door, hard and fast.

Our kisses deepen, tongues tangling, hands roaming. Zero to a hundred in four seconds flat. The space between us dissolves, but I can't get close enough. My desire for her ratcheting up with each sweep of her tongue across mine. Each time she bites down on my lower lip, a twinge of lust shoots straight to my dick.

I'm about to lift her up and carry her into the cottage when she kisses me softly, more hesitantly. Pulling back, she looks conflicted.

Maybe she doesn't want this after all. I've assumed we're on the same page, but science has taught me never to assume.

"Hi," she says, breathless.

"Hi." The world around us spins. Her eyes lock on mine. "You okay?"

"Very okay."

"Okay, good."

She closes her eyes and tips her face up to mine once more. The words are just a breath on her lips as she says them. "I'm just having a hard time going slowly. I know what you said, but—"

It's all the permission I need to do everything I've been dreaming about for days.

"Fuck, Junebug, we have all night to go slow. I want you hard and fast, and I don't want to wait."

Lifting her up, I angle her hips against me, and she wraps her legs around my waist. She leans forward, and our lips meet again —passionate, hungry. No hesitation.

I push her against her front door and let my hands trail down her legs and back again, feeling every curve of her thighs under the thin fabric of her dress, desperate to strip it off.

"Where's your key?" I ask against her lips.

She fishes around in her pocket and places it in my palm. I fumble it into the lock with one eye open, unwilling to break the kiss for anything.

The door springs open, and we tumble inside, me holding her hard against my body and her burying her face in my neck. It's dark in the room, but I've been in her house enough times to know my way around a little, so I move in the direction I think will take us to her bedroom.

"Yeah, down this hall," she purrs against my ear while my insides are consumed by lust. Careful not to bump her against any walls, I make my way to the bedroom, where a bright white blanket catches the moonlight through a window.

Lowering PJ onto the bed, I survey her body from head to toe, salivating over which part of her I want first. My brain fires on all cylinders, and I feel momentarily lost in the choices. And I plan to devour it all.

"So fucking sexy…" I pull off each of her shoes and toe off my own.

She looks at me with hazy eyes, and I'm overwhelmed by how much I want her. "So. Fucking. Sexy."

I crawl up her body until I reach the soft skin of her neck. She purrs with approval as I kiss a trail down the curve of her neck to her shoulder.

Pushing her dress up over her hips, I slip my hands underneath. I caress the warm skin of her stomach and run a finger over the outline of her bra. Her nipples go hard under my touch, and my cock responds in kind.

"Keep talking, hot scientist." She lifted the hem of my shirt, and I yank it over my head. Her hands dance along my ribcage and settle on my pecs. Man, I love the feel of her hands on my body. I've imagined it so many times when I was in the shower in the cottage across the way, taking myself in hand when I wished it was her.

Arching herself up from the bed, she kisses a trail down the center of my chest and licks each one of my abs. Delicate and hungry at the same time.

The groan that's been caught in my throat all night tells her everything about how it feels.

"I want to bury my face between your thighs…" I tell her, peeling her thong over her hips and down her legs.

Her hands are still moving, unbuckling my belt and popping the buttons on my jeans. "I thought I was the one undressing you." Not that I mind this one bit. Having her fingers dancing over my skin makes my breath hitch.

She reaches across to her bedside table and tears open a

condom. I take it from her and roll it down my length, feeling like a high school kid who'll barely last ten seconds.

"You promised me hard and fast, so let's go."

It's all I need to hear. Lowering myself on top of her, I gaze down at the combination of curves and strength that turns me on every time we're together. We go from zero to a hundred in about four seconds. Her dress flying off, tongues melting against hot skin, her hot, sexy curves everywhere.

"I want to fuck you with my tongue. I want to taste every part of you—" I breathe against her neck, needing her to understand that I want to go slow, but I can't. I just fucking can't with her. Not right now.

She cuts me off with a finger pressed against my lips. "Later. I need you inside me. Now."

My cock aches for her. My whole body aches. I want to admire her. I've never been this hard for a woman in my life, and this one is slowly rubbing my length against her soft, wet heat until I feel like I might explode.

I slide slowly inside her, giving her time to get used to my size before I move again. "Mmm," she moans against my lips.

Then she pulls me hard against her and her hips rock up. There's no chance of going slowly now.

"Yes, PJ…"

"Yes," she pants against my neck.

So beautiful, this woman. So damn pretty coming apart beneath me, and I can't stop staring at her.

She's different from anyone I've ever met, and not just because she doesn't give a shit about my bank account. Her radiance comes from within, and her easy, joyous spirit is so genuine that it makes me want to be a better person.

Every time I move, I feel the electric hum under my skin. And as she grinds beneath me, making slow circles and taking me in to the hilt, I become more and more certain of one thing—I won't be able to walk away from PJ Corbett with my heart intact. Now that I'm inside her, I don't ever want to leave.

I hold on as long as I can, reaching down to stroke her clit and get her where I want her to be. "God, Colin..." she cries out, and I'm right with her.

Pumping hard and fast, I feel her hot, tight muscles clenching me, draining every drop as I come hard.

Hard and fast and fucking amazing. And only the beginning.

"That was only a hint of what I want to do with that hot little body of yours." I prop myself on my elbows and gaze down at PJ's flushed face, her lazy smile telling me she's on board.

"Okay." She lets out a long, satisfied exhale. "Now I'm ready for slow."

CHAPTER
Seventeen

Colin doesn't need to convince me to stick around for round two. Not when the first orgasm I've had in years blew my damn mind.

Blew. My. Mind.

And then he takes me to places I've never imagined. He covers my mouth with his, gently kissing me like we have a week just for this. He tips my chin to the side and angles his mouth to deepen the kiss.

I nip at his bottom lip and feel a wave of heat roll across my skin when he groans.

He kisses the curve of my jaw, stopping every few seconds to take a gentle bite and soothe it with his tongue. I sigh and let my eyes drift shut, imagining how it will feel to have his lips and tongue in other places.

And I want him in all of those places.

I'm still reeling from our first round, still half-dizzy and barely coherent, when Colin slides down my body, licking my stomach and leaving a trail of kisses over the swell of my hip before flipping me over and centering himself beneath my legs.

"Sit on my face, sweetheart."

I suck in a breath when I feel his tongue run along the sensitive skin of my inner thigh.

*He's not going to…*My eyes go wide. "Are you sure?"

He tips his head up and meets my gaze, a wolfish gleam in his eyes. "Yes, Junebug. I'm more than sure. Unless you don't like it. Then you need to tell me."

"It's just…I've never…"

His eyes widen briefly before a sexy smirk washes over his face. "Well, then you're going to right now."

I'm afraid I'll crush him. Or suffocate him. But I'm also really curious about how it will feel to ride him this way. My curiosity—and downright hunger for him—wins over.

"Okay." The word comes out as breathless and desperate as I feel.

"Good."

So, so good.

Yes, in my few relationships before now, men have gone down on me. But I never felt like they were really into it. And they definitely weren't into it after they'd already come inside me. And they definitely didn't want me to sit on them.

But Colin? He is *into* it.

His hands splay across my hips, and he uses only his tongue to ease into my center. Immediately, a sigh rolls out of me, and I wrap my hand around a pile of blankets.

He's decadently slow and thorough with his tongue, and each stroke brings me higher until I'm moaning his name and losing focus.

"That's my girl," he says between swipes of his tongue.

"God, that feels amazing…" I don't know what I'm saying. I'm just *feeling*. Everything.

He sucks my clit into his mouth. "Colin, my *god*…"

"More. Come for me, Junebug." How is his voice saying that ridiculous nickname so hot and sexy? I decide it's the best nickname in the world. Every time he says it, it will bring me back to this moment.

And then I stop thinking because his fingers ease inside me, and he finds the perfect spot. And I mean the perfect spot. My back arches as he hits the trifecta with his tongue circling my clit and his other hand working my nipple.

"Holy shit, are you for real?" The words tumble out, and I can't even feel self-conscious about them anymore. I don't care if I sound like the world's most orgasm-drunk groupie if he'll just stay exactly where he is.

"Yes. I'm for real, and I'm not stopping until you come again."

He takes me higher, up to a place where light and colors cloud my vision, and then I'm falling, cresting the peak.

I grab his hair and hold on while my body rides out the best orgasm of my life. Eyes still closed, I try to speak, but all that comes out is, "Mmm."

Colin rolls me to the side and moves slowly up my body, planting kisses on every curve of my waist and swell of each breast. My nipples were already hard, but he licks them into tight peaks until they ache with delicious pain.

Then he's inside me again, moving at a languid, seductive pace. "You're a goddamn drug, PJ. I can't get enough."

My garbled half agreement is all I can come up with because *he* is a drug, and I'm already craving days and weeks of him.

I wrap my legs around him, and he groans, still moving slowly, deliberately. And like the orgasm-drunk groupie I apparently am, my body responds to every shift in his movement.

"God, PJ…"

"I know. It's…I can't even…"

He laughs at my inability to articulate a thought, but soon he's grunting one-syllable nonsense and moaning my name.

I come undone beneath him in waves as he's biting out a curse.

The two of us lie there, chests heaving, bodies glazed with sweat, until our breathing starts to slow.

Completely spent, I lie with my head on the pillow as Colin rolls to my side and tips my chin up to kiss me. All I can think about is a way to make tonight even better.

"Hey," I say, staring into Colin's eyes. "Would you be up for a grilled cheese sandwich?"

This could go one of two ways—Colin could think my post-sex snack idea is ridiculous, and I'd have to accept that we have our differences. Or he could think I'm a genius, and I'll have another reason to fall for the guy.

He laughs, and I feel grateful—and a little nervous—that he's chosen door number two.

———

Being the youngest kid, I learned to make easy dinners for myself when my siblings were at sports practices or out with friends, and I was left hanging with only our nanny for company. Grilled cheese has always been a personal favorite, and I see no reason to stop eating it just because I'm an adult.

Fortunately, Colin seems to like my version, which features shredded cheese on the outside of the bread, fried in butter. Sitting on a stool in my kitchen in only boxers, he is in the middle of eating his second one.

"So you're a hot scientist with a brilliant mind and a sinfully gorgeous face. How are you not dating a model or something? And don't tell me that tall, attractive women aren't your type because then I'll know you're lying."

I'd been wondering about this since the day we met, and none of the articles I'd scrounged up about his personal life told me anything. I wasn't about to ask my brother.

"They're not."

I hold a scolding finger up. "Stop. I said not to lie."

"I'm not lying. I never thought I had a type." He leans back and looks me over from head to toe. The heat of his gaze spills over every part of me, setting me on fire. How does he do that with just a look?

Colin's voice is a lust-charged growl. "But now, I'd have to say that curvy, smart-mouthed, unspeakably sexy women are my type." He dips his head toward mine as though he needs to tell me a secret no one else can hear. Only there's no one anywhere near us. "And you just blew that type out of the water because I've never seen anyone sexier."

I'm not expecting the compliment, and it makes me blush. I swear, I spend most of my time around Colin sporting a shade of red on my face that's somewhere between a ripe strawberry and a beet.

"Okay, um…" I try to feign a bit of chill, but I have none. He watches the scarlet crawl across my face, and a wicked smile forms as I open my mouth and close it again because I'm tongue-tied.

He reaches over, cups my cheek in his hand, and plants the softest kiss on my lips. "I don't know what other sinful scientists do, and I don't really care. You are my type, and I want to be with you."

"Well, lucky me, being here right when you decide to hide out from your life."

"No. Lucky me." His gaze is soft.

"So explain it to me. What is your life like exactly?"

I don't mean to sound so naive. My family has made a good living in the wine business, but most of the family wealth is reinvested back into the company.

"Probably not all that different from yours." He stares out at the acres of vineyards I look at each day, and the muscles in his face relax. I've seen it happen to hundreds of people who come to spend the afternoon at the vineyard. Something about being under a cloudless sky in the fresh air and breathing in the scent of grapes ripening on vines extracts every ounce of stress like a French press coffee maker. All that is left is gratitude for the setting.

"Actually, it's really fucking different," he amends. "First of all, I stare at the white walls of an office building all day. This—this is magical."

"It is. I never take it for granted. When I was in college, I had jobs around campus at food service places, and I hated it. Not the work itself, but the lack of windows that could open."

"Exactly. That's the problem with where I work." He looks off into the distance as though picturing it.

I cock my head and study him. "This may be a dumb question, but since you're the boss and all, why don't you set up shop in a place you like? Aren't there astrophysics labs with windows that open?"

He blinks a few times in that way I've come to understand as how he formulates thoughts before speaking them aloud. "There are some limitations with the kind of work we do. It lends itself to the basic Silicon Valley model of an open-plan workplace with modular desks that move around. A lot of natural light comes in the windows of the bigger workspace, but our labs can't have windows because of the work we do." He moves his hands in the shape of a cube as though his office is just that size. Somehow, based on how he downplays everything else about himself, I get the feeling his office is rather large.

"A lab, like one telescope and a desk?" I turn my face up to his innocently.

The corner of his mouth tips up. "Are you giving me shit about my lab?"

I mimic the cube shape he made a minute ago. "If *this* is really the size of four football fields, then yes."

He says nothing, but the flush across the back of his neck tells me it may even be the size of six football fields. I love catching him in these moments of embarrassment about his success, mainly because he downplays everything about his hot nerd brain all the time.

"Do you want to see it?"

"See what?"

"My lab."

A laugh bursts from me, and I pull mocking depth into my voice. *"Hey baby, want to come see my lab?* Is that how you get all the hot chicks?"

Somehow, he manages to turn his momentary embarrassment into a hot guy smirk, and I feel it in my bones. I like this man and can't find the tools to convince myself I don't.

I'm in trouble, but I push that thought away for now.

"Not *all* of them. Not yet." His smile is a weapon, and I can already see I won't make it out alive. "Let's do it. Let's take a little test drive."

"In your car?"

His lips quirk to the side. "No. Of my life. Come back to the city with me for a day, and I'll show you what I do for fun."

COLIN

"So you're basically a reluctant billionaire," PJ says when she catches me cringing at the helicopter that's arrived to fly us down to Silicon Valley for our day in the city.

"I feel like that makes me sound like an asshole."

"Well, let me give you a little quiz, and we'll see. A, do you give money to charity?"

"Yes, I have a charitable foundation set up with a full-time staff in charge of reading grant proposals."

"So you're using your money to help other people."

Squinting, I tilt my head at her, trying to read what she's saying. "Yeah...that's generally what charitable giving is all about."

"Sure, of course. Unless you're funding planet-destroying technology or giving all your money to con artists."

"Ah, that kind of 'philanthropy.' No, that's not what the foundation is about. But thanks for trying to keep me on the straight and narrow."

"I'm a giver."

The helicopter rotors whip around, sending ripples of wind scuttling through the grapevines. I catch PJ looking at her peaceful daily backdrop stirred up and marred by the trappings of my world, and I hate the idea of what she sees.

I signal to the pilot, who flips open the passenger door, and I hurry PJ along. We dash across the grassy field, and I step onto the step and into the helicopter. Then I bend down and extend my hand to help her inside.

Holding my breath, I watch PJ take in the helicopter's interior. From the way her eyes go wide, I can see she was expecting something more like a barebones news rig. This one has polished wood interior, plush gray carpet, seats wrapped in butter-soft white leather, and a separate cabin where the pilot sits.

Instead of making a crack about the luxe conditions, PJ shrugs and rolls her eyes. "I flew in one of these yesterday. Whatevs."

Our pilot gives us headsets, which blunt the noise of the rotors and allow us to talk to each other, but I'm more concerned with hurrying things along.

I lean over to secure PJ's headset and signal to the pilot to lift us into the air. The faster we get out of here, the less damage to the idyllic scene around us, which I've been disrupting for a week and a half with my presence.

Flipping the switch on the headsets, I tune us to a channel only we can hear, knowing the pilot is probably listening to air traffic control dispatches on his channel. If he needs to communicate anything, he'll give me a wave through the glass, and I'll switch back to his channel. It's a protocol I established the first time I rode in one of these so I could use the time in the air to conduct business. I needed to be certain that any important conversations weren't overheard.

Hearing PJ talk about information leaks proved why my paranoid instincts were right. People are always listening, and there's no guaranteeing who can be influenced to share some juicy tidbits with a reporter.

"I feel like such a jerk. Does the wind from the helicopter

damage the grapes?" Surely, Archer would have told me if it was a problem.

She slides closer to me on the seat and talks into the headset. "It's okay. We get high winds out there sometimes. The grapes are hearty."

For the first few minutes of the short flight, we alternate pointing out landmarks as we fly over them—the Vallejo wildlife refuge, the Golden Gate Bridge, the clock tower on the UC Berkeley campus.

I opt against telling PJ just how sexy she looks, sitting primly with her legs crossed on the high-backed seat. I decide not to tell her how desperate I am to slide her legs apart and spend my time between them. But I could show her…

She's looking out the window as we fly over the southern end of San Francisco, right over Oracle Park, where the San Francisco Giants are playing a day game. With my arm wrapped around her shoulders, I pull her closer to me, angling her back so it's resting against my chest.

Sliding my fingers across the warm skin of her bare legs, I gently lift the upper leg off the bottom one so both of her feet are on the floor. When I slide my hand higher on the delicate flesh of one inner thigh, her eyes shoot to mine.

"Relax," I mouth to her, watching her struggle to steady her breathing.

"Here?" she asks, eyes flaming with warning and excitement.

I shake my head slowly and move her so she's leaning against me again. "Not gonna fuck you in the back of a helicopter with the pilot two feet away," I growl into the headset. "But he needs to keep his eyes on the skies, so what he doesn't know won't hurt him…"

My hand moves farther up her thigh, and her body relaxes into mine. A tiny hint of a sigh hits my ears through the headset, and my heartbeat ratchets up in my chest. I want to rock her world. If she's never sat on a man's face, then for damn sure, she's never had an orgasm in a helicopter, and I want to be her fucking first for everything.

I can get awfully far like this, with her seated right next to me, legs parted just a bit. I can probably get her off with a finger or two. The pilot will be none the wiser.

But I want more. When I first looked at stars and planets through a telescope, I didn't see something out of reach. I saw a goal. And I imagined how I could get there.

So I know there's a way to stay out of our pilot's sightlines and give PJ everything I want her to have right now. Up in the sky, hovering over the world.

Leaning forward, I brush her cheek with my lips. I let my tongue draw circles against the soft skin of her neck until I hear a quiet moan. It comes straight into my ears through the clear channel of the headset, and the sound of her pleasure shoots straight to my dick. I don't need to study physics to understand the connection between those straight trajectories.

Edging her legs farther apart, I rub a finger against her core, feeling how wet she already is through her panties. "I know you wore this dress for me with this in mind, didn't you?" I keep my voice low, talking through the headset. The connection is so intimate despite the loud noise just outside our bubble.

She sucks in a breath as I push the flimsy whisp of lace aside. I'm desperate to touch her. "Are you wet because you like the helicopter?" I can't keep my cheeky grin in check, and she elbows me.

"No."

"What's that?"

I slide my finger through her slick folds and watch her eyes drift shut.

"No," she pants.

"Why are you so goddamn wet, Junebug?"

Another sigh. "Because I like you."

I nod, brushing the curve of her neck with my lips and kissing the underside of her jaw. Each time I kiss her, I nudge the headset aside, but it's annoying the shit out of me, so I break off the mouthpiece and fling it to the floor. I can give her all the dirty talk she wants when we get to my office, but right now, I intend to use my mouth to devour her.

Sliding to the floor, I know I'm out of the pilot's line of sight. I've never been more grateful for a private luxury helicopter, and I intend to make good use of the ample floor space in front of PJ's chair. I'm effectively blocking her from view on the chance the pilot looks back. But he won't. He's in charge of flying a billionaire client, and he's not about to jeopardize that by losing focus. Even for a second.

Nor am I. Focus is the one area where I excel, and it's about to serve me very well.

PJ leans back on the seat, her hips swiveled so I can get exactly where I need to be in the small space we have. I reach up with both hands and grip her hips underneath her skirt. Her skin is soft and pliant under my hands, and I dig my fingers in, wanting to possess her in every way I can.

It's different than I've ever been with a woman, wanting to feel her pleasure more than my own, but it's like a drug. Knowing she doesn't want anything from me makes me want to give her everything.

I can't get enough of the little sounds she makes when I touch her, and I'm fucking grateful that the headset was made of cheap plastic so I could break it in half and still have her sounds filtering through my ears.

With two fingers, I slide her lace thong down her legs. Crumpling it into a ball, I stuff it into the hip pocket of my jeans. Maybe I'll give it back to her. Maybe not.

I listen to the sound of her heavier breaths coming through the headset. It fuels me to part her legs a little bit more so I can look at her. All pink and perfect beneath my hands.

I rub her clit with my thumb and feel her body quake. Another swipe, harder this time, and she moans. Again. And again. Her moans fuel me, sending lightning shocks through my body, dead-ending at my dick.

Leaning in, I replace my fingers with my tongue. Rolling over her clit. Feeling new jolts of pleasure each time she feels them.

Sliding a finger inside her, I keep working her over with my tongue. Lapping up every drop.

Her moans turn to cries, and I feel her hips shudder beneath my hand. She clenches around my finger, and I slide a second one inside. So tight, so wet for me.

"I—Colin, I can't—"

"Yes, you can," I say against her flesh, wanting her to lose control, wishing for her to let me be the one to get her there. I could do this every minute of every day just to experience her feeling this good. It's a high I'm never going to achieve, even if I put an astronaut on Mars.

At that moment, I realize how gone for her I am.

I've never put anything above my dreams of exploring the red planet, and it shocks me for a moment to realize I just did. And to realize it doesn't bother me one bit.

I'm also very glad I've done away with the mouthpiece of my headset because otherwise, I just might tell her everything, which would be a giant mistake.

We have an expiration date when I return to work, and it's nearing rapidly.

With my fingers deep inside PJ and my tongue circling her clit, I regain my focus. She grips my shoulder with one hand, and her fingers rake through my hair with the other.

"Colin—"

I inhale her sweet scent and listen intently as she comes undone beneath me. It's the best sound I've ever heard in my life.

———

It doesn't take long before we hover over the landing pad atop the AstroTech building. It's painted with a black and blue bull's-eye, which I happen to know the pilot doesn't need in order to land the helicopter. He expertly lowers the bird onto the roof with barely a bump when we touch down.

A minute later, the rotors begin to slow, and I reach over to unbuckle PJ's seat belt. She still has the same dreamy look plastered across her face, and I take a moment to kiss her back to reality.

"You okay?" I can't erase the smirk from my face at the sounds I'll have forever etched in my brain. Every damn time I ride in this helicopter until the end of my days, I won't be able to unfeel her orgasm.

She nods and kisses me in response. I grab her hand and make my way around to where the pilot exits the copter. He nods at me, his expression stoic and professional. If he has any idea what happened behind his seat, he has the good sense not to try to *bro* me with a wink. Good thing because I'd fire him for it.

When we get inside the elevator that takes us down to the lobby, PJ turns to me, concern lacing her brow. I don't like the look of it, especially compared to the bliss I witnessed for ten minutes over San Mateo.

"What's wrong?" I ask, pulling her close, our hands caught between us. I raise them up so they're over her heart.

She worries her bottom lip with her teeth.

"Penelope June, what's up?"

"Is that, like, your thing?"

"Is what my thing?" I feel like I should know what she's talking about, and not knowing makes me feel dumb in a way I hate.

"You know, what we just did. Do you go down on women in your helicopter? Is that, like, a *thing* for you?"

I can see that laughter is not the response she's expecting because she presses her lips together and tries to back away from me. But I have her where I want her, and I don't intend to let her go.

"You're laughing? Nice." Her brow furrows, and I know I need to turn this around before she gets the wrong idea.

"PJ, relax. No, it's not my *thing*."

She manages to wrench her hand out of my grip and turns enough so that she can cross her arms. I wish I wasn't so turned on by how feisty she gets when she's annoyed because it's making me reluctant to clear up the confusion, and that makes me an asshole.

I'm used to people thinking I'm an asshole, but I don't want to be an asshole to her. Not ever.

"PJ, I swear. That was for you. Only." I quiet my voice and wait for her shoulders to relax. The wheels turn in her head, and I can see she's still calculating something. She doesn't fully believe me.

"How did you time it so well? Are you just some kind of expert on women's bodies, so you know you can get me off in the time it takes to fly here once you've passed the Golden Gate Bridge?"

The wheels clank into place in my brain, but I feel dumb again. This time, for a different reason. I rub a hand over my face, wishing it could have the effect of wiping the slate clean and rolling back time to a few minutes earlier.

"No, that's not what happened up there. It wasn't about calculations or timing or some *thing* I have about women in helicopters. You are the first. And that's because you're the only woman I've ever wanted so badly that I couldn't wait until the damn bird landed to get inside you. And trust me, as far as timing, I just got lucky."

She inhales a deep breath and lets it out slowly. All the muscles in her shoulders and neck unclench, and she drops her arms by her sides.

When the elevator doors open, I reach again for her hand. She looks down when she sees I'm handing back her panties. Her eyes meet mine, and she raises an eyebrow. Bending down to slip them over her feet, she works the scrap of fabric up her legs slowly, lifting her skirt to show me every bit of what she's covering up before dropping it over her hips and folding her body against mine. I exhale a shaky breath and wrap my arm around her shoulders, pulling her close.

This woman.

"Sorry. I didn't mean to go all paranoid on you. It's just…you know I'm…this is new for me. I'm not used to this much…I'm not used to feeling this good."

I have so many things I want to say to that, so much venom for the men who came before me for not giving PJ every damn thing she deserves, in the bedroom and outside of it. But I also realize they did me a favor because I get to do all those things for her. For the first time.

"Well, I hope you're up for getting used to it because I want you to feel this good all the time."

"When I'm with you, I do."

CHAPTER
Nineteen

"We have a noon reservation," Colin says, striding down a quiet hallway that looks untouched except for giant framed photos of telescopes lining the walls. The gray pile carpet crunches beneath my feet, and the air smells like fresh paint.

Holding my hand, Colin shuttles me along at a brisk pace as though we're late for wherever we're going. "Reservation for what?"

"Lunch." He looks at me. "Sorry, I assumed you'd be hungry. Guess I should've asked."

"No, lunch is good. When did you make a reservation?"

He holds up his phone. "The magic of technology. All the cool kids are doing it."

I roll my eyes, but I'm intensely amused. Not by his dorky humor but by how comfortable he seems here. Since we left the elevator, we've walked down several hallways, turning so many times I doubt I could find my way back if I had to. The building is huge and sprawling, but even though it's clean and spartan, it doesn't feel sterile. No idea how he manages to accomplish that, but it's one more quality that's uniquely Colin. One more quality I really like.

"Is this area new? It feels like no one's ever walked on this carpet."

"Yes. We just built this wing for our new labs."

"I'm surprised no one's here on a Tuesday. Didn't you say you work every day?"

"Yes."

"Are you the only one who works here?"

"No. I told everyone not to come in today. We have the place to ourselves."

I'm dumbstruck. "Colin, isn't that, like, millions of dollars in lost productivity?"

He shrugs, and I know he's chilled the fuck out because he actually doesn't seem that concerned. "I'll make it up."

We turn down another hallway that looks a lot like the first one. He pulls open a door and stands back so I can walk inside. "Welcome to my office."

He smiles like a kid staring at every snow cone flavor in the world.

I guess I was expecting—I don't know—four walls, a computer, and a desk? His "office" is a lab containing several enormous telescopes, row upon row of tables with microscopes, computer screens lining the walls, and a glass-walled area that looks like a shower stall.

"What happens in there?" I point at the stall, which is lit by yellow bulbs.

"Clean room conditions in the next room." Colin points at a set of windows separating this lab from another one. "To go in there, you need to gown up. We'll save that for another day."

All I can think is that I want to have sex in the clean room, and I wonder if that makes me a terrible person. It would probably ruin hundreds of millions of dollars of equipment, to say nothing of the research, but my mind goes where it goes. And right now, it's thinking that if Colin blew my mind in the helicopter, there's no telling what he could do in a clean room.

As if he can read my dirty little mind, Colin shakes his head. "Not in there." His eyebrows bounce as he glances around the lab. "But if one of these lab tables suits you, I'm in."

He leans against a clean white lab table and crosses his arms. It's impossible that a man could look this hot standing in a science lab, right?I rein in my horny desires and turn to face him. "Later. Turn me on with some science facts, baby."

He laughs and pulls me in for a kiss.

"You are extremely beautiful. That's a fact."

"Sounds like an opinion."

"Nope. Fact. Because facts exist on their own without needing to be proven."

For the next hour, he tours me around the lab, explaining how everything works. "The telescopes show us where we're headed, but we can simulate the conditions here and see how matter behaves."

"Give me an example."

"The environment on Mars is radically different from what we experience on Earth, but we can recreate the conditions here in the lab and see how atoms, molecules—even plant life—behaves under those conditions."

"So you're basically building a mini-Mars here."

"Basically…" He tilts his head from side to side, considering the veracity. He swallows. "I guess, yeah." His hesitation tells me I've vastly oversimplified his life's work, but the smile lines around his eyes and his boyish grin prove he's okay with that.

"I know I just dumbed it down."

"Not really." He takes my hand and leads me toward a different door from the one where we entered. This time, we're in another hallway, but it's shorter and leads to a set of doors, which Colin opens using his phone. "Come. We'll head back here at night and look through the telescopes, but I need to feed you."

The doors open to an empty indoor parking lot, save for one

shiny black Porsche sitting in a prime spot. It beeps when Colin unlocks it and guides me to the passenger side. Opening the door, he plants a kiss on my lips, which turns into a longer, deeper kiss. I debate telling him we should skip lunch because this kiss is all the sustenance I need.

He pulls me closer, trapping our clasped hands between us and slipping his other hand along my cheek and into my hair. Angling my mouth against his, he delves deeper, winding his tongue around mine and sucking my bottom lip until my body trembles.

Kissing a trail across my cheek, he elicits another sigh from me.

"Junebug…" he rasps against my ear. I nod against his lips. I feel everything he's feeling. It's so good that I want to tell him we can do this forever.

But I don't say anything like that.

The feeling has no place in our time together. There will be no forever for us, and we both know it. He's taking a break from his life, and soon, he'll go back to it.

Instead, I turn my face to kiss him once more. Lightly, sweetly. The kind of casual kiss you do right before you hop into the passenger seat of a Porsche and race out of the garage to head to lunch.

"I thought we were getting a burger or something." I stare at the tiny seashells dabbed with horseradish cream, stone crab, and slivered almonds sitting on a bed of brined lemon slices and caviar.

"You wanted to see what my life is like. This is lunch." He spreads his hands over the table, gesturing to the tiny breadsticks in a glass vase, the perfect orchid floating in a silver bowl, and the twin glasses of prosecco from the bottle our server brought us "on the house."

"What does that even mean? You *have* to eat tasting menus every day? Come on."

He smiles ruefully and looks at the table. "I'm making myself sound like poor Eloise in the penthouse or something."

"Just a little. Why can't you eat a sandwich instead of sampling San Francisco's most expensive molecular gastronomy?"

"No, I can. On a normal day. There just aren't a lot of normal days. Getting the funding for the space project is a round-the-clock job, and I have to go to a lot of lunch meetings with venture capitalists and other investors. Plus, I speak at a lot of sympo-siums and things about climate change and technology. This is pretty standard fare."

"Ah, okay. We have a seasonal tasting menu at Butter and Rosemary, but I mainly only eat there when we have events."

His eyes light up like I've discovered a new chemical element. "So you see why I enjoyed your grilled cheese."

I do see. He lifts his prosecco glass and takes a sip. Then he lifts the seashell from his plate and slurps down the little appe-tizer. I do the same, feeling my tastebuds come to life when the combination of flavors hits. "Wow, not gonna lie. That's the bomb."

Colin laughs and refills my glass of prosecco from the bottle in a silver bucket next to the table.

I like it, and I hate it at the same time. The luxury and sheer extravagance of the meal is fun as an excursion from real life, but when I think about Colin doing this all the time, I feel sad.

Knowing him the way I do now, I can see it doesn't suit him, and I can't believe he has so little agency over his life and his free time that he can't even enjoy it most of the time.

"I get why you'd want to slum it at the movie theater and eat popcorn and Junior Mints."

"Hey, in no way was that slumming it. I consider our combina-tion of movie treats the highest of haute cuisine."

"Good." I swirl the prosecco in my tall flute and watch the

bubbles rush to the top. They look like little kids racing to win, each one being chased by a new upstart.

Our server sweeps our empty plates away and replaces them with slivers of yellowtail crudo with a ponzu glaze, edible flowers, and shaved radishes.

"I feel like I should be eating this with tweezers." I look around my plate, where three forks sit, waiting for this new course.

Colin looks right at home here, deftly using the proper fork for each "amuse bouche" our server brings to our table before we even look at a menu of three possible tasting configurations. When we arrived, he shook hands with the maître d', who offered to seat him at his "usual table," which is in a private corner with a view of the Bay Bridge through a giant floor-to-ceiling window. We can't see the other restaurant patrons, and they can't see us.

I imagine Colin holding court with investors, giving them his impassioned take on why Mars exploration is "vital for the future of humanity" and sipping soda water from the same flutes.

Thinking of this other Colin who has charmed the world with his visionary ideas makes me feel like I'm with a different person than I've grown to know over the past couple of weeks, and I'm not sure how I feel about it.

Even though he says he'd rather eat a burger or shove his hand into a bucket of popcorn in a small-town movie theater, this is his world. The real world. Not the fairy tale place where he's been hanging out with me and lifting my body to heights I've never imagined.

This is where he resides. And he'll return here in a few short days, and I'll return to my world.

Nothing is new there. I need to reel myself back in and remember to enjoy the here and now. Like I always do.

"Hey." He reaches for my hand on the table. When I look up, the creases have deepened across his forehead. The last time I saw him look this concerned was when Mallory caught sight of us at the movie theater and snapped a photo. This time, his concern is focused on me. "What's wrong?"

It's then that I realize my own forehead has creased. I've been looking out the window for who knows how long, mulling the ways I don't fit into Colin's world.

"Nothing. Sorry. It's just interesting seeing the real you after seeing the vacation you."

He sits back against his chair, frowning.

"This isn't the real me. I think you've gotten to know me by now. These are just the trappings of my everyday life, and it's all really centered around work. We talked about that."

The restaurant is bustling, alive, and festive, with every table filled on a Tuesday. We're in a touristy area of San Francisco, and I can almost feel the warm weather through the large windows with vistas of water and hills to the east and south.

He scoots his chair closer, so we're sitting almost next to each other. "I needed you closer," he explains as though he's speaking a plain, universal truth, and my heart expands against the walls of my chest when I feel the warmth of his arm drop around me.

Leaning my head against his muscled shoulder, I inhale the scent of him, all woodsy and fresh. With each exhale, I feel calmer. Finally, I decide to go for broke, baring my deepest insecurity to a man I don't think will judge me, even if he doesn't fully understand what I'm about to say.

"I guess…I worry that you might be bored."

He leans away, eyes blinking with incomprehension. "Bored?"

A big part of me regrets opening a can of worms that should probably remain tightly shut, but something makes me feel like I can trust him to understand this part of me.

"You're obviously brilliant. I saw where you work, and it's not like you're playing with LEGOs there."

"No. Although that would be fun." He's still blinking at me, confused.

I take a cleansing breath and tell him the rest. "I know I'm not a genius. I'm just...normal. So I hate to think that you're having to dumb down your thoughts or conversations to suit me."

He frowns, and I'm desperate to erase the lines around his mouth and eyes. He looks more hurt than upset, and that bothers me even more. "How could you possibly think that?"

I shrug. "I don't know. It's just that I really like hanging out with you, and I want to make sure you're stimulated enough."

His eyebrows bounce. "Oh, I'm plenty stimulated with you."

I roll my eyes at the double entendre and give him a playful punch in the arm. "Not what I meant."

"I know, but I can't allow you to think that I'm anything but stimulated—in every possible way—when I'm with you. The crazy whip-smart thoughts in your brain, your sassy sense of humor, your fierce competitiveness..." He leans closer and kisses a trail up my neck. Then he whispers in my ear, "Your incredibly hot, sexy, very stimulating body...I'd take you right here if I could..."

A chill shudders through my body, ending at my core. Electricity hums in my veins. I want this man more than I've ever wanted anything in my life.

I've never been one for public displays of affection, but I'd let Colin lay me on the floor of the restaurant and have his way with me right now.

"C'mere." His voice is gravel under metal gears, and I think he wants me to move closer to him. But he's on his feet, hand extended.

I look at him warily. "Where?"

"Just come."

His fingers are warm honey wrapped around mine, heating my bones as he leads me through the restaurant. Sneaking a look at his face, I find him resolute, jaw hardened, a muscle ticking in his cheek. He grips my hand like a lifeline.

Weaving between tables, Colin says nothing, but I get the sense he knows exactly where he's taking me. We haven't paid the bill, but I assume that somehow he has that covered if he intends for us to leave right now in the helicopter.

But then he slows, carefully guiding me past the restaurant kitchen where a couple of chefs look up and acknowledge him with a tip of their heads. "You know them? I'm impressed."

Turning his face to the floor, Colin looks sheepish. "I invested in the restaurant, actually."

"Oh. Cool. Nice that they let investors get to know the chefs."

We move quickly past the open kitchen and down a darker hallway. "Something like that," he mumbles. Before I can ask him to elaborate, Colin shoves his hand into his pocket and fishes out a key. He uses it to open the lock on a door with a plaque that reads "Office." He pushes the door open and backs through it, pulling me with him.

"Do they give all the investors keys?" Maybe it's the wine we've been drinking, but my brain is slow to figure out why Colin suddenly seems like he owns the place.

"I own the place."

"You—?"

I don't have a chance to ask anything more because Colin lets the door slam shut, leaving us in near darkness. The only light seeps under the door through a wide crack, casting shadows around the room. I can see a desk with a chair behind it and a bookshelf, but the rest of my assessment is cut short when Colin's lips crash onto mine.

Gone are the light touches and gentle hints of affection he showed me at our table. Everything now is want and need and desire.

His mouth devours mine with intensity. The hungry gaze is the one he reserves for the chessboard.

I return his passion in equal measure. Tongues tangling. Bodies pressed hard until there's no space between us.

Walking me backward, Colin puts his hand flat on my back and lowers me to the empty surface of the desk, his mouth pulling away from mine long enough for him to see what he's doing.

I'm breathless and heaving, but I want answers. "You own… the restaurant?"

"Yes."

He doesn't seem interested in talking about it, though, because a moment later, he lowers himself on top of me, and his lips return to mine. He kisses me hard, teeth digging into my bottom lip.

I reach up and pull his lip between my teeth and suck on it before letting him go. Leaning away, I ask again. "Why didn't you tell me earlier that it's yours?"

Holding himself above me on his hands, Colin lets out a long sigh. "You really want to talk about this now?"

A part of me wants to pull him close and continue what he started, but a bigger part wants answers. It's the piece of me that feels like this could be more than a temporary fling. The piece of me that has been feeling a pull toward Colin all day long and wanting to know him better.

"Kind of. You brought up something interesting right before you started kissing me. It's hard not to want information."

Sliding down my body, Colin stands between my legs, which are opened wide and dangling off the edge of the desk. Rubbing a hand over his face, he groans. "My own fault, I guess. I can't just dangle a juicy fact in front of you and expect to kiss the thoughts from your mind."

I prop myself up on my elbows and look at him. "You almost succeeded." I still sound breathless, my heart racing in my chest. "I want both."

He smiles. "I love that about you."

And then my heart stops. Just for a beat before it starts thudding like a bass drum.

It's just a crumb. Just a mention of the L-word in passing. Many other people have professed to love little things about me here and there. Friends lob little missives like that all the time.

But coming from the cerebral, brainy Colin who chooses his words carefully and is sparing in his praise, it feels like a nugget of gold has landed at my feet, and I can't stop staring for fear it will vanish as quickly as it appeared.

Colin doesn't seem moved by his admission because he keeps talking. "People need money for a lot of their projects like opening new restaurants or buying office buildings or helping startups, you know…start up. I have money. So I end up mucking around in a lot of different shit."

He splays his hands out to the sides as though it's enough of an explanation. In some ways, it is.

"Do you own a lot of other shit?"

"Some." He gives me a wry smile. "Is that enough information to satisfy your brain for now so I can make you come on this desk?"

His directness makes me smile. He's so direct and intentional when he speaks, and even if I don't know what he has planned, I understand him well enough to know he has a plan. I also know it's something I'm going to enjoy. A lot.

I nod, leaning back down on the desk as he pounces on me like a wolf. Licking his lips, Colin dives in and sucks the sensitive skin beneath my ear. I hear myself moan over his delicious breath against my ear. Then I feel him hard against my center, and I start to lose touch with all of my senses except touch.

Because damn, he feels so good.

His hands work the hem of my skirt up over my legs and pull my panties down, where they dangle from one of my feet. I fling them away and go to work on his zipper. Before I get very far, Colin pulls me up from the desk and flips me around.

My hips hit the edge of the desk, and I leaned forward to brace myself on my hands. From behind me, I hear the zip of his jeans and the rumple of fabric falling to the floor. Then his large, strong hands grip my waist and his hard length nudges between my legs.

I expect to feel him thrust once or twice and pound into me for a quickie before the next course.

Instead, he drops to his knees.

The cool air hits between my legs as he holds my skirt up around my hips. Then his tongue sweeps up along my inner thigh and finds my clit. I gasp when he closes his mouth over the sensitive flesh and sucks gently.

Then, not so gently…his tongue makes circles, and one finger slides inside. I can feel how wet I am for him as his breath hits my skin, and I shudder from the chill.

Every nerve ending feels so highly sensitized that it doesn't take me long before my legs are quivering. My whole body lights up under his touch as he continues his ministrations, taking me higher.

"God, Colin…" I pant, not fully aware of anything except the feeling between my legs, which is so, so good that I cry out as he pushes me over the edge.

Then I'm falling through a cascade of light and dark and feeling and sensation. Trying to ground myself and feel everything about this moment at the same time.

That's when Colin thrusts slowly inside me, replacing his fingers and his mouth with the weight and thickness of his cock. As he fills me, I moan again. This time, I'm joined by his own growl of satisfaction.

"So fucking tight, PJ. I'm so damn hot for you…"

He pumps harder, and his hands slide up under my sweater, massaging both breasts as he pounds me from behind. Steadying myself against the desk, I ride out the orgasm I didn't think could continue like this. But like everything about Colin Hathaway, this too is a surprise.

One I don't want to end.

———

Seated back at our table, the only hint of our field trip to the office is the fact that our next course has been served. That, and a slight rumple of Colin's hair. I'm sure mine is a nest of curls, but I'm too distracted staring at the handsome man across the table from me to care.

I slide the filets of sole around on their little sea of butter sauce and take a bite of a fried squash blossom with a honey glaze.

Every morsel is delicious, but they pale in comparison with the appetizer I just experienced in Colin's office.

He spears a bite of fish and swirls it in the sauce before popping it into his mouth. I can't stop staring at the beauty of his face, placidly glowing in the light just outside the windows. I follow the afternoon sun's glow down across the San Francisco Bay, where it paints a long, bright stroke against the water.

It reminds me that I should leave my small-town community more often.

"Thank you for the tour." I point in the direction of the kitchen, where we moved quickly past the chefs on our way back. "Do you do that a lot?" I give him a cheeky smile, hinting at the many women who would sacrifice a kidney for the treatment I just received.

Colin doesn't look amused. A muscle in his jaw clenches and his eyes narrow.

"No."

I wait, but he presses his lips together as though preventing himself from saying more.

"O-kay…" I wonder if I've made him think about an occasion where he brought another woman there, and it didn't go well. I'm still formulating what to say next when he grabs my hand. His grip is strong, as though I'm dangling from a ledge, and he's the only one who can reel me in. His chest swells as he takes a deep breath. When he lets it out, his face calms and he brings my hand to his lips, kissing my knuckles and letting his breath warm them.

Somehow, the warmth of him sends chills down my spine. A delicious combination of fire and ice that's so addictive.

"I don't do that ever," he says in a quiet tone that would put fear into soldiers on a battle field.

"Okay—" I start to say because he seems upset, and I'm pretty sure I caused it with my flippant remark.

He puts a finger against my lips to stop me from speaking.

"I don't fly women to the helipad of my office and show them the rovers and spacecraft that are still in development. I don't. And I never take women to my office in the restaurant and go down on them. Not ever. I'm doing these things with you and only you. Because you make me want to see what life looks like outside my little bubble. But I only want to do them with you." He stares so long into my eyes, and my heart starts hammering so hard that I think I might need CPR in another minute.

But he kisses me instead. It's a life-giving kiss, and it seals the deal.

If I thought there was any chance of getting through Colin's time at the vineyard without falling hard for him, the odds just fell to zero.

I want him for as long as he'll give me, even though I know our clock is ticking.

CHAPTER
Twenty

COLIN

I couldn't have planned it better if I'd hired an advance team of professionals to snowplow the way to a perfect date. Taylor Swift just happened to be playing at the stadium near my house this weekend.

I just happened to have a few investors who worked for the touring company responsible for booking her concerts.

The rest was just phone tag and calling in a few favors.

"I didn't bring a change of clothes," PJ said when I told her our day in Silicon Valley would continue into the evening.

I'd already thought of that. I had my assistant help with that part because I don't know shit about women's fashion, and by the time we arrived at my apartment to freshen up for our evening plans, she'd delivered four outfits for PJ to choose from, as well as a pair of sequined cowboy boots for me.

What kind of man would I be if I wasn't willing to put on sparkly boots for the woman I don't want to let walk out of my life in a few days? I've been resisting the thought all week, but with the expiration date on our time together looming, my brain won't let me resist it anymore.

I just didn't know what to do about it. PJ has so much on her plate with her dad's illness and the company finances. The last thing I want to do is get in her way as she navigates how to handle the guy who's making a play for Buttercup Hill and deal with debts no one understands.

I just want her.

"What the heck are these?" PJ asks when I hold up four hanging bags and offer them to her.

"I think you look great the way you are, but if you feel like changing clothes, these are a few options."

Her jaw hangs open. "Are you serious? Did you...buy me clothes?"

"Not exactly. My assistant did it. I hope I got your size right."

"What size did you tell her?"

"I said you were a foot shorter than me with curves I can't stop staring at, a tiny waist, and a hot little ass."

PJ rolls her eyes, but she can't help cracking a smile. "Based on that, I'll be very interested to see what she came up with." She takes the hangers and lifts the plastic that hangs over the clothes.

The first outfit is a red pantsuit. The second is a frilly long dress that belongs on the cover of a romance novel. There's a short sequined dress that's instantly my personal favorite. And a tee that says, "Who's Taylor Swift anyway? Ew."

I'm about to call my assistant and rake her over the coals for choosing the last one when PJ bursts out laughing. "Are you serious with these? Are we going to a karaoke night? Is that what you high rollers do on a Tuesday night around here?"

She's still laughing when I take out the cowboy boots and hold them up. "We are not going to a karaoke night."

Looking from the boots to my face and back again, her eyes flash as she puts the pieces together. "Wait, you didn't—" Almost like saying the words will make them untrue.

"I did."

"We're going to the concert?!" Her voice hovers somewhere between a shout and an ecstatic squeal. I nod, and she jumps into my arms.

———

"She's amazing." It's easily the fifteenth time PJ has said this in the five minutes since we left the concert. "And so are you."

Mission accomplished. The smile that's been plastered on PJ's face as she sang along to every song for over three hours is reward enough for the ache in my toes from these damn boots.

I took them off the minute we got back to my car in favor of some running shoes I keep in the trunk.

"So you liked it?" I feign innocence as I flip the turn signal to get us onto the freeway.

In response, she throws her arms around my neck and kisses my cheek.

Yeah, mission accomplished.

We've skated out of the parking lot in record time, thanks to some VIP passes that were thrown my way by the investors who provided the concert tickets. Behind us, car horns honk and throngs of Swifties glide through the immense parking area, where they'll probably spend the next hour jockeying to drive out.

Sometimes I feel guilty about the privilege I have based on wealth that seems unwarranted. The truth is, I'd be doing what I do without a financial reward. I just like the work. But that's not something I'm going to say to investors. Or anyone. These past few weeks have gotten my priorities back in line, and I plan on keeping my head down and my mouth shut when I go back to work next week.

Showing PJ around the lab has me jonesing to get back there. I didn't realize how much I've missed it. The only thing remotely close to the adrenaline that races through my veins when I walk into the lab is the way I feel with PJ. And if I'm honest, being with her is even better.

That scares the hell out of me because my fascination with science has sustained me for most of my life. I never questioned whether there could be anything else that might get my juices flowing. Now, faced with a single person who exceeds every possibility I ever imagined, I feel a little unmoored.

Astrophysics has been the answer for me, and it's served me well. What's more, it's served the larger community well. Putting a dent in that for my own selfish pleasure is irresponsible.

It's why I'm starting to hate that my time with PJ has an expiration date. For the first time, I'm letting my emotions get ahead of my rational sense that I need to stay focused on work and only work.

But what if…what if PJ and I didn't have to end? What if I could have both?

I'm wrestling with these thoughts as we exit the freeway near the lab. I have one last thing I want to show PJ tonight, and as far as I'm concerned, it's the best thing out there.

When we pull back into my parking spot, PJ tips her head against my shoulder. "Thank you so much for an incredible day. I know you like the simple things, but all the fancy shit makes a hell of an impression."

I kiss her temple and let myself imagine for a moment that she and I could be permanent. It's just a momentary fantasy. No harm in that. Then I pop the locks and walk around to the passenger side to open PJ's door.

She sways against me in the elevator as though she's still hearing Taylor's music in her head. When we reach the top floor and I guide her down the hallway, she casts me a side-eye. "Isn't the helicopter that way?" She points in the direction where we entered the building this morning.

"I have one more thing to show you before we fly back." I guide her to the observatory, which is equipped with our largest, most powerful telescopes.

The room has dim lighting to make for better viewing, and

when she sees the telescopes, she nods. "Okay, this may be even better than the concert."

That's the moment when all my lustful feelings toward her from the past two weeks mushroom into something so much more. Or maybe it's when I allow myself to acknowledge them. I know how much she loved the concert, but to react the way she does to the idea of stargazing before we've even looked at anything seals the deal.

This woman is mine. Even if she doesn't know it.

"Come." Taking her hand, I lead her to the gamma-ray telescope and click a remote control that slides the domed roof open for night viewing. "My lab is situated here, on top of the hill, for a reason," I explain, hoping she recalls the scenery when we landed earlier.

I guide her over to another telescope, this one over ten meters in size, watching her round eyes fill with anticipation. "This one has mirrors that correct for small distortions in the atmosphere, so the images look especially sharp. Let's start with this one."

I adjust a few knobs and let her have a look. The scope is pointed at Saturn, visible in the early night sky at this time of year. "Oh wow!"

She backs away, expression agog. "I know. When you first see those rings, it's pretty unbelievable. But there's more."

We spend the next two hours looking through the telescopes, viewing black holes and talking about the behavior of small red stars called dwarfs. It's been a long time since I've been in here with someone who wasn't a scientist or an investor, and showing her what fascinates me about astrophysics reminds me of how much I love my job.

And viewing the stars with PJ confirms that I love something else—her.

I point the final telescope toward the summer sky constellations and let PJ stargaze for a while. I know the effects of looking skyward and letting my mind dream and wander, but it's not until I hear a quiet sigh from her that I know she gets it.

She turns to me and encircles my neck with her arms. "Thank you. It's been a great day."

"It has." It's been a great couple of weeks, which is why I find my brain on overload. Only this time, I'm not thinking about space missions and the quest to reach Mars. I'm thinking about how to keep PJ Corbett in my life for a little bit longer. Or even forever.

Twenty-One

PJ

It was no secret in our family that I got special treatment for being the youngest. At a young age, my siblings gave up trying to deny it was true. Beatrix was the favorite, but I was the baby who our dad couldn't say no to, evidenced by trips for ice cream at Baskin Robbins.

It was usually when our mom was visiting a relative, and our dad would make a big show of "rescuing" us from the team of nannies who took care of us even when our mom was in town. We knew he liked them and relied on them, but when it was his turn to pile us into our family minivan, he rebranded himself as a valiant knight riding in to save us.

We'd tumble out of the van, and our dad would grumble things about us being a ragtag band of misfits unfit for the world outside our house, but we knew that was his way of saying he loved us.

I'd give almost anything to hear him say it now.

"Last week, I only stayed fifteen minutes, and that seemed to exhaust him. This may be a quick trip," Beatrix says as we walk the path to the largest building on the vineyard property, a stately white mansion with columns in the front, gardens that wrap around both sides of the house, and potted red geraniums hanging above the second-story porches.

"Coming," I say, lagging a couple feet behind her in my joggers, gray sweater, and a scarf wound twice around my neck. It's warm out this morning as usual, but I'm always cold in my dad's house, so I come prepared with extra layers.

There's no telling exactly when our dad will be the most lucid, so we sort of hover in a suspended state of readiness. When Dad's nurse thinks he'll recognize us, she calls, and we come right away. The only downside is that today it meant skipping my normal latte at Sweet Butter and, therefore, my chance to see Colin.

Thinking about him has me so distracted that I don't notice I've slowed down to a dreamy crawl.

"You okay?" Beatrix snaps me back to reality.

"Yeah. Just worried about how he'll be today."

"Only way to know is to go."

She's right, but that doesn't make it any easier. When my dad looks at me, I'm not even sure he recognizes me most of the time. Sometimes he looks downright frightened when I walk into the room, like I'm a stranger who might do him harm.

I can only imagine how easy it would have been for someone to take advantage of his frailty, even without knowing the extent of his dementia.

But back when he drove us five miles over the speed limit down the main road in Napa Valley, we thought our dad was the king of everything.

When we got to the ice cream shop, Dad would always go in order of age, allowing Archer to pick his flavor first—always rocky road, always in a sugar cone—and moving down the line. Jackson went next, needing to look at every bin of ice cream in the case and taste a few before deciding. Nine times out of ten, he picked mint chip, but he always made a big show of debating the others.

Beatrix always chose vanilla and asked for a second scoop of a different flavor. Dad would allow it if she chose to have her ice cream in a cup, like somehow it was so much healthier if she gave up the cone for the second scoop.

Then came Dash, who couldn't resist the pink, sickly sweet bubble gum ice cream and who always picked out the multi-colored chunks of gum to save for last. He'd chew them up into a giant wad and taunt the rest of us with his dessert after dessert.

When it was my turn to pick, my dad would lift me onto his shoulders because, at age two or three, I couldn't see into the cases. He'd read all the flavors to me and give me side commentary on the ones he liked best. "Mocha almond fudge is a classic. You can get vanilla anywhere, so I'd pick something with a little caramel or nuts. Daiquiri ice looks better than it tastes." I'd solemnly listen to his advice, even though it was mostly the same every time, and then I'd reliably point at whatever was the most colorful, generally the rainbow sherbet. I'd ignore the chorus of doubt from my siblings, who'd always tell me that sherbet wasn't really ice cream.

"Don't listen, Penny. It's real ice cream to me." My dad would often order himself a scoop of the same thing just to prove it was the best. That annoyed my brothers, who were always jockeying for attention.

They held it against my dad for years, but now, we're all in the same boat, watching him slowly slip away. Equal opportunity loss.

Now, being the youngest gets me nothing, not a glimmer of additional recognition when I walk into his bedroom with my sister, who is with me today when I visit. Dad's doctor suggested we visit in pairs—something about making it easier for him to recognize us without overwhelming him. I don't know. It hasn't seemed like it's helping.

Beatrix and I hike up the stairs to the second floor of the mammoth house where Dad and the nannies raised us after one too many affairs with Napa's single women drove our mother to move out. The seven-bedroom home has cathedral ceilings on both stories, making for an extra-long winding staircase. It used to entertain me as a kid to send stuffed animals down the curving banister and see which could get the farthest before falling off.

Holding the banister now, I feel like those days were a lifetime ago. I only come to this house to visit my dad, which colors the experience with sadness.

Dad's nurse, Betsy, waits for us outside his bedroom door with her brown chin-length hair framing her owlish face. Her round eyes and arched brows tell me more about what to expect than she could with words.

"Not a good day?" Beatrix speaks my concerns out loud. She knows the drill. It's rarely a good day, just degrees of bad or worse.

Betsy tips her head from side to side as we approach. "Morning, ladies. He's doing okay this morning, all things considered."

"Meaning?" Beatrix's heels click-clack across the parquet floor as she approaches, arms crossed over her crisp white blouse and black buttonless jacket. I, on the other hand, am wearing sweatpants. My dad used to scorn me for it—"Always dress to impress, even if you're the only one who knows it"—and maybe a part of me wants my slovenliness to shock some recognition into him.

"He's tired even though he slept all night. He knows who I am, so I'm optimistic he'll recognize you," Betsy says quietly, ushering us through the double doors that lead to my dad's bedroom suite. Painted pale yellow, it's a bedroom and a living room and an office all in one. It's bigger than the entire cottage where Colin is staying.

That thought brings my mind back to Colin, and I wonder what he's planning on doing today. I can't help being acutely aware of how little time he has left before work and life will take him back to Palo Alto. Three days, to be exact.

"Trixie, good morning." My dad's voice emanates from deep in his belly, and he's always had the ability to command a room. It heartens me to hear him call my sister by her nickname. I follow her into the room, and his eyes land on me. "How's my Shiny Penny?"

It's a rare moment of clarity, and I know Beatrix feels the same gratitude I do that we're here for it.

"Hey, Dad." My sister goes over and kisses his cheek. I can't help it—I want a hug, and he indulges me.

He has his breakfast spread out on the writing desk that sits opposite the king-sized bed, which has about fourteen decorative pillows against the headboard even though he just slept in it. Gold threads run through the fabric of the duvet cover and the pillows, all shades of yellow, giving the room a pale glow.

Betsy opens the window shades enough to let in some sunlight, but just barely. My dad squints at the change, and I watch his face flush. Small things like this sometimes set him off into a confused state, but I know the natural light is good for him. The moment passes, and my dad seems to adjust.

"How are the cabernet vines looking? Ready for picking?" He sits in a swivel chair at the desk and folds his hands over his stomach. Betsy butters a piece of toast for him, but he glares when she slides it toward his hand. "I'll eat when I'm hungry."

"It's only August, so it's too early yet," I tell my dad, knowing he loses track of time.

"Ah, August. So we wait. I'll ask your brother about it."

"Yes, Archer will be able to give you a better sense of the sugar levels." I intentionally say his name to help Dad recall of which brother is in charge of winemaking now.

Our dad used to go into the different vineyards daily and pick a few grapes from different growing sections. He'd bring them back to his lab and test their sugar and acid levels to gauge when it was time for picking. Now that's our brother's job.

"Archer," he says. "That's not the brother I meant. The younger one."

Beatrix and I share a look, concerned he's getting confused. Often, when it starts, the thoughts meander even farther away, so

I'm hoping we still have some time with him today before that happens.

"Archer is handling the wine making," I tell him gently, hoping it will remind him of what he already knows rather than upset him for getting it wrong.

He shakes his head. "I know. I told Jackson the same thing. He knows what I mean." My dad's blue eyes pierce the space between us like lasers. He looks absolutely certain of what he's saying, so I nod and tell him I'll speak with Jackson about it.

Dad picks up the toast and takes a bite. Chewing slowly, he watches us. Then he slides a plate of strawberries and sliced peaches toward us. "Hungry?"

I nab a slice of peach, its juices dripping down my chin when I bite it in half. "Mmm, they're perfect right now."

Beatrix sits in the armchair opposite my dad and tells him about the upcoming events at the restaurant. "We have the big fundraiser at the end of the month. Should do gangbusters for the new arts center."

My dad nods and engages her in chitchat about the menu changes at Butter and Rosemary, and for a moment, it feels like a normal conversation between a father and daughter. A wave of calm washes over me, and I almost get a little teary because I know the feeling won't last.

I'd love to use this opportunity to get some advice from my dad about how to handle Trevor Stagwood, but I know the mandate for these visits—all of us need to capitalize on any moments of lucidity to find out where and why our dad spent so much of the winery's money.

"We're pulling together paperwork, and we don't have anything on the investment you made last year. Do you have records of the money you spent?" I grab another peach slice and sit on a couch at the foot of the bed. It too has several yellow throw pillows. I know for a fact that my dad doesn't give a fig about throw pillows, so I wonder who chose them. They can't be left over from when he was married to our mom, but this isn't the time to ask about it.

"Records?" He squints in confusion, but he still seems lucid.

"Yes. Did you invest in something, buy something, pay someone off in a lawsuit settlement? I need any documents you have." Each of my siblings has come to our dad with different versions of the same request and sometimes we get a new crumb of information. Here's to hoping.

He scowls. I know he doesn't like this subject, but it's best to be direct. I don't know how much time I have before the veil will fall, and he'll usher me from the room. It's happened too many times to count with each of us. "I told your brother what to do with the money. He knows."

But my brothers don't know.

"Are you sure? Can you remind me what you told him?"

He throws a dismissive hand my way. "Talk to him."

"Dad…what is your connection to Duck Feather Winery? Did you tell someone there about our finances?" With his deteriorating mental state over the past few months, there's every chance the leak came from him. And who knows who he might have told if Trevor got wind of it.

"I said talk to your brother."

"Why can't you just tell me? If you talked to people about selling, we need to know."

"I feel fine, thanks."

My heart aches because right here, right now, I'm sure he does feel fine, but that wasn't my question. I move to where he's sitting and hug him fiercely. I meet my sister's eyes and she nods. "Okay, Dad. It's good to see you. Love you."

"Going so soon?" His voice is gruff, but I doubt he's annoyed, mainly because he's already moved on to the stack of newspapers on his desk and is fanning them out, studying them intently. He's read three papers a day for as long as I can remember, and it's still part of his daily ritual, even if half the time he doesn't know what he's reading.

"Bye, Dad," Beatrix says, leaning in to give him a hug and kiss his cheek. He barely acknowledges her, now absorbed in meticulously turning the pages of the newspaper one by one. His eyes look a bit less sharp, and I tell the nurse to keep us posted on how the rest of his day goes. She nods.

Beatrix follows me down the stairs, and I gaze at the shiny banister, wondering why anyone bothers to polish it to its current sheen when my dad only leaves his room for the occasional walk, and even then, he takes the elevator.

"Why'd you ask that?" Beatrix asks as soon as we're outside. My face feels hot from the combination of hope and despair I feel each time I see my dad. I wish there was a way out of this for him, but his symptoms are only going to stay in a holding pattern or get worse, so we're told.

"What?"

"Why'd you ask about selling? Do you know something?"

"I just wanted to see what he remembers."

"Who else knows about our finances? Did more people approach us besides Trevor?" The suspicion in her voice hits me like an out-of-tune instrument.

"Relax. No one knows anything. Paranoid?"

"I don't like being left out of important decisions when we each had to take out loans to keep us afloat."

"No decisions have been made about anything. Stop worrying."

She starts walking faster, as though it will get her someplace where important decisions are made. Instead, she just kicks up little bits of gravel, which inevitably end up in her low-heeled pumps. She growls and stops to take her shoes off and shake them out.

"Relax," I say again, unsure whether I'm talking to her or to myself.

CHAPTER
Twenty~Two

PJ

"Trust me, I'd so much rather go hiking with you," I tell Colin when he intercepts me outside Sweet Butter as I'm leaving with my latte. But after Beatrix and I left my dad's, she insisted we have a family meeting the following morning.

"I know it's a workday. No pressure." Colin looks like a different person than the one I met his first day here, awkwardly ordering coffee and wincing at the idea of two weeks off. His shoulders have dropped, he's learned to rock a hoodie like no one's business, and his eyes look bright from sufficient nights of sleep, despite our shenanigans.

"We have the event tomorrow, so I think everyone wants to get our ducks in a row." I don't realize that my own shoulders hover near my ears until Colin's steady large hands land on me and gently press my shoulders down. He massages the sore muscles, and I melt into his touch. "How are you so good at that?" I moan.

"It's easy to be good at things that make me happy."

I want this, the easygoing way we are with each other in the vacuum of solitude. No one is here to judge him for taking time away from the day-to-day grind at AstroTech, and I'm outside the critical glare of older siblings who'd judge me for "bedding the billionaire."

"Listen, I've been thinking about tomorrow…" I tip my head up, and Colin's lips meet mine in a kiss I can't resist.

"I'm thinking about right now," he murmurs against my lips.

He makes me smile. "That too, but as a publicist, I'm not sure it's a good idea for you to come to the event at Butter and Rosemary. The optics aren't good if you're photographed hobnobbing with wine country elite instead of running AstroTech. Plus, I'll be busy trying to make sure the right people get photographed for the right media outlets and deflecting attention from questions about our finances…"

He shakes his head. "This is an important night for you. You'll manage all these media wasps like a champ, and I want to be there to see it."

His words strike a deep chord within me, warming me from the inside out. No one has ever had the kind of faith in my ability to do my job well—the way I know I can do it. Selfishly, I want him to be there, even if he's across the room drinking wine with my brother.

A heavy sigh rolls from me, and I'm surprised at how relaxed I feel at the thought of him having my back at the event.

And even…after the event?

We haven't discussed whether we'll see each other after he returns to Palo Alto, and this isn't the time. With the event weighing on me, I need to make a good showing in front of my siblings and handle the media ops like the pro I know I am.

He points at my cup. "Got your fuel, I see."

"Wish I had time to kick your ass in chess. That might relax me."

He grins. I know he likes my wisecracking. I know he likes me. The problem is that what I'm starting to feel for him goes way beyond liking him.

Can I love a man after just two weeks?

"I'd play you, no problem, but will it mess with your mojo if I kick your ass?"

I pat his cheek. "Wouldn't go down that way."

"I so want to prove you wrong."

I smile. "Maybe the meeting will be short, and I'll come back, and we can play."

"Hope so. Bring the A game I know you have, and your family won't know what hit 'em."

This guy…I love that he sees the best in me.

I carry that light with me all the way into the meeting with my siblings, fearing it will vanish the moment I walk in the door. Hoping it won't.

———

Inside the old barn, Beatrix stands in the industrial kitchen with her arms crossed. Hair pulled back into a ponytail, eyes hard, she looks from Archer to Jackson to me with suspicion. Somehow, Dashiell escapes her glare.

A spread of sandwiches and pitchers of lemonade sit on the table untouched. We don't bother eating the snacks or exchanging niceties because Beatrix launches right into the reason she called us together. "Are you all holding out on me? Is there anything about our finances I don't know?"

Archer pours himself a cup of coffee from the urn that keeps it hot for our employees all day long. "You mean, other than missing millions of dollars? God, I hope not."

She turns to me pointedly. "PJ was asking Dad if he talked to anyone about selling. What do you know that I don't? Are we selling to Duck Feather? Did you guys go there without telling us?" Now she's including Dash in her accusatory glare.

I hope my return stare conveys the betrayal I feel for being called out. I hate that she doesn't trust me. "We haven't gone. We haven't had time." Feeling my cheeks redden at the thought of why I haven't had time, I look at the floor and hope Beatrix doesn't take this moment to out Colin and me.

"Let's do it this week," Dash proposes to me. I nod.

"And as to my questions, the Trevor thing has been bugging me, and I want us to be prepared since we're hosting half of Napa at the restaurant tomorrow. We want to be prepared if more potential investors plan on ambushing us."

Beatrix visibly relaxes, her shoulders dropping and her features settling into calm. "Oh. Okay. That's a good point."

"Sheesh, sis. We need to stick together here. I was planning on sending a memo to you all with talking points ahead of the event. I think we should use this as an opportunity to subtly feel out potential donors without them knowing that's what we're doing." Emboldened by my conversation with Colin, I feel like I have a seat at the table. My ideas have merit.

"That's not the worst idea," Archer intones, arms crossed. From him, it's like high praise. "We could use the event as an opportunity. Every conversation is a potential piece of information."

Jackson nods. "The reality is we may need some investors to stay afloat, so we should take a close look at everyone from that perspective."

"I hate to think we'll need investors, but he's right," Archer says. "And I'll do anything to keep this place out of the hands of Trevor Stagwood. That guy chaps my hide even when I don't see him. I couldn't handle having him anywhere near this place."

"I'll handle him." I meet each pair of eyes at the table, looking for agreement. "Kill him with kindness and send him on his way."

I get a few nods of agreement. A small show of faith. It's all I need.

Twenty~Three

COLIN

When I walk into the event at Butter and Rosemary, I can see that this is not a situation where I can kick back and relax. Too many people are snapping pictures with their phones, and a few news photographers make the rounds.

PJ was right—coming to this party could paint me in a bad light—hobnobbing with wine country elite while hiding from my mistakes. But I want to see her. More than that, I want to support her on an important night, and that makes me reckless.

I arrive with Archer, who guides me out to the restaurant's patio, where several rows of wineglasses sit on a deep wood bar. Each section of glasses sits in front of a bottle of Buttercup Hill Reserve wine, either cabernet, chardonnay, or sauvignon blanc.

It's darker out here, and there are fewer people. I feel a bit less exposed, but some guests seem to recognize me. I've gotten good at picking up on the signs. There's a little point of a finger here. A little attempt to take a selfie with me in the background there.

Most of the time, I'm meeting with investors or scientists if I'm not in the lab, so even if I end up on someone's social media feed, there aren't any salacious details to report. Or even to speculate.

Here, I know it's a different story. The optics aren't great when I rub shoulders with wine makers and wealthy property owners who like to have a winery in their portfolio, along with a private jet and a ski house. Even if I'm not here to purchase a winery, there's guilt by association.

AstroTech's stock still hasn't bounced back, so I shouldn't do anything to stir the pot.

"You good?" Archer asks, handing me a glass of red wine.

"Thanks. Yeah, I'm good. Cheers."

Archer holds his glass up for a toast. "Nice having you here these past couple weeks. Sorry I haven't been able to spend more time with you. Winery's kind of a shit show right now, and we're trying to come up with a plan. Tonight's kind of a low-key mingle to gauge interest from potential investors."

"Oh, really?" I feign ignorance even though PJ filled me in. "How do you feel about going that route?"

"I don't love it, but it might be worth trying to find the right pair of hands in order to keep the business out of the wrong ones."

"Understood."

"Yeah, you get it. Investors muck up the works sometimes, and they come with their own interests and requirements, but sometimes it's necessary."

"Exactly."

I hear PJ's laughter coming from somewhere inside the restaurant. It's like windchimes calming my nerves in the late afternoon breeze. I can't see her, but knowing she's near enough for me to hear her drives home the feeling I can't shake—that I want more of her.

I should say something to Archer about PJ. He's my oldest friend, and I owe him my honesty. At the same time, he seems so utterly wrecked by his dad's health and the financial troubles at the winery that I don't want to flip him out tonight.

Maybe he'd shrug and tell me he was just blowing smoke when he said to stay away from his sister. After all, we're grown-ups. But tonight, with the high stakes of the evening laid out so clearly, it's not the right time.

A hint of a smile creeps across his face as he surveys the healthy crowd. This is the same guy I've known for half my life, the one who was always my wingman when I wasn't being his. I know he wants good things for me, and I feel a little bit guilty that one of those things is his sister. But we don't always get a choice, and my heart chose her.

I'll tell him. Just not right now.

From across the patio, I see PJ square her shoulders when she sees me talking to Archer. She puts on the serious work face she thinks she needs to be taken seriously.

When she reaches us, I grab a glass of wine from the bar and hand it to her. It's the sauvignon blanc I know she likes. "Thanks," she tells me before turning to Archer. "You making the rounds?"

"Yeah, and I still hate the idea of any of these people butting in where our business is concerned. Especially Trevor Stagwood. Is he here yet?"

"Not sure, but I promise I'll handle him. I've got this."

I want to put my arm around PJ to reassure her that I believe she's absolutely got this, but instead, I subtly press my hand to her lower back.

Her eyes shoot to me and she flinches, but Archer doesn't notice. Guy has a shit-eating grin on his face as he sees something inside the restaurant.

"What just gave you a hard-on?" I ask.

Archer wraps an arm around each of our shoulders and gives us a squeeze.

"Mallory Rutherford. She always talks a good game about wanting a bigger footprint in Napa. Maybe it's time to see how serious she is."

He continues smiling at us as he backs away, leaving us alone on the patio. A few other people stand in groups chatting, but it's far less crowded than the madhouse I can see just inside the restaurant.

Photographers' camera lenses are aimed everywhere, and smiling groups are captured for the society pages of magazines and newspapers. It's not my world, but living amid tech billionaires gives me enough of a view of it at home.

A tuxedo-clad server walks past with a tray of ahi tuna appetizers on fried wontons, and I turn to grab a couple on a napkin for us.

"Aw, there she is! I've been looking all over for you." The deep male voice doesn't faze me until I turn back and find my view of PJ blocked by a slicked-back head of hair and a guy in a brown suede sport coat.

I circle around to find that he looks about a half dozen years my junior and has PJ buttonholed in a corner. He wraps an arm around her waist and pulls her against him. She tips her head up to kiss him on the cheek, but I see the stiffness in her gesture. She doesn't like him.

He returns her gesture—slowly and intentionally. Even though it's a cheek kiss, it's too long. Too intimate. Then he gazes into her eyes.

Who the fuck is this guy?

"Tuna tartare?" I offer the appetizer to PJ and tilt my head at the new guy because she either needs to introduce us very quickly, or I might punch his lights out. Maybe this is the infamous Trevor.

"Ooh, thank you." She slurps the tuna off the wonton and crunches into it. A dribble of sauce runs down her chin, and the douchebag who still has her in his grip reaches over and wipes the drip with his finger. Then he fucking licks it.

I glare at him, and the words rip from my throat uncensored. "Take your fucking hands off her."

He turns slowly to face me, eyes wide in mock innocence. He takes his arm from around her, thereby saving his own life. He puts up his hands like I still might shoot him. He's not wrong—I might.

"I'm sorry. You are…?" The boredom in his voice irks me.

PJ wraps her hand around mine, instantly calming the fire in my veins. Slightly. She steps forward, forcing me to move away from the guy I still want to clock with my fist. "Colin, this is Trevor Stagwood. Trevor, Colin."

I glare at Trevor. He looks at me, unimpressed and slightly confused, until a light bulb seems to sputter to life in his dim brain. He smiles at me and nods. "Hey, nice to meet you. You're the space guy, right?"

I grind my teeth so hard I'm pretty sure the people in the restaurant can feel the vibration. PJ interjects before I tell this tool of a man that there is no such thing as a "space guy," unless he's talking about the character from *The Lego Movie*.

"He's an astrophysicist. His company launches spacecraft. They're going to Mars." The pride in her voice pulls at my heart.

"Oh, cool."

Yeah, it's really cool, you douchebag.

I don't want to go full Neanderthal and pull her into my clutches, but…well, maybe I fucking do. Moving to the other side of PJ, I put my arm back where I wanted it before I had the poor judgment to turn away for an appetizer. Then I pull her closer and stare into her eyes. "You were too far away." Just for emphasis and to piss this guy off, I kiss her. Friendly at first, then deeper, with all the pent-up possessiveness this guy unleashed in me. I don't fucking care who sees.

When we break the kiss, PJ looks a little dizzy. Good.

She looks at me, then at Trevor. "Um, so…"

The guy doesn't take the hint. "Yeah. Anyway, Peej, if you have time, I'd still love to continue our conversation from the other day." He smirks as though the conversation was about anything other than business. I smirk back because I know the truth.

He's not getting any sort of hint by my possessive grip on PJ, but fortunately for me, she doesn't seem to mind being plastered against my side.

"Tonight's a crazy night for me since we're hosting. Can't talk about any of that now."

He nods, grinning at her like the memories are particularly vivid and sweet.

"Sure, sure. We should get drinks soon. Get into it."

"Sure, yeah." She clinks her glass against his and turns away from him. I wish she didn't sound so enthusiastic about having drinks with this dickwad, but at least we're now out of his orbit.

"Sorry about that," she says, grabbing two skewers with cherry tomatoes, mozzarella, and basil from a tray. She offers one to me and pops a tomato into her mouth.

"That's your potential investor?" I struggle to keep my tone light. Inquisitive. Like I'm barely interested in Trevor and really disinterested in whatever plans they'll make after I'm no longer in town.

"You heard Archer. Over his dead body."

"He seems he'd be okay with that if it meant spending time with you."

"Yeah." Her laughter tells me there might be something to it.

"So I'm not wrong."

"We dated once upon a time, but *that* didn't go well." She rolls her eyes as though we both understand how not well it went. All I can think about is that this man was with her—kissed her, touched her, had her in a way I've been pretending was all mine— and now I want to murder him.

It's not rational. Of course I know intellectually that she's had relationships before I waltzed into town. I know I'm not her first.

But until Trevor showed up, I could convince myself that no other men existed for her before now. I could believe that the look in her eyes each time she comes is mine alone.

I struggle to keep my he-man instincts in check when all I want to do is jump on a table, beat my chest, and tell everyone I gave PJ three orgasms last night.

"Oh yeah?" The croak in my voice betrays how not-casual I feel.

"Yeah. It was years ago."

PJ is twenty-six years old, so it couldn't have been that long ago, though if she's talking about some junior high school crush, I need to cool my jets.

"He seems like an ass," I say through my teeth. I stare across the vineyard as though I have X-ray vision or something and can see in the dark. Because she's smart and already knows me, PJ doesn't buy it for a second.

She turns and looks me dead in the eye, taunting me. "You were glaring at him like you wanted to eat him for dinner."

There's no point in trying to deny it. "Yeah. The second he touched you, I felt a jealous streak a mile long. Not a good look."

"Actually, I kind of loved it." She licks her lips, flirty.

I swallow over a lump in my throat because I'm falling so hard for this woman. Despite all my warnings to myself and my carefully built walls to block out relationships, she's obliterating them one by one.

I don't know what it means for my future, but I'm not going to do a damn thing to get in the way.

"Yeah?" I'm still holding her hand, so I take the other one and bring both to my chest. "I don't like to come in second place. You might as well know."

She nods slowly and stands on her toes so we're eye to eye. "I already knew."

This time when I kiss her, I don't give a shit if Archer comes over and shoves me. I don't care what social media sites post the pictures. They can pound sand. I only care about being with her.

It may come back to bite me in the ass when I like her too much for my own good and I have to leave, but right now, I'm all in.

She breaks the kiss, and her eyes sparkle, a naughty gleam dancing in her pale blue irises. "Please don't eat Trevor for dinner."

I nod slowly like I'm in a movie dream sequence. The air around us feels warmer than a few minutes ago, like we're being hugged by the dog days of summer. "I wouldn't do that. Mainly because I'm not a cannibal."

Locking eyes with me, she finishes her thought in a sexy rasp. "You could eat me instead."

Her words land in my chest, rocket around for a second, and dead-end at my dick. "Here?" I look around, ready to roll if there's a nook on this patio where I could get away with it.

"No. Not here." Someone inside catches her eye and waves. "But later."

"How much longer do we need to stay?" The desperation in my voice sounds like the ache I feel.

She laughs, tossing her head back so the moonlight snakes through her hair and dances across her face. Nothing lovelier on Earth.

"Give me an hour." She kisses my cheek and moves inside to deal with her work responsibilities. I'll give her an hour.

And if I'm being honest, I want to give her so much more than that. I just have no idea how that will work when I go back home.

CHAPTER
Twenty-Four

PJ

It doesn't feel like we're being careless when I suggest leaving Buttercup Hill and grabbing breakfast in St. Helena. Sure, it falls outside of Colin's "safe zone" for staying hidden from the public eye, but we're still in Napa Valley, after all, and no one pays that much attention to who's eating breakfast with whom and at which bakery.

Or so I think.

Maybe the fallacy in my reasoning comes from not eating breakfast in St. Helena very often myself. If I did, maybe I'd know that eyes are always watching. I'd know that precisely these types of bakery runs are how people know this guy's wife was spotted very early in the morning with that guy's former lover. It's how this person's ex decided to advertise that he moved on to that younger woman after his wife threw him out for cheating.

But I'm not thinking about any of those things because my brain is still on hiatus after private helicopter rides, stargazing, and private boxes at concerts and tasting menus. And early morning sex. And orgasms.

I suppose I could blame my lapse in judgment on all of those things, but I suspect that the multiple orgasms are really to blame. And yet…so worth it.

"They have good coffee," I tell Colin, not thinking twice about grabbing his hand and leading him from the car to the bakery entrance. I don't think twice about standing on my toes to kiss him while we're in line.

No one is paying attention to us.

Except that I have it backward. It's me who's not paying attention to anyone else. Thus, the problem.

"So, like, a double shot, half-caf oat milk latte wouldn't be out of the question?"

I clap a hand over my heart. "Look at you. My baby has left the nest. I feel so proud."

He smiles, treating me to the dimple I love. "Thanks to you, I can order coffee anywhere in California and sound like I know what I'm doing."

"Yes, but never order half-caf. You can handle all the caffeine, Colin."

His arm wraps around my shoulder, and I stand there smitten, my thoughts circling through my brain on repeat: how can this feel so good, and how am I going to patch my tender heart back together when it ends?

Colin will only be here for one more day. Neither of us has mentioned it, but it hangs over every kiss and every brush of our hands against each other when my siblings aren't looking. Even if Beatrix knows, my brothers are still clueless, and I intend to keep it that way.

No good ever comes from them knowing who I'm kissing, and I'm not about to lose a moment of sleep or great sex worrying about what they think about it.

But being in my little lust bubble with Colin doesn't make us invisible. And I should know better. I should know that gossip is a local pastime around here and remind myself I'm canoodling with a billionaire.

Even though he seems like a nerdy pal when we're playing chess and walking around the Buttercup Hill property.

Even though Colin and I came to St. Helena to see the movie last week and barely interacted with a soul.

Even though running into Mallory Rutherford barely registered on my radar because we're old family friends, and she's basically harmless. Maybe it should have.

Maybe she's the reason several paparazzi are lurking in St. Helena when Colin and I leave the tiny brunch place next to a high-end clothing store and take a moment to stare at the window display.

I've been here dozens of times, and even though the area is always lively, it's mostly full of locals picking up a few pastries or waiting in line for a latte. If the occasional paparazzo is here, it's for an A-list celebrity who wants to be photographed. I should know. I've courted enough media photographers when we've had events at the winery to understand how this works. They don't show up unless someone tips them off that there's a story. Or a reason to show up with long-lens cameras.

It should occur to me that Colin hiding out in Napa is just such a story, but I've been so blinded by the intense feelings that have been growing by the day that I've blocked the big flashing warning lights from my field of view.

But they're coming into full focus now.

"Colin!"

"Colin Hathaway!"

Two photographers jockey for attention outside the bakery. We're not far from my car, but they happen to be blocking the shortest route there. Maybe they know that. Or maybe they just got lucky.

One guy scratches his scruffy beard and focuses his lens from a few feet away, walking backward as Colin and I move toward the car. He's already taking photos before I realize it.

Shaking myself back onto high alert, I instinctively move in front of Colin, knowing I'm too short to fully block him, but feeling protective nonetheless.

He puts a hand on the small of my back, and I want to melt into him. Instead, I dig in and let my publicist instincts rule my actions.

"Excuse us. Could you move, please?" I hold a hand out in front of me and walk us directly into the path of the photographer, who's moving backward and needs to look behind him to avoid tripping.

That's when I grab Colin's hand and pull him into the street, outside the immediate view of the photographer.

It seems the best way to protect Colin from unwanted attention is to use myself as a human shield. So that's what I do.

"Colin, over here!" The other photographer now has a cell phone aimed at us, and I like that even less than the big camera. Anything he captures on his phone can be uploaded instantly, and I'll have no ability to control who sees it. So I pivot and move to block that photographer's access with my body.

"Head down," I tell Colin, grabbing his hand and pulling him farther into the street. He's wearing a baseball cap, but it doesn't do much to obscure his face. I look back at him, and he ducks his head down as instructed.

I can't imagine why these people want photos of him so badly, especially when his company announced that he'd be back at work on Monday. The media frenzy over the things he said a couple weeks ago is old news.

I'm so busy puzzling through how and why the photographers know Colin is in town and trying to prevent anyone from getting a good picture of him, that I'm not even thinking about myself. I've never been the subject of interest, so there's no reason I would be now.

People on the sidewalk are starting to take notice, and a few of them have their phones out, though I doubt they know what they're looking at.

Swinging the passenger door of my car open, I block Colin as best I can until he's inside before slamming the door shut and jogging over to my side.

It barely takes me ten seconds to turn on the ignition and put the car into gear. In another minute, we've swerved around the first photographer who I see in my rearview mirror taking pictures of the back of my car. Ridiculous. What the heck does he think he'll do with those?

"Does this happen to you a lot?" I finally look at Colin who seems just as confused as me.

"Not really. I usually go from lunches to meetings and back to my office. But I guess maybe I got people interested by running my mouth and disappearing." He rolls his eyes like it's the dumbest thing ever.

Huffing a laugh, I can't help my amusement at his lack of media savvy.

"You think?"

He shakes his head. "It does happen…sometimes." He says the words slowly like he's admitting a dark secret.

"Yeah, not surprised people want to take your picture. You have a nice face. You could capitalize on it, you know. Sell calendars or whatever."

He stares at his lap for a moment before reaching for my hand. "I didn't think it would happen here. Sorry."

I squint at him because he can't be serious. "Why are you sorry? I'm the one who didn't do a better job of keeping you out of the public eye when you're supposed to be laying low. It's not going to make you look like a saint if you're out cavorting in Napa Valley."

"Worth it."

"What?"

"All the time I spend with you is worth the risk of ending up in someone's social media feed. Yes, I might look like a jerk who's vacationing in Napa when I should be making public apologies, but I'll get to that on Monday. For now, any heat I suffer, any shit I take from my PR team is a small price to pay. You're worth it. No question."

My heart, which has already been slowly breaking in two, cracks open a little more for this man. And with the idea that he'll be going back to his regular life tomorrow, I can't keep out the feeling of sadness I've been fighting.

"I don't want you to go," I blurt. As soon as the words are out of my mouth, I regret them. Not because I want to hide the truth but because it feels like I'm putting a burden on Colin by saying them.

The only noises I hear are the tires rolling quietly on the asphalt and my own breathing, which sounds like I'm sucking air through a snorkel underwater.

Not for the first time in my life, I wish for an edit button in the real world. All the prior times I wished I could take things back pale in comparison with how much I want to pull these words out of the atmosphere and replace them with white noise. Maybe Colin can figure out how to do this someday in his physics research, which he'll be doing far, far away from me because I'm sure I've scared the hell out of him with my possessive neediness.

I don't dare turn and look at him for fear of what I'll see in his eyes—confusion, detachment, fright.

So I keep my eyes on the road, paying special attention to each crossroads, looking both ways at the stop signs, exaggerating my careful driving skills in a town I know like the back of my hand. Anything to avoid the disastrous aftermath of six words I shouldn't have spoken.

"I..." I shake my head when he opens his mouth but has nothing to say. If I could bury my face in my hands, I would, but then I'd crash into something, and that would increase my mortification. Probably.

"Forget I said it." The words rush out in a rescue mission to help him avoid having to make me feel better with his own carefully chosen words. "Just...can we forget it?" I make a quick circular motion with one hand. "Rewind. Erase. Whatever."

"No, I don't think I can."

I exhale a frustrated breath. "Because you have a photographic memory. Or whatever. But just try, okay?"

"No, I mean, I don't want to erase them. I have to go back to work, but I'd like to see you again. I know we haven't talked about that, but I don't feel like we're finished. At least…I'm not, and I'd like to see where this goes."

I'm about to turn onto the road that crosses through Napa to the main road where Buttercup Hill sits, but instead, I pull to the curb and shut off the ignition. Turning to Colin, I search his face for signs that I heard what I think I heard. He looks back at me, the barest of smiles playing on his lips.

"Yeah?" I ask.

"Yeah."

"Okay, I could drive down for dinner one night."

He frowns and rubs a hand over his face, as though considering the reality of what I'm proposing. "That's nearly a two-hour drive."

"I know. I'm not saying I could do it every day, but sometimes, maybe."

He looks a little less convinced than he did a moment ago. "I could work in the car and come up here."

I consider whether this makes any sense at all. Honestly, it doesn't. As much as I like him, it doesn't.

He reaches for my chin and dusts one finger beneath it. "It's not that crazy. We could try it. I want to try."

"I know you said you don't do relationships," I remind him.

"I don't. But I'd like to try one with you."

My heart flutters in my chest, and I let out a shaky exhale. "You would?"

"Yes, but I might not be good at it. I don't have a lot of practice, and there's a lot at stake in my job. No room for errors, and so far, I haven't made any."

"Good on you. But Colin, what about you? Don't you want to

be more than a machine who works around the clock to satisfy shareholders and pay people's salaries?"

"I never used to. It used to be enough. More than enough, actually." He looks sheepish, brushing a lock of hair out of his eyes. Then he reaches and tucks a stray strand of my own hair behind my ear.

"And now?" I get the feeling he's holding something back. Maybe it's wishful thinking.

He inhales a deep breath and lets it out slowly. Then he nods. "Now that I see what I've been missing, I want more. With you. I want it all."

My heart hammers in my chest. They're the words I've been waiting to hear, and I can't believe he's saying them.

"I want that too."

"Let's try to make this work. I don't know what it looks like to try to see each other. I mean, we're a two-hour drive from each other, and I work around the clock."

"There are weekends."

"I work weekends. But there's a helicopter. And I don't work every night."

A part of me wants to protest that a few nights aren't going to be enough for me. I already feel like I miss him, and he hasn't even left yet. But I understand how busy he is and how much rides on his space exploration—literally billions of dollars. I can't be selfish, even if I want to be.

Another better part of me wants to take whatever he's offering because I can't bear the thought of letting him walk away. The past two weeks with him have been better than any time I've ever spent with a man, and I want more of him.

And yet…there's my self-respect. I know I deserve better than someone's odds and ends of time after he's done satisfying himself and everyone else. Being the youngest in the family has taught me that I need to look out for myself because sometimes I'm the only one who will.

"Okay, let's try," I tell him, loving the way his eyes light up at the promise.

My gut tells me I'm making a mistake, that it won't be enough and I'm short-changing myself out of what I know I want.

But I do it anyway.

If he wants to have it all, I want to be the one to give it to him.

COLIN

I don't think either one of us could have anticipated the shitstorm that followed my impromptu makeout session in front of PJ's former flame, followed by the paparazzi outside our coffee run in St. Helena. But as a scientist, I feel especially bad for not factoring in the risk factors, the world's propensity toward chaos, and the ability for normalcy to change at the speed of light.

In other words, I was willfully oblivious to how a few photographers could fuck everything up. That's the problem with letting my heart make decisions for me instead of reason and facts.

"Let's grab you a couple cases of wine to take back with you," PJ says, leading me toward the brown barn.

"Why don't you bring them yourself when you come to spend the weekend with me?"

"We can do both." She smiles at me and looks down at the screen of her phone, but then something stops her in her tracks. I don't immediately see why she's stopped until I catch up. Standing in the middle of the lobby, where several winery guests wander around, taking in the memorabilia on the shelves and waiting for tours, PJ looks like she's seen a ghost.

"Everything okay?" I whisper, out of earshot of the guests.

PJ shakes her head and indicates that I should follow her up the stairs. Moving silently, PJ stares at her phone, scrolling through screen after screen, her face pulled down into a scowl. "Shit. Shit!"

I don't interrupt as she continues scrolling, instead taking out my own phone which is vibrating in my pocket. What appears on my home screen doesn't make me feel any better.

"Is this what you're—"

"Don't," she reprimands. I don't see anyone anywhere near us, so I don't understand why she's lowered a cone of silence, but I obey and follow her into her office. She shuts the door behind me and balls up her fists, pressing them into her eye sockets. "Oh, we're so fucked."

"The pictures from earlier?" I want to make sure we're worrying about the same thing, though I'm more worried about her reaction than any harm to myself. Then again, that sort of oblivion to the impact of social media is what got me into my current mess.

"No, I mean, yes, but there are others. From you kissing me at the winery event. Are they all over your feed?"

I shrug. "I don't really have a feed, but a few people have sent stuff to me." I'm downplaying, trying not to freak PJ out since she already seems very freaked out, but the messages I've received in the past few minutes are anything but positive.

She scrolls from page to page on her phone, the lines on her forehead growing deeper, her scowl turning into an angry bark. "They're such assholes. How can they accuse you of being tone deaf just for getting photographed getting coffee?"

She knows the answer, but I say it anyway. "Because I'm in Napa Valley, where some people buy wineries like other people pick up private jets."

PJ slumps into the soft cushions of a burgundy velvet couch

opposite her desk. Above her, an open window lets in enough fresh air to make me aware of the sheen of sweat across my brow. I still can't decide whether I'm more concerned about my potential media problems or her reaction to them.

"I feel terrible. I should be helping you avoid the media storm, not contributing to it." She reaches for a pink metal water bottle on her desk, uncaps it, and slugs down half its contents.

I walk over to the couch, sit beside her, and put my hand on her knee. Her leg feels tense under my hand, so I gently massage it, hoping she'll slow her roll. "You didn't contribute to it. I'm as much at fault as you for not doing what I was told. It was my idea to kiss you in public and to go out for breakfast, remember?"

"Still, I should know better. This is my job, after all." She goes back to scrolling on her phone even though I feel certain she's seen the worst of it. I gently put my hand over hers and guide her to put the phone on the couch between us.

When her eyes meet mine, I see worry and indecision that she hasn't shown in the time I've known her. "Here's what you're going to do. Talk to your PR people, tell them you're working with me as a consultant, and the photos were of the two of us after a meeting. Make sure they punch holes in the gossipy stuff about you being spotted at a movie theater and restaurants and all that. It's just hearsay since these are the only pictures."

She looks around her office, the wheels spinning in her head a mile a minute. "Tell them to play up the angle of you and Archer being college friends. Make sure they communicate that you aren't here touring wine caves, drinking thousand-dollar bottles of wine, or looking to buy property. The optics of you flitting around Napa only look bad if you don't control the message."

PJ opens her mouth, surely to launch into another set of rules and publicity tactics, but I gently place a finger over her lips. Her large blue eyes blink at me until I remove my finger and replace it with a kiss. Only then does her body relent, leaning a little more softly against the couch cushion.

"Relax. It's going to be fine. I'm going back to work on

Monday, and I'll say all the right things in the right places to put this in the rear view. Can we just...try to enjoy the last day together here?"

Nothing changes in PJ's eyes, but she finally nods her head before resting it on my shoulder. She exhales a long breath, and I finally feel her body relax underneath my arm around her shoulders.

This. *This* is what I've been missing from my life for all the years I've spent putting astrophysics in front of every other priority. And for the moment, this, having a woman find solace in me, is all I want.

I love her. I want more than two weeks with her, but I'm in uncharted territory. When it comes to space exploration, the feeling of the unknown thrills me. With PJ, it makes me nervous because I'm worried I'll screw it up.

But I'll deal with all that on Monday. For today, I have everything I need right here.

CHAPTER
Twenty-Six

COLIN

I could have guessed how things would go when I returned to work.

After two weeks away, all the pressures and excitement about the upcoming launch came back at me in spades.

At first, I didn't mind at all. I was hungry to feel useful, and months of prepping for the next space mission left me exhausted and happy at the end of each day. PJ and I talked on the phone and FaceTimed at night, so it was easy to keep my optimism high. We'd make this work. The week would fly by, and we'd see each other over the weekend.

The good thing about loving my work is that I've never been upset about spending sixteen hours a day on it.

When the first weekend rolls around, I cringe at what I need to do. "I'm so sorry. I want to see you, but I've fallen so far behind that I need to catch up. It wouldn't be fair to you if I'm half distracted by work," I tell PJ when I have to break the news that I'm canceling our plans.

"I get it. You're doing important work. We'll see each other next weekend. Right?"

I assure her that we will. "I miss you so much already. Can't wait to see you."

Then I get back to work. It's all-consuming, but I can't fully get my mojo back, and it concerns me. A part of me is distracted thinking about PJ, picturing her skin under my hands, needing the closeness of her.

I'll see her in just a few days, I tell myself, and I'll get the hang of the elusive work-life balance. I need to make it work, not just because I love her, but because I need to prove to myself that I won't let the same thing that happened to my marriage happen again.

It can't. It won't.

———

"The maître d' of Cevice called to confirm tonight." My assistant Kate hovers in the doorway of my office, where I've spent most of this week.

I should be ecstatic about the dinner reservation with PJ because it's the best part of a week that has mostly gone to shit. Only, I forgot about it until just now. I close my eyes to block out the reality that in just a few short weeks, I've gone from professing my desire to make it work no matter what to forgetting we have plans.

It's not that I don't still crave PJ's touch, her smile, her calming presence in my life. In fact, I want them more than ever. But work, as usual, has other plans for me.

"Shit."

"So…I should cancel?" Kate chews on her thumbnail, waiting for my response. I can hear the chipping of nail polish, and my desire to have her leave my office beats any other thoughts.

"No, not yet. I'll work it out. Thanks." When I look back at my computer, Kate takes her cue to leave.

The space launch is a mess. I know I'm driving everyone crazy with my exacting standards, and it's making it nearly impossible for us to stay on schedule. I've micromanaged all the things they accomplished while I was gone.

I don't like the carbon emissions of this project, and my conscience won't let me send the thing into space until I can make it more environmentally friendly.

I haven't been in the lab much this week because I've devoted all my time to working on chemistry problems. I shouldn't even be worrying about the emissions because we have enough government credits to launch without changing a damn thing. But that's just dollars changing hands. We're still damaging the planet, and that's something I'm finding harder and harder to stomach.

Hours go by while scientists come in and out of my office with proposals that aren't good enough. I keep sending them back to the drawing board as the clock ticks down to our launch day.

Finally, I face facts and ask Kate to cancel our reservation. No way will I be able to enjoy dinner with PJ if I have all this crap on my mind. I'll call and explain, hoping she'll understand. Again.

"Hey Colin, can you come take a look at something?" Chuck, my chief technology officer, looks excited when his blond head pops into view. "We may have a solution to the emissions issue, but it requires a little rebuild."

I'm out of my chair in a heartbeat, rushing to the lab where the rebuild my team has in mind looks great, but it's not little. "How long will this take to implement?"

A dozen pairs of eyes look back at me, and no one seems certain. "We'll get going ASAP, but I can't guarantee we'll be able to stay on schedule," Chuck says.

I nod. "Let's put more people on it. The schedule has to stay, so let's get to work." I jump in with both feet and spend the rest of the day in the lab. The idea that we can build a greener product makes me the happiest I've been in a long time.

The hours fly by, and I'm surprised when Kate pokes her head into the lab to tell me PJ is waiting in my office.

Shit.

I forgot to call her and cancel. And now she's driven two hours for our date. Kate ushers her into my office, and I take in her pretty dress and hair falling in smooth waves. I'm standing here in the same gray Henley I've been wearing all day and the jeans that are my uniform. I'm wearing glasses instead of contact lenses because I didn't spend the extra two minutes to put them in this morning.

She takes one look at me, and her face falls. "Is this still a good time?"

"Sure. Yeah." I know I don't sound convincing, especially because my computer keeps beeping with incoming messages, and I get distracted by the onslaught.

"Maybe I shouldn't come. It seems like you've got a lot on your plate."

I start overthinking. Is she responding to what she believes I want, or is she looking for a way out? With no way of knowing, I have a knee-jerk desire to protect myself. I should give her an out.

"Whatever's best for you."

"Um, okay." She sounds unsure. "But this isn't about me. I was trying to do what's best for you."

I'm an asshole. She just drove two hours to see me, and I'm waffling and making her feel like I don't want her when the exact opposite is true.

I close my eyes and inhale a breath. When I let it out, some of the panic has subsided. "No. Come." I take her hand and lead her upstairs. "Let's go look at some stars."

After fifteen minutes in the quiet of the astronomy lab, I've calmed down. Even though I'm still working through calculations for our upcoming space launch, I'm happier now that PJ is here. So happy that for a minute, I almost forget about space at all.

It's a good thing. And also dangerous because, damn, this woman makes me want to forget about everything I've ever cared about. I'm in love with her. A total goner. It thrills me and freaks me the hell out.

"Let me tweak the focus so you can see it better." Standing behind PJ with my arms around her, I peer through the telescope and adjust the dials. The focus is good, but I want it to be perfect. I want her to see what I see.

"It looks pretty great to me."

I laugh because she hasn't even looked at the view of Mars I have in the scope, but when I pull my gaze from the telescope, I find her peering over her shoulder at me.

"And even better now." She turns in my arms and kisses me. I forget all about Mars and million-dollar lenses and ten years' worth of work in an instant.

It's all desire, longing, hunger. When we break the kiss, PJ inhales a shaky breath that matches mine.

"I've missed you, Junebug."

"Ah, me too. But we're being silly. It's only been a couple weeks."

"A long fucking couple weeks." My voice is a low growl against her ear, and she sighs. I nip at her ear and trail kisses down her neck. I feel her go limp against me as she tips her head back to give me better access to the soft, sweet-smelling skin at the base of her throat. Kissing her there too, I'm ready to shove millions of dollars' worth of telescopes aside and take her right here in the middle of the lab.

But she's here all weekend, and I need to slow my roll.

"Okay, tell me what I'm looking at." PJ positions herself like a quarterback getting ready for the snap and looks through the lens.

I know the landscape of Mars by heart since I've been staring at it for months. Even though she can't see me, I point at the sky and narrate the path the telescope will follow, based on how I've programmed it.

"This is where we've been exploring for the past year. You can see the rover moving through the dust. It's gathering images, but

I'm mainly using it to map the terrain for future spacecraft to land."

"That is so cool. Does it move all the time, or are you controlling it?"

"It's programmed to move all the time, but I can tell it to change course or focus on specific things."

"Wow. It's…spectacular."

PJ's wavy blond hair catches the moonlight beaming through the open hatch of the observatory. In her loose-fitting dress, PJ casts attention away from the curves of her spectacular body, which is just fine with me. I don't need any other man ogling her.

I wrap a hand around her hip and pull her against me. I flick a lever on the scope to move it upward, knowing exactly what PJ will see. Her gasp tracks with the vast display of stars that will never fail to blow my mind when I see them.

"The Milky Way. Have you seen it before through a telescope?"

"No, just on camping trips when I was a kid. And it was kind of hard to see, if I'm honest."

I nod against the crown of her head, lost in thought. "A week from now, we'll be airborne." I've said it to myself so many times it feels like a mantra.

"Are you nervous?" She pulls away from the telescope to look at me. "Probably not, right? For you, flying a mission is like delivering a pizza."

Her faulty assumption has me stuttering. "N-not at all. Are you kidding? I've been on pins and needles for weeks."

"You don't show it."

She turns to kiss me, and the nerves disappear. All I feel is her enveloping me in her scent and soft curves.

"I should go," she murmurs against my neck. It's not what I'm expecting her to say, but she looks up at me and nods. "You're launching in a week. I know you invited me for the weekend, but you need to focus without me distracting you. And I want to distract you."

"I want that too."

"I don't want to take you away from the things that bring you joy."

"You are one of those things."

She smiles. "I'm gonna go. We're good. Do what you need to do at work." I know she's doing what she thinks is best for me, but all she's doing is driving home the reality that I can't balance work and a relationship. This—seeing her for a couple hours every few weeks—is not balance.

And yet, I know she's right. I do need to focus on the launch. I see our future dissolving before my eyes, even though she's right here reassuring me we're still good.

It doesn't feel good.

"Okay…yeah."

The fact that she understands me so well scares me a little bit. I'm completely off kilter when it comes to her, and yeah, it scares the fuck out of me.

I picture her driving back to Napa and running into Trevor in St. Helena. I fucking hate that guy, but I hate even more that he has a better chance of seeing her this week than I do. I'm losing control of the situation and don't know how to reel it in.

Instead of telling her any of this, I push the thoughts aside and try to refocus on the launch.

We walk downstairs slowly, stopping every minute or so to kiss under the low-voltage lights. I start to steer her toward the parking garage, but she stops me. "No, I found a spot on the street."

So we go there instead, and I watch her drive down the quiet road toward the freeway. A part of me regrets letting her leave, but I have work to do. It's what I know best.

A painful ache throbs in my chest when she's gone, but I also feel relieved because sticking to science is easier than trying to find balance in my life. I've never been good at it, and I'm not good at it now.

I'm walking back to my office when two reporters ambush me

outside the AstroTech building. One more reason I don't ever leave through the front door. For all I know, these people camp out here on the daily.

"Colin! Are you off the market?"

"Are you dating PJ Corbett?"

The voices drown out my thoughts, which had just returned to thinking about the upcoming launch. Now I'm back to gossip fodder, and I hate it.

"Is it serious?"

"Are you more focused on your love life than on your launch?"

"Would you live on Mars with PJ?"

Such. Stupid. Questions.

I'm angry with myself for letting her leave instead of pushing work aside and fighting to have her here all weekend long. I see the trajectory of us flaming out just like my marriage did because I've learned nothing.

When faced with love, I let my work rule the day. Again. I don't deserve her.

The same flame of frustration rears up as when I blurted my thoughts over a month ago, but apparently, I've learned nothing. "It's nothing. She's nothing to me. End of story."

It's me who's nothing, incapable of pulling my gaze from the starry sky long enough to hold onto the best thing I've found. She was right in front of me, and I let her walk away.

Turning away from them before they can snap more photos, I pull open the door of my building and hurry inside to the safety of my lab. But the words have left my mouth, and I already regret them.

Especially because I know that in the world of social media, they'll live forever.

PJ

My heart is on the floor.

It was bad enough that Colin canceled two of our last three attempts to see each other over the past three weeks. Now I understand why.

Because I'm "nothing" to him.

My social media feed burned this morning with that clip of Colin glibly telling some reporter that we are nothing. Squares with what most people in my life seem to think about me. Frivolous, sassy, social media maven who doesn't know how the real world works. I just thought he saw me differently.

"I hate seeing you beat yourself up over this," Dash says as we drive to Duck Feather Vineyard. He's trying to be supportive, but it feels like older brother pity, and I hate it. I hate being the younger sister who's a mess. Again.

"It's fine. I'm fine."

"You're not fine."

"I will be. If freakin' Colin would stop texting and calling me."

"He trying to apologize?"

I shrug. "Don't know. Don't care. I'm done."

Fortunately, Dash is so easygoing that I barely notice the ten-minute drive to the vineyard. He rambles about wanting to learn to surf and offers me a latte I didn't notice sitting in his cup holder.

"Picked it up from Sweet Butter. Heard you haven't been in this week." He doesn't ask why, and I don't offer my sad story about not having the stomach for the place because it reminds me of Colin.

"Yeah. Been busy."

The glance he casts my way is the only indication he knows I'm full of shit. Other than that, he goes out of his way to talk about anything but Colin, and I wonder if my sister sent out an all-points bulletin to the others, telling them to leave me alone.

When we arrive at Duck Feather, the driveway curves around and takes us under an archway with the winery's name spelled out in capital letters with a duck pond beneath it. One duck, tail feathers in the air and head underwater, sits next to a floating duck on the logo.

"How have we never been here?" I mutter, looking around at the scattered oaks and haphazardly planted rosemary bushes. It doesn't have nearly the manicured look of Buttercup, but it's much smaller and charming in a rustic way.

When we reach the front of the tasting room, we find a single door leading to a small gift shop chock-a-block with everything from bathing suits to stiletto heels. Unlike our gift shop, which mainly sells wine, wine openers, charcuterie boards, and anything wine-related that we can stamp our logo on, this shop has just about everything but wine-related items.

"Never had a need," Dash says, looking around. "Guess it hasn't been here long. Less than a year."

"What was here before?" I rack my brain to recall.

Dash shrugs. "Land?" He snaps his fingers, realizing. "Oh, wait. It was that small winery that imported grapes from Sonoma. Weird place?"

I vaguely know what he's talking about, but a lot of the smaller wineries come and go. Some are vanity purchases by wealthy people who don't really want to be in the business of farming, so they sell the place after a couple of years. Or they rebrand and hire other people to run them. So there's lots of turnover.

We exit the gift shop and wander down some outdoor pathways leading to a small vineyard I recognize as cabernet grapes. The vines are well-manicured—all most too well-manicured, which tells me they don't farm organically here. Not a crime. Not uncommon.

Dash points up at some handmade road signs pointing in different directions—toward the vineyard, a small apple orchard, and the tasting room. They have different street names like Hayden Lanes, Tollman Meadows, Bergen Avenue. None of the names have any meaning to me other than Hayden Lanes, which was a riddle Jackson couldn't solve after our dad mentioned it. But it's brought us here now, looking for answers.

"Hopefully, the owner's here. Let's ask in the tasting room." Dash turns and walks a few paces ahead of me. We've done some research and come up empty. The winery is owned by a corporation with an accounting firm as the only named contact. We don't even know the owner's name.

In the small tasting room, we're greeted by a guy who looks like he's about my age, maybe a couple years older. He's stacking cases of wine against one wall and tips his head at us. "Hey guys, you looking to buy some wine?"

Dash takes the lead. "We were hoping to talk with the owner. Any chance of that happening?"

The guy stands to his full height, and he's tall like Dash. He gives us a canned smile, designed neither to welcome nor offend. "What's this regarding?"

I take a step forward and extend my hand. "I'm PJ Corbett. We're neighbors down the road." I point in the vague direction of our winery, but if this guy's been around the wine business for more than five minutes, he'll recognize my name.

His smile fades slightly. "Hello." He moves a few paces away and leans on a wooden bar where several bottles of Duck Feather wine are displayed. "So you're from Buttercup Hill."

"Yes. Is the owner here? We just want to introduce ourselves since we've never met, and we're neighbors, like I said."

The guy doesn't budge. It gives me a chance to study him. Dark hair brushed off his forehead, tanned skin, dimples when he smiles. Dressed in faded jeans and a chambray work shirt over a tee, he looks fit, like he spends time working out—or maybe working in the vineyard. There's something familiar about him, and I think back to the winery events we've hosted. He must've come to at least one of them.

"Yeah."

The way he leans against the bar with his arms crossed reminds me of my brothers. I guess it's a universal guy thing, that smug assessing posture. Dash must see some kinship because he takes a step forward, crossing his arms the same way. "Yeah, meaning the owner's here?"

The guy points at himself with two thumbs. "Graham Garcia. I own the joint."

I don't know why it takes me by surprise that he's the owner. Maybe it's because he's bustling around the tasting room, not sitting in an office somewhere. Maybe it's his chill demeanor. He doesn't seem nearly as stressed as we all are, but maybe that's because his vineyard isn't in debt.

"Have we met before? At Buttercup Hill?" I know his name hasn't been on our guest lists, but something gnaws at me.

He shakes his head. "This is a first."

The words hit me like a rock plummeting to the depths of my gut, bottoming out everything I took at face value a moment earlier. It's the words, sure, but also the tone—a deep boom that reminds me of only one person—my dad.

I sneak a look at Dash to see if he's seeing what I am. His eyes go wide, and he takes a step closer to me. "You okay? You look pale."

Shaking my head, I don't know what to say. The longer I look at Graham, especially as he stands toe-to-toe with Dash, the more certain I become. He's part of our family, no question about it.

And suddenly, it all makes sense. If our dad made a big investment in Duck Feather because its owner is his son—albeit not by our mother—then all of his advice to me about "talking to your brother" is even more logical.

"Kingston Corbett is your dad," I say, not a doubt in my mind.

Slowly, the remainder of the smile fades from Graham's face, and he swallows hard. His Adam's apple works in his throat just like Dash's does a few paces away. Dash reaches for my arm and pulls me closer to him protectively. He's now turned the shade of pale I imagine he sees on my face.

Graham nods. "Yes. He's my dad."

An hour later, my siblings are gathered in Archer's living room, and it feels like a contest over who is more pissed off and who can be louder about it.

"So Dad had an affair. Is that what you're saying?"

Dash puts his hands out defensively. "I don't know. It's not even for sure that we're related, though Peej seems to think it's a slam dunk."

"I just said he looks exactly like our family, which he does. And it makes sense that Dad would maybe give an extra son money to start a winery."

"You think that makes sense?" Archer's face is so red it looks like he just came back from a long run in the cold.

I take a step away from him and lower myself to the couch. I'm too emotionally drained to get into it with him. Or anyone.

Beatrix paces the room in a pantsuit, not a hair out of place from her tidy bun. "So that's where the money went?"

"It makes sense with the paper trails I've been following, actually," Jackson says. "The only thing we can't know is whether Dad made the decision under duress. Did this Graham kid seem to know about Dad's dementia?"

"We didn't stick around to find out. As soon as he said he was Dad's, we got the hell out of there. We needed to regroup."

Jackson nods and rubs a hand over the beard he's been growing. "This is so fucked up. I have no idea what any of it means, but I do know that."

I look from one sibling to the next, and it seems like we have a consensus there. And after another hour of going through the same facts as we know them, we're no farther along.

CHAPTER
Twenty-Eight

COLIN

My front door is open when the elevator dings, and Archer exits on the floor of my apartment building. I hear his voice before I see him because he doesn't come directly into the living room, where I'm sprawled on the couch.

Instead, I hear the faint tinkle of ice cubes hitting glass and the rumple of a chips bag being opened. It reminds me of my trip to the grocery store with PJ, and I immediately feel sadder than I already did.

"Here, seemed like you might need this." Archer strides into my living room and hands me a glass of what looks like scotch on the rocks. He has a bag of Doritos and a bag of Wavy Lays tucked under his arm and his own drink in his other hand.

I take the proffered drink and sip it, grateful for the oblivion it might bring. My life has been a shit show ever since the night PJ went back to Napa and I stupidly trashed our relationship to that reporter.

She hasn't taken my calls, which is probably a good thing because I didn't really know how to make things better. Even though it was just the recorded greeting on her voicemail, I wanted to hear her voice.

"I dunno. Does scotch turn an asshole into a guy with work-life balance?" I take another sip, hoping it does. "Guess, if nothing else, it blunts the fact that I ruined things with your sister. Oh, I'm in love with her, by the way. And I know you told me to stay away from her, so if you're here to rake me over the coals for not listening, you can fuck off."

Archer says nothing. Sitting in the navy wingback chair across from the couch where I'm hunched over my drink, he stares at me. "I should do that, but I won't."

"How magnanimous not to kick me when I'm down."

He plucks a large chip from one of the bags and offers it to me. I decline and lean back against a furry beige pillow. "It's not that. It still gets my hackles up that you pursued something with her behind my back, but…we're not in college anymore. She's a big girl."

"For what it's worth, I wasn't just fucking around. I fell for her. Then I ruined it, as you know." When I called Archer after my newest media spectacle went viral, it was to apologize for the photos he'd no-doubt seen of me with PJ and the awful way I treated her.

He grunted and listened like the solid friend he is and promptly insisted I helicopter him down to visit.

"I think you're being too hard on yourself."

I shake my head. "I thought I could make it work. I wanted to. Desperately." I feel a catch in my throat and hide it by swallowing another mouthful of scotch, relishing the burn in my throat.

"You really love her?" He gives me a wary side-eye.

I nod. "But I'm not built for love, apparently. I'm a workhorse, and you can't teach this old pony new tricks."

"Aw, hell. Is this where I have to convince you to be with my goddamn sister?"

"No." I drain the last of my drink and pad over to the kitchen for the bottle. When I return, Archer is on the couch where I just was. I stand over him, waiting for him to move his dumb ass.

"Do you mind?"

"Actually, I do. Sit in the chair." He points at the stiff-backed chair I hate. It's rigid and uncomfortable and doesn't allow me to slump like I want to. But I sit and pour myself another drink.

"Why?"

"Because it's as uncomfortable as shit, and that way, I know you'll pay attention." Archer sips his scotch and grabs a wavy chip. He crunches on it and talks as he chews. "I love my family more than anything, and I'd guard PJ with my life. But I don't want to guard her against love. Does she feel the way you do?"

I nod. "I think so. At least before I shot my mouth off."

He grimaces. "Yeah, that was a bonehead move, but let's assume you can get past that. Why do you think you're not built for love?"

My eyes go wide because it's that obvious. "Clearly, you see my track record. I sabotage it because work is everything to me. I can't let up or things fall apart."

"Do they?"

"What do you mean?"

"I mean, you spent two weeks at the winery, and the place did just fine without you. So do "things" fall apart, or is it just you?"

It's the question I've mulled since I first laid eyes on PJ Corbett, asking myself if I could have everything I want and eventually talking myself out of it.

"I don't know."

"Don't you?"

I want to throw my glass at his head for his rhetorical questions, except that he's probably right. "I guess…it's hard for me to accept that they don't need me as much as I thought. And also… it's hard to accept that I could be this happy."

"With my sister." He confirms what I'm still hesitant to believe.

"Yeah."

"Then I think your choice is clear. Accept it. Ease your grip on the work treadmill and trust that things won't fall apart. You can look at the stars all day long, but Earth is where it's at. Get the girl, for fuck's sake."

He's right. I know he's right. The problem is in my head—and in my big mouth that can't stop saying the wrong thing. There's got to be a way to fix things, but that's not Archer's job. He's already done the heavy lifting.

He stands up and dramatically gestures to the vacant couch, and I lug my sorry ass over there. But I don't slump. I move to the corner and put the pillow on my lap. It's a big couch, so there's room for Archer on the other end.

"You're a good friend, Arch."

"The best." He could be the same guy standing at that salad bar. Still cocky, still a loveable asshole.

"Now tell me what's up at the winery. How can I help?"

He lets out a long sigh. "You can't."

"Don't be so sure. Give me all the details."

Archer shakes his head and leans back on the couch like he's been dealt a blow. "Well, you're not gonna believe this, but we have a half brother." He goes on to tell me about Duck Feather Winery and the new financial conundrum at Buttercup Hill.

"Listen, if you're giving me your blessing to make out with your sister, maybe I can return the favor."

He listens. He grimaces. But he doesn't seem to hate the idea.

"Okay, maybe. No promises, but maybe." He looks exhausted by the conversation. "Now, I'm going to top off this drink because I need to get the image of you kissing her out of my head. That's fucking necessary."

I laugh. "Tell her I miss her, okay?"

He shakes his head. "Tell her yourself."

Twenty-Nine

COLIN

"I have an idea for you." Paul, my publicist, rubs a hand over his goatee and looks at the view of downtown Palo Alto through the plate glass windows of the AstroTech conference room.

"I feel like wars have been lost and companies have gone bankrupt after a person uttered that statement."

"Yeah, probably."

"Yeah, I'm not sure I'm interested."

I still love this view, a bird's eye of the world. But Archer's words stick in my head. "You can look at the stars all day long, but Earth is where it's at."

People work in the labs and cubicles throughout the building, but no meetings are scheduled today, so the two of us are alone in the large room equipped with a massive table, video conferencing equipment, and two dozen chairs.

Yet it's the view that captivates us. "This is why I first got interested in astrophysics, you know?" I'm more talking to myself than to him, so it startles me when he answers.

"You wanted to look at city streets from the fifth floor every day?" Missing the point, as usual. If he wasn't so good at his job, I wouldn't work with him because he doesn't really understand me. Maybe that's precisely what makes him good at his job—he's all about the work, objectively looking for solutions to my problems and angles that benefit the business model. He doesn't give a shit about me, my love for astrophysics, or my feelings.

"No, I wanted to look at the sky."

"Can't you do that from pretty much anywhere?"

I should fire him on the spot. I hate working with people who don't get it, but I'm too damn worn out to care right now. It strikes me again that this isn't normal for me. Coming to the lab and thinking about spacecraft on Mars is my jam. I don't need anything else.

Well, that worldview is shot to hell.

"Okay, I'll bite. What's your idea?"

He clears his throat and cues up something on his phone, which he holds up for me to see. It's an Instagram reel with the volume on mute, but I can see a woman talking and gesturing to the camera.

"What's that?"

"Chantal Winters."

I spread my hands and shrug. "Don't know her."

He holds his cheeks between his hands. "How is it possible that you're one of the most successful men on the planet, and you've never heard of Chantal Winters? She's only the biggest celebrity interviewer out there."

"Maybe I'm successful because I don't sit around watching celebrity interviews," I say dryly.

"You ought to be watching her."

"Fine. Whatever you say." I hate the idea that he's right, but I know enough to leave open the possibility that he knows more than me in this area. Maybe I need to get in better touch with popular culture. Maybe it will help the next space mission, although I can't imagine how.

"Noted."

"I made some calls, all under the veil of secrecy, of course."

I roll my eyes at his dramatics. "What's that supposed to mean?"

"I can get you an exclusive interview with Chantal."

A laugh peels from my throat. It surprises me because it's the first thing I've found amusing in weeks. I guess I owe Paul something for that.

"Why in the world would I want to do that?"

He explains his reasoning. Then he explains it again, standing up with his arms waving. "For weeks, you've been telling me that your friend over at Buttercup Hill does my job better than me, and while I call bullshit, she may have a point. Maybe it's time you opened yourself up and talked about everything. Tell people about your desire to go green, make yourself sympathetic. Be smart and forward-looking, and people will eat it up. Just...say what you need to say. I'm not saying it's the right decision, but we've tried it the other way, so..."

The reference to PJ sets off a drumming in my chest that I haven't felt in weeks.

I miss her.

I want her.

There's no debating that. But instead of listening to those feelings, I let them scare me. I ran back to the haven of work when I should have been running toward her.

So, if I'm going to spill my thoughts to a celebrity interviewer, there are a few important things I need to get off my chest. And none of them have anything to do with astrophysics.

PJ

I don't know what I was thinking. Maybe I've said that before, but this episode of self-delusion really takes the cake.

Somehow, I allowed a tiny thought to enter my head like a seed planted in fertile ground. At first, it was just a vague whimsical wish that Colin Hathaway, billionaire astrophysicist, would have room for me in his life.

I should have nipped that thought in the bud rather than letting it germinate and take root. Okay, enough plant analogies.

The point is that I allowed myself to think—and then, to believe—that the whisp of a relationship could survive in the real world. Sure, it felt so easy and right when he was hiding out at the vineyard in vacation mode. Who wouldn't make an ideal date and an even more perfect fling?

Bluebirds flitter in and out of the tiny square houses mounted on the tops of the vines outside my house. I can hear them twittering, happy in the morning light. They suck.

I tried with a yoga class and an afternoon hike yesterday. I tried with a glass of wine and a bubble bath the night before. I tried by burying my head under my sheets and blankets and blocking out the world.

The world came a-knocking bright and early in the form of my brother carrying a latte. But for the coffee, I might have turned him away. Not that he gave me a choice, walking past me and turning to survey my oversized, raggedy tee and baggy sweatpants.

"You look good." His sarcasm doesn't even bother me because nothing bothers me. I'm already in the pit of despair after letting my heart have its way with me. Stupid, stupid.

This is what I get for thinking I could make a relationship work with a smart older man who was never going to take me seriously.

"I know, I'm a mess." I can't even look Archer in the eye. Everything he warned me about has come to pass, so I need to own my mistakes.

"You're not a mess. Get that out of your head." The words are kind, but his deep voice makes it hard to discern the tone. He sounds angry, and I figure I deserve it. He did warn me to stay away from Colin, after all.

"I don't even care enough to argue with you."

Lying on the small couch in my house, I shake my head and throw an arm over my eyes. The daylight feels too perky, and I can't keep up. I'm not expecting my brother to walk over to my supine body and lift my arm from my eyes. Why isn't he taking the hint?

"Sit up, Peej."

I ignore him.

"Fine. Do what you want."

"I want to lie here and wallow, and you should let me be the disaster we all know I am. I'm tired of trying to prove to all of you that I'm capable when clearly you were right all along."

I hear a long, frustrated exhale, but I don't bother looking at Archer. He can be as frustrated as he wants with me, but he's the one who chose to come into my house today.

"PJ..." Archer slumps against the back of the sofa as though I've slugged him. "I'm an asshole."

"Well, at least we're in agreement about that. Maybe you could lighten up on me for once in your life. Cut me some slack. You have to know my intentions are good here. I'm not trying to screw everything up for you. Or your best friend."

He shakes his head. "No, that's not it."

I wait for him to explain because, as usual, he's an enigma. A grumpy enigma. Now it's my turn to slump in my chair because I'm all out of fight. If he wants to tell me once and for all that I'm the family screwup and read me his long list of evidence, I'm not sure I have the wherewithal to defend myself.

I'm not sure I care what he thinks.

In fact...for the first time in my life...*I do not care.*

It feels like a breakthrough. Because it is. It's the first time I've ever come to terms with the concept, and in an instant, it makes me feel lighter. I could just...not care.

It would take some doing and a lot of practice. I'm sure I'll backslide and have some knee-jerk reactions to things he says, but...I could push through and remind myself not to care.

And the idea of it feels pretty fucking good.

Trying it on for size, I level my brother with a stare. "I don't care what you think."

He blinks a couple times. I see a muscle tick in his jaw. He swallows and his Adam's apple works in his throat.

He doesn't look happy about my obstinance, but I don't care. There it is again, the idea that I can cast off my brother's opinions and be okay with it.

I lean my cheek on my fist, waiting for him to figure out that I'm over him and leave me alone. "Good."

"What?"

"You shouldn't. You should be your own person, Peej. She's awesome."

"I don't understand those words."

Finally, he shakes his head. "Let's start over. I didn't come to rake you over the coals about anything. I came here to see if you're okay."

"What?"

He nods and leans forward, elbows on his knees. Looking up at me from under his baseball cap, I have a fleeting recollection of Colin wearing a hat like this one on our hike. I banish it from my mind and focus on what my brother is saying.

"I saw Colin last night."

Just hearing his name forms a pit in my stomach. But I can't stop the exhilarated rush of endorphins it brings at the same time.

"Why?"

"He called me. And then I went over there."

"Why?"

Archer's eyes soften, and he gives me a closed-mouth smile. Sympathetic. Concerned. "He's a fucking mess, Peej."

Of all the ways I could imagine Colin Hathaway being described, this is not on the list. He's an astrophysics genius who has the universe, quite literally, in his hands. "Stuff with the Mars mission?" It has to be that. If something went south, he'd be upset, of course. I just can't understand why Archer is coming to me with this information. What does he expect me to do about it?

He takes a sip of his coffee and puts the cup on the table in front of him. "No, not that." He waits as though it's a game.

"Am I supposed to keep guessing?"

"PJ, the guy is in love with you, and he's a wreck about how he ended things. He's...I've never seen him like this. It's worrisome."

"What do you want me to do?" I'm still not understanding because Colin didn't mince words. "He said we were nothing. He's right."

"He fucked up."

"So why can't he tell me himself?" My voice pitches up, but I can't help it. "He sends you as his emissary? And you just...take orders?" It doesn't seem like Archer. Then again, they've been friends for a long time, and maybe I don't know anything about either one of them.

Archer gets up from the couch and paces around the room. I like him better like this. He has so much energy it actually feels weird to see him sitting down. "He didn't ask me to talk to you. In fact…he asked me not to."

"I'm confused. Are you here to tell me that, once again, I screwed something up?" Even though I don't really care, I still sort of care a little bit. Rome wasn't built in a day.

"PJ, I don't think you're a screwup. Get that out of your head."

"Ha!" It comes out of my mouth as more of a noise than a word. It's a gasp of disbelief because he can't be serious. "I call bullshit. All you've ever done for my entire life is treat me like the little kid who doesn't belong at the grown-ups' table. We're only ten years apart. I work my tail off for the vineyard, and I'm good at my job. And all you see is a screw-up who's not good enough for your friend."

Archer's chest puffs up as he inhales a deep breath. I half-expect him to yell when he lets the air out because I'm still so confused about this conversation. "It was never about you not being good enough for my friends. You've got it backward."

It takes me a minute to do the math and figure out what he's saying. I'm still looking blankly at him when he elaborates. "He's not good enough for you. None of them are." Archer looks ready to murder the next man who comes in the door and looks twice at me. I'm familiar with the look, and I can't help but laugh.

"Something funny?"

"The expression on your face."

"I always assumed it was because you thought I was doing something wrong by flirting with your friends."

He relaxes a tad. "At some point, it was. But PJ…that's when we were kids. It's not the case anymore. Not at all. Now it's about them not being good enough for you. End of story."

"Even a hot astrophysicist who's your best friend?"

Archer shrugs. "What can I say? I have high standards. But I'll make an exception for him."

My chest feels tight from the surge of emotions. I don't know if it's because I misunderstood my brother's motives all these years or because he's giving me a sign of encouragement about Colin. Not that it's up to him…

"He was pretty clear about where he stands. I'm a distraction."

Archer shakes his head. "That was a lifetime of thinking about the world one way. He's working on changing it."

I love hearing it, but I still have my doubts. People don't change so easily. "I really hope you're right. But I'll believe it when I see it."

"I know. You're smart that way." Archer stands. "Just make sure you're not so locked into your own way of thinking that you don't allow something new."

With that, he's out the door, leaving me with his instructions and a new view of myself. And the realization that maybe the problem all these years hasn't been how my siblings see me—it's how I see myself.

COLIN

I know I'm taking a risk. Fortunately, this is not new territory for me.

In the weeks since I last saw PJ, my mind has emptied of the very thoughts that drove me to build AstroTech into what it is today. It's strange to think about a single person more than I think about the mysteries of the universe, but I chalk it up to one mystery of the universe I may never understand completely. Even if it's the only thing I know for sure—I want this woman more than I've ever wanted anything.

More than I wanted to build a multibillion-dollar company. More than I wanted to explore the far reaches of space. More than anything.

Period. End.

Instead of scaring the hell out of me, this fact now delights me. Because it's finite. A single tangible desire. If only I can convince her that we're on the same page, that I won't cut and run the second my feet get put to a media fire.

After all, she's the one who advised me how to handle it.

As I sit in the hair and makeup chair, two women fuss over me, dabbing concealer under my eyes and combing my hair. I hate it, but I don't say anything.

"Look at that. No more dark circles under your eyes. So much better, right?" One of the women tilts my chin up so my face catches the light. I notice a glow on my skin that must be due to the layer of makeup she's been slathering on for the past half hour.

I can't wait to be done with this whole performance so I can wash my face, put on a baseball cap, and salvage what I can of my romantic life.

A few minutes later, I sit alone in the green room of the Chantal Winters show, where I've agreed to an interview. Plucking a mint from a bowl on the table, I make a mental note that the walls are actually green. Would have thought it was just a metaphor, though I wouldn't know what for.

The show's first guest is the governor of California, and his segment with Chantal plays on four TV screens that cover the wall to my right. For a moment, I lose myself in watching the talking heads on the screens and tell myself that it will be easier to do an interview with a reporter than it is to address a room full of investors.

But I'm not so sure about that. Investors are all on my side. We all want AstroTech to succeed, and for years, it has. I worry that a reporter will try to punch holes in whatever I say and make me look bad.

Maybe this wasn't such a great idea. There's a reason I've been "media shy" all these years. It's not just about hiding my personal life and the mistakes I made there—it was just good business sense.

I check my phone for the twentieth time since the Town Car dropped me here. I need to make sure no one needs me for anything at work, and the fact that there are no texts or messages proves what I should have realized years ago—the company I built can function without me being involved in every decision every damn minute.

Overhead speakers play music, which I've been ignoring until now, when a Taylor Swift song comes on and gets my attention.

The song rockets me back to the concert, when I knew I was happy, but I didn't know why. The guy who sat there with PJ that night couldn't have possibly known what he needed to be happy like that all the time. Not until he pushed her away.

My eyes dart around the room, suddenly feeling like what I'm about to do is a ridiculous stunt that shouldn't be necessary to prove what I already know—that I love Penelope June Corbett, and I want her more than I want anything else.

It's enough just to tell her that.

In a momentary fit of panic, I take a tissue from a holder on the table and scrub the makeup off my cheeks. This is all wrong. It feels like an ambush when what I need to do is drive to Napa and talk to the woman I—

"Colin."

Tissue suspended in my hand, I stop moving.

I'm losing it. I'm hearing PJ's voice in my head because I'm so damn desperate for the real thing. I'm actually hallucinating because now I feel like I can smell the lemony shampoo she uses, and it knocks the air from my lungs.

I need to get a grip.

Just like that, I feel the grip of a hand on my shoulder. I've always turned to science over anything mystical or spiritual because I prefer to believe in things I can quantify, but right now, I believe in this life force telling me to stop spiraling and get a grip.

"Hey. Are you okay?"

The voice is closer to my ear, and now I feel the hand run from my shoulder down my arm. A moment later, PJ sits on the couch next to me and my lungs have a hard time drawing breath.

Turning to look at her, I feel the need to place a hand on her cheek so I know I haven't fully gone mad. But it's the sweet curve of her face and the warmth of her skin that I feel, and for the first time in weeks, I feel like I could be whole again.

"You're here." Stating the obvious is all I seem capable of, and she smiles.

"Yeah. What the hell were you thinking?"

The wheels in my brain grind slowly through all the possible mistakes I've made and all the reasons a person could ask me that question. There are too many for me to choose only one. "I'll need you to be more specific."

"Archer told me you invested in Buttercup Hill to keep us from defaulting on our debts. You're a part owner."

Oh, that.

It seemed like the least I could do since I could afford to help my oldest friend and his family stave off bankruptcy by signing on as a silent partner and shoring up the winery's finances. When Archer told me about his new half brother, it sealed the deal. He'll have enough to deal with there without worrying about money. No one has to know I'm involved.

Except that, apparently, he told his sister.

"True."

"Why, Colin? If this is some kind of ploy to make things up to me after you pushed me out of your life—publicly—I'm not biting. And if you don't understand why, you don't know me at all."

"Junebug…" I reach for her hand, but she snatches it away.

"Don't." I wish that this fiery side of her didn't make me love her even more because I need to take this seriously. But I love her so damn much, it's all I can see.

"It was never about that. I was never trying to do that. Please believe it."

She lets out a long, slow exhale and bites down on her lip.

"Please, PJ. Even if you don't believe anything else that comes out of my mouth, believe that. I would never try to buy your love. I want to earn it."

She blinks hard. "You lied to me."

I reach for her hand again and feel her start to tug it back, but I hold on. She relents and lets me intertwine our fingers. I've missed the warmth of her so much that it makes my heart ache. I need to make things right, and she's here, giving me one opportunity. I can't blow it.

"I never lied to you. No. God, PJ, I love you so much."

Her eyes go wide. "What?"

I shrug. "It's a fact. I love you, PJ. I lied to everyone else about it because I wanted to keep it to myself. I didn't want to share you with the public. And I'm sorry because I know I hurt you in the process."

Her expression softens, and she squeezes my hand. It's a tiny thing, but it's enough.

I feel a semblance of my equilibrium returning, even though this woman can knock me off balance just by smiling at me. I inhale the first full breath I've taken since PJ walked out of my office on that day when I thought I knew what I needed.

"I don't know how to ask you to forgive me. You didn't deserve how I treated you, and I know you believe people don't think you're enough, but I'm here to say that couldn't be farther from the truth. You're more than enough. You're everything."

She nods. "Thank you for believing that."

"PJ, I believe it with all my heart." My words aren't convincing enough, and I've already proven to her that I don't believe. She has no reason to trust me when I showed I didn't trust her. I'm just hoping she'll do it anyway.

"I'm going to work on believing it too."

My brain buzzes with ideas I've had over the past few days since Archer left my house. "I'm not planning on working weekends anymore. Period, end. And since I'm a part owner of Buttercup Hill, I'll need to spend more time there. And if you can work remotely sometimes, I'll send the helicopter and set up an office for you at AstroTech or in my apartment—"

She cuts me off, raising her hand. Her laughter is the prettiest sound I've heard in weeks. "Slow down. I believe you. It's not the number of hours. It's the quality of the time we spend together, so we'll start by working on that. Okay?"

"Sweetheart, don't you know? Every minute I spend with you is quality. All of it."

I'm about to pull her into my arms when there's a knock on the door.

The twenty-something PA with the blond braids who escorted me peeks her head in and gives me a thumbs-up.

"They're ready for you, Mr. Hathaway."

"Colin," I correct her. I don't want to be the unknowable, unreachable asshole who makes people afraid. I don't know when I became that guy, but he's not me. I turn and grab PJ's face, cupping it in my hands. I pull her toward me and kiss her. It's a hint of all I want to give her and a promise of everything I haven't thought of yet.

——————

I can tell Chantal is disappointed. So far, our interview has consisted of pleasantries. We've talked about the facts and the biographical information people already know about me. She could be reading my Wikipedia page for all the uninteresting stuff we've covered.

She's tried a couple times to delve deeper, but I'm nervous about baring my soul. So I keep pivoting whenever she asks something that digs too deep.

"You made some statements on social media that got you into trouble. How did that feel?"

"Oh, I did the necessary penance, staying out of the limelight and returning everyone's focus to astrophysics."

Pivot.

"You're famously secretive about your personal life, but some recent photos have gotten people excited."

"Correct. There were photos."

She frowns. I sit calmly.

Pivot, pivot, pivot.

"You've spent some time in Napa Valley recently. Anything you'd like to tell us?"

I'm all ready to answer her question with another bland, nothing response that won't get me into hot water later, except that…I can't.

I can't pivot and stay calm and collected now that the idea of marriage bounces around in my brain. And PJ is sitting in the green room a few meters away. And if there's anyone on the planet I can imagine marrying, it's her. For once, I have faith in myself—that I won't run at the first sign of some new shiny thing at AstroTech.

The confident smile melts from my face, and I look at my hands splayed out on my thighs. When I meet Chantal's gaze, I see her expectant yet wary expression as she tries to give her audience a good interview while I've been reticent and stubborn.

And I relent.

"I'd like to talk about the future of space exploration as I see it. And I'll explain why I said what I did a few weeks back. You see, I've been worried about the carbon footprint of our company, and I know that spouting my mouth off wasn't the way to bring about change. For that, I'm deeply sorry."

Chantal's face softens but her eyes sharpen. The journalist in her senses this is about to become a good episode.

"You haven't apologized publicly before now, correct?" Chantal leans forward slightly, enough to show she's interested in what I have to say. She's good at her job. She meets my gaze, offers me a sympathetic half smile, and tries to make me feel comfortable enough to say more.

Even though I can see what she's doing from an intellectual perspective, it doesn't fail to draw me in. I nod. "This would be the first time, yes."

"So why? What's changed?"

I nod as though this is the first time I've considered the question. I can help her build tension. "In some ways, nothing. I've always cared about the environment. It's why I got interested in science in the first place. I'm passionate about our natural world, and I want us to be able to explore beyond the boundaries of our planet. I don't think anyone who's followed the exploits of Astro-Tech would be surprised by that."

Chantal nods. "You've made a business of it. And the world is watching."

"Exactly. So, to me, that's the perfect time to say something I've needed to say for a while. I do think we need to do better when it comes to how we treat our planet, and that extends to space exploration as well. I stand by my comments from a few weeks ago. We're making some changes to the spacecraft that will make our next launch carbon neutral. It's a big deal. And I wouldn't have been able to make those changes if I hadn't gone off the rails and upset everyone. But…"

I shift in my seat. I'm a little uncomfortable, but I'm also helping build some drama because I want people to pay attention. I understand this television moment for what it is. My pause will make people invest in what comes next. I can see it in Chantal's sparkling eyes.

She waits, leaning forward a tad more.

"I regret the way I said it. I should have been more thoughtful. And I don't offer these opinions lightly. In the past few weeks, my team at AstroTech has been redirected so we can fulfill the promise of being cleaner and greener, while at the same time profitable. In order to back that promise and give investors a reason to have faith in me, I've bought back shares of the company in order to bring our stock price back to what it was on the day I spoke out. If I can't make good on my promise to be greener, I don't deserve my personal wealth. And I was told by someone very wise that I should own up to my mistakes, so that's what I'd like to do now."

I stop and let the words land. Chantal's mouth twitches. I didn't tell the person who pre-interviewed me last week any of these things, so Chantal is unprepared with answers. To her credit, she rolls with it.

"That's…quite a gesture."

She's right, but it's not the way I want to end the interview. I've come this far, and seeing PJ in the green room drove home exactly how this all needs to go down.

"Yes, and all of the specifics will be released in great detail in a statement from AstroTech. But there's something else."

Chantal's eyes light up again. "Yes?"

"I wanted to answer your earlier question. And that is to say that I can't think of a better reason for doing the right thing than love."

Chantal's lips twitch as she tries to figure out what to do with this nugget of information. Her lips twitch as she formulates a final question.

"You sound like a man who may have found what he's looking for in that department."

I swallow and let the smile drift across my closed lips, but then I shake my head. "I love space exploration and the possibilities of the human race if we open our minds. And yes, I've also found love in my personal life."

Chantal looks like a puppy. If I tossed her my mic, she'd probably catch it in her teeth. But I don't do that. "Yes?" She scoots to the edge of her seat.

"The woman I was spotted with, PJ Corbett, is a woman I love more than space exploration itself, and that's been my life's work, so…you can see why I'd want to keep that away from public consumption. Which is why I denied the rumors when they surfaced. But she deserves better." I look into the camera, hoping PJ can see the interview on the monitors in the green room. "She deserves it all."

Chantal swoons. She actually leans back in her chair and puts an arm over her forehead like I've just knocked the wind out of her. "That's the most romantic thing I've ever heard."

I really hope so.

CHAPTER
Thirty~Two

PJ

Two Weeks Later

Colin's interview has gone viral, and because he talked about our relationship, the attention has spilled over to Buttercup Hill. We've had so many daily visitors coming for tastings and tours that we've had to double our staff.

Domestic and international orders for wine have tripled in a week.

It's certainly not going to be enough to shore up our finances after our dad gave our half brother millions of dollars to buy Duck Feather Vineyards, but Colin is still determined to be the silent partner who keeps us afloat.

Now that I know he's doing it for the right reasons, it's easier to accept.

Having a brother, on the other hand, is still a lot to handle. I don't think any of us can really wrap our brains around the fact that our father had an affair with Graham's mother, who may have even worked for Buttercup Hill at the time. Graham says he doesn't know much because he doesn't have a relationship with her now, but we're not about to drop the issue.

Archer has extended an olive branch and invited him over to Buttercup Hill to meet us all, but he's turned him down so far.

"Is Colin coming for dinner tonight?" Beatrix bustles through Butter and Rosemary carrying a charcuterie platter, and I follow with a basket of bread. She's hosting our family dinner tonight, but we're eating at the restaurant because she hates to cook.

"Yes, but I think he's running late." The space launch went off without a hitch last week, and he's still fielding media calls about it. I've been giving him advice on how to handle the publicity, and he's become a media darling almost overnight. He says just enough to satisfy reporters, and then he walks away and regains his privacy.

Colin sometimes uses the helicopter to come up to Napa during the week, but weirdly, there's even traffic in the skies. Sometimes he has to wait for air traffic controllers to give him the thumbs-up to fly.

Most of the time, he makes it here in time for dinner or a late-night grilled cheese sandwich, which I know he likes as much as I do.

I drive down and spend weekends with him. The two-hour drive flies by, and I'm always happy to sneak off to Colin's lab and look through the telescopes at the stars.

"No big deal. It's just family." We climb up the top two stairs and push open the door to the rooftop terrace of the restaurant. There's a private area where we'll have our dinner away from the other restaurant guests.

But that's not where Beatrix goes. I follow her to a regular table off to the side that's set for eight. "Oh, we're eating over here? Is there a private party in the back?" Not that it matters. My siblings are loud, but if we're eating with the rest of the diners, maybe I'll be spared another game night, and Colin and I can go back to my house early.

He spent last night in Palo Alto, and I miss him.

"Yeah, private party. We're over here."

I follow her back down the stairs, where we retrieve individual plates of salad from the kitchen. We each balance several dishes and make our way back upstairs. Beatrix is funny in some ways. She's not interested in cooking dinner herself, yet she refuses to let the staff at the restaurant serve us when it's her turn to host the dinner. Carrying everything up to the roof herself makes her feel like she's doing her share of the work.

After a few more trips, we have everything set up for the first course of dinner, including wine and all the place settings. The table looks good, and Dash and Archer arrive together in the middle of a heated discussion.

"I don't want to have anything to do with the guy," Archer insists, crossing his arms.

Dash shrugs and brushes a lock of hair off his forehead. "Don't think he's going anywhere anytime soon, so I just say we deal with him sooner rather than later."

I already know they're talking about Graham. It's all any of us has talked about for weeks, but we agreed to let the financial issues settle out with Colin's investment before we stir anything up with our father or our new half brother.

"I'm still too angry." Archer looks up when Beatrix steps right in front of him and uncrosses his arms. She reaches up and smooths the crease between his brows and pats him on the shoulder.

"I know it sucks. We're all in it together. Can we agree not to talk about it tonight? I want it to be nice."

"What's so special about...? Oh. Okay." Archer looks at the table she's set up and presses his lips together. He's been so much grumpier than usual since he learned about our father's affair that his weirdness barely registers with me. I just feel sorry for him.

I have to admit, my sister sets a pretty table. Purple orchids in bud vases sit at each place, and a drawing pad and pens are set up for Fiona, whose voice I can hear at the bottom of the stairs.

"Last one up's a rotten egg!" Her voice rings out before the pounding of feet on the stairs. If I had one-tenth of that girl's energy, I could move mountains. A moment later, the messy cascade of blond hair appears at the top of the stairs, followed by Jax and Ruby, who look worse for the wear after chasing her.

"Okay, that makes seven out of eight." I check my phone for a text from Colin.

"Do you have an ETA?" Beatrix asks.

"No, but that's normal for him when he gets wrapped up in something at work. We can start without him, and I'll text him to shoot us a smoke signal when he's close."

Everyone takes their seats around the table except Beatrix, who looks down at her own phone with a frown.

"Everything okay?"

She lets out a long breath. "Just an issue with the private party. Apparently, they're upset about something." She frowns and looks mournfully in the direction of the private terrace. "I just don't have it in me at the end of a long day to deal with it…"

The fixer in me springs into action, newly empowered by the idea that my siblings do think I'm capable and pushing myself to own it. "Let me handle it. Go have a glass of wine. I'll make sure everyone's happy over there and be back in a sec."

She looks gratefully at me and nods. "I could use a break. Thanks, sis."

I straighten the neckline of the red sundress I put on earlier with Colin in mind, knowing how much he'll enjoy taking it off me in one swift motion, and tuck my hair behind my ears. I know I don't have a prayer of looking as polished as my sister, but I'm put together in my own way, and it's about time I started believing that.

The private terrace is separated by a wall of potted plants and three steps to another level. When I slip past a little olive tree in its terra cotta pot, I have my eyes peeled for some sort of entitled troublemakers, and I'm ready to conquer whatever issue at hand.

Only…there are no troublemakers. Unless I count Colin, who looks like the very best kind of trouble, sitting at a table for two in a crisp navy sport coat over a pressed white shirt. With his hair slicked back, mischievous eyes sparkling, and the hint of a smile, he's everything I want to have for dinner.

"My family's eating on the regular terrace tonight," I explain. "There's a private party here."

I expect him to stand and follow me back to where my siblings are probably digging into the charcuterie platter and fighting over the aged gouda, but he doesn't budge.

"Yeah. This is the private party. Table for two."

He stands and walks over to me, extending his hand. When I reach out to take it, I find my own hand shaking. "Just...us?"

My brain can't compute what's happening. I don't understand why we're having dinner here when the rest of my family is a few yards away. It feels momentous, but I know we don't have anything to celebrate. We've only just figured out how to make our relationship work. We've only committed to that.

And yet...that feels important.

"Just us."

"Okay..." I glance in the direction of where I can hear Beatrix's cackle over the din of the rest of the diners. I feel a little wistful to be missing the fun, but when I look back at Colin, something shifts inside me.

This is where I want to be.

"Is it okay?" He guides me to my chair and pulls it out for me. Before he pushes it in, he leans down and kisses me. Soft, just a hint at what his kisses are capable of eliciting from me.

"Yes, it's very okay," I tell him as he walks around to his side of the table.

"Good. I just thought...we should have some time alone. We can join your family in a bit, but I was hoping we could just be us first."

"I like that."

"I'm working on balance, so maybe this is what it looks like." Colin takes a bottle of sauvignon blanc from the bucket where it's chilling and pours each of us a glass. He lifts his for a toast, but instead of clinking my glass with a quick "cheers," he clears his throat.

"Balance is important. And I like looking at you, so we're all good here," I tell him.

"Junebug, I never thought I'd find true love. I didn't think I was even worthy of it…" He suddenly looks younger, more vulnerable, with his hair slicked back and his face clean-shaven in the moonlight.

"You *are* worthy. And I love you, Colin Hathaway, so you'll need to accept it."

"I love you so fucking much. And I don't have a big speech prepared to drive that point home. It's just a fact. And facts exist on their own without needing to be proven." He smiles and I remember the first time he said those words to me at the lab.

"Someone brilliant told me that once."

"He didn't realize it at the time, but he was talking about you." Colin takes my hand and kisses my knuckles. Intertwining our fingers, he rests our hands on the table. We each take a sip of wine.

I blush, not because I'm embarrassed but because Colin Hathaway warms me from the inside out.

"So this is it. Just us two, having dinner. In love." It's impossible not to smile when I look at him.

He grins back at me. So easy now. "I remember the first time I saw that smile. It had something to do with squirrels."

"Who knew that was a family of squirrel matchmakers? We owe them at least a burrito or two."

The easy jazz music spills over from the other part of the rooftop, and the dinner chatter and clink of silverware on plates add to the music.

A server comes by with an appetizer of prawns and chilled avocado, setting the plates down wordlessly before moving off. Beatrix is good at her job. I make a mental note to thank her—and the rest of my family—later on. For now, I only want to be with one person.

"How did you know this was exactly what I needed tonight when I didn't even know it myself?" I ask, looking into Colin's eyes.

"Because I know you, Junebug. You're all I want. I look at you and I see the future."

His eyes are locked on mine. This man, who gazes at stars every day of his life, thinking about the possibilities of what's out there, is looking at me. It suddenly seems so simple.

"I see it too."

Love feels so complicated when you can't find it. So elusive. But when it's here, staring at you from across the table, it's... simple. It's perfect.

Epilogue

PJ

Three Months Later

It's become a bit of a tradition for Colin and I to have dinner alone on the rooftop of Butter and Rosemary before migrating to the larger outdoor dining area to hang with my family. Colin hasn't missed a single Sunday in three months—always arriving right on time by helicopter—and our commuter relationship is stronger than ever.

As soon as Colin loosened the reins on himself and cut back on his hours, I saw the smile return to his face. He began taking hikes again, even from his place in Palo Alto, And I loosened my own set of strictures once I began to see that my siblings have full faith in my ability to do my job. It's amazing how much more energy I have now that I'm no longer fighting a battle that was mostly in my head.

"He's not here yet?" Archer asks, looking over my head as though he can see past the potted plants to the private dining area.

"I'm early."

Archer was the one who suggested the dinner tradition. "Good. Just glad you two are still putting in the effort. It's important to make time for each other," Archer says, grabbing a breadstick wrapped in prosciutto from a charcuterie board on the table in the corner. He's acted like a doting father since learning of our relationship, and it warms my heart, especially since our own father didn't recognize me the last two times I visited.

It's a cooler night, so most of the guests at the restaurant are dining inside. We have the whole patio to ourselves.

"You don't mind us showing up late for dinner?" I pour myself a glass of wine and lean against the patio rail. I showed up a little early because Dash said he had some news.

"Nah, I think it's good. Important to set boundaries with meddling family members." He doesn't seem to include himself in that description, which makes me laugh.

"Hey, oh good, you're all here." Dash catches his breath after running up the stairs to the rooftop. His face is flushed like maybe he ran here from his house.

"What's the big news?" Jackson has his arm around Ruby, who holds up her glass of chardonnay to toast with mine. Our glasses clink, and I look past her to see Fiona busily picking all the pitted olives from the charcuterie platter and putting them on her fingers. Ruby and I share a look, both besotted with that girl.

Beatrix comes over from where she was admiring the sunset over the vineyards. "Yeah, don't keep us waiting. Are you here with industry gossip or personal gossip?"

Dash gives her the playboy surfer smile that's won the hearts of women countywide, and even my sister blushes a little at his charm. "It's both."

"Okay, come on. Spill." Archer isn't normally the one eager for gossip, but now that we're not in dire financial straits, even he's mellowed out a bit.

"Mallory Rutherford just asked me out. In a text."

Jackson's groan cuts through the night air. He puts his arm around Ruby protectively, and I recall that she was once jealous of Jackson taking Mallory to an industry event. It's ancient history now that they're in love, but my brother doesn't have many good things to say about Mallory.

"I know, I know. She's not your favorite," Dash says, still grinning. The guy can convince any woman he wants to go out with him, so I can't imagine why he's so jazzed about Mallory. He's never mentioned her before.

"She asked you out?" Beatrix clarifies, jutting her hip to the side and crossing her arms.

"Yup. You know the rumor that her family is thinking of selling some property. And we need more cabernet grapes if we want to grow the business, so maybe it's not the worst thing in the world if I show her a good time and earn a spot in line to buy more land. Especially since we don't know what this Graham dude is up to."

"Don't do it," Jackson says.

"Why not?" Dash looks like an eager puppy about to lose his chew toy.

"She's a nightmare. She'll come onto you and make you feel things you'll regret later on, trust me."

I catch the glimmer of a frown on Ruby's face until Jackson pulls her close and wipes away the expression with a kiss. "All in the past, Ginger," he says. "You're my future."

Dash shrugs. "Sounds like fun to me."

My siblings continue to debate whether Dash should date Mallory and spin theories on why she suddenly asked him out. I don't get to engage much more because Colin texts that he's already at the private table next door. "Okay, you guys. Save some of the gossip for me. I'll be back after our dinner in a bit."

They barely acknowledge my exit, but I no longer look at situations like that as proof they don't take me seriously. They're my family. I know they love me and mostly see the best in me. But more than that, I see the best in myself.

I hear Beatrix cackle at something Archer said as I make my way past the potted plants that separate the two dining areas. Colin stands by our table in a dark suit, which is unusual for him unless he has a board meeting. I don't recall him having one today.

"Oh my gosh, you wouldn't believe the conversation happening over there…" I make a beeline to where he stands holding a bunch of late summer peach roses tied with a raffia string.

"Hi," he says, ignoring my gossip.

"Hi." Seeing him makes me smile so widely that my cheeks hurt. I can't help it. This is what happiness feels like, and I'm not willing to rein it in one bit. His eyes hold mine, and I forget all about what I cared about thirty seconds ago.

"Everything okay? Did you just come from a meeting?" I gesture to the suit.

"No, I wore this for you."

I look down at my long linen dress under a bulky cardigan. It's fine for dinner, but no match for his attire. "I would have dressed up…"

"You look beautiful."

Colin looks serious, maybe even nervous, when he lowers himself to one knee in front of me. "Just you and me, hopefully for a very long time."

My heart, which was already zinging around in my chest at the sight of him looking so delectable, now starts hammering like a woodpecker on crack. "Colin…is this? Are you…? God, why do I have such a hard time forming sentences around you?"

He laughs. "You are one of the most wise and articulate people I've ever met, PJ 'Junebug' Corbett. And if I make it hard to form words, it's only because we don't need any."

I nod slowly, my breathing beginning to steady as my heart gets fully onboard with what's happening. And I love it. "Maybe just a few. I love you, Colin Hathaway. That's it. Those are the only important words."

"God, PJ, I love you so fucking much."

The poor guy has been on one knee for a while now, and I'm starting to worry that it's really uncomfortable. "Ask me, Colin. I promise I'll say yes."

"PJ, you're it for me. I love you more than I love the infinite possibilities of the universe because I see infinite possibilities in you. In us." My whole body collapses in a giant sigh. "Will you spend your life with me? Will you be my wife?"

I nod. "Abso-fucking-lutely."

He produces a ring box and opens it. I don't know what I expected an engagement ring from Colin to look like—I never allowed myself to imagine it. But this ring with its beautiful solitaire diamond that looks like a star in the sky is the most beautiful, perfect thing I can imagine.

He slides it onto my finger, and a giant round of applause breaks out behind us. I turn to see my siblings lined up with Fiona on Jackson's shoulders. He puts her down, and she runs at me, screaming, "I love happily ever afters! Yay!"

"Aw, sweetie." I bend down to where Colin is still kneeling and pull her into my arms. His arms encircle us both. "You're so right. I love them too."

Fiona wriggles out of my grasp and soberly tells me, "I need to give you some space so you can kiss." I look at Jackson, who's rolling his eyes with the biggest grin on his face.

Then I turn to Colin, who looks at me with so much love that my heart melts. And I'm fine with that because my heart belongs to him.

"Kiss. Him!" Fiona squeals.

"You heard the lady," Colin says, cupping my chin in his hand. When our lips meet, I know it's right.

I know it's forever.

-v-

Thank you so much for reading Love You Anyway! I really

hope these characters touched your heart—they owned me while I was writing them, and I didn't want to let them go!

Dying for a peep into their happily ever after? Join my mailing list to have a BONUS EPILOGUE delivered right to your inbox. I'll only send you the best stuff—new release info, exclusive sales, and a monthly free romance from one of my author friends.

Ready for Dash and Mallory's story? You can reserve your copy NOW! Read on for a sneak peek!

Acknowledgments

Readers, thank you. I know there may be only three of you, but I love each and every one. You make it possible for me to do a job I love.

Jesse and Oliver, future heartbreakers—make all the messes you want, and I'll love you anyway.

Thank you to my beta readers Leah, Amy, and Meagan for keeping me in line. And Jenny Sims for top-notch edits (was I supposed to hyphenate that?).

Thank you Echo Grayce for the gorgeous cover x 2—I'm so impressed by your work and your kindness.

The team at Valentine PR is lovely and amazing—thank you, thank you.

Bloggers and bookstagrammers—thank you for embracing my books and exposing my writing to readers. I couldn't do it without your help. Glad to have you in my corner.

And to my fellow authors: you lift me up. Love you.

Website: https://www.www.stacytravis.com

Email: stacytraviswrites@gmail.com - tell me what you're reading!

facebook.com/stacytravisromance
instagram.com/stacytravisauthor
bookbub.com/authors/stacy-travis
goodreads.com/stacytravis
tiktok.com/@stacytravisauthor

Also by Stacy Travis

The Summer Heat Duet

1. The Summer of Him: A Mistaken-Identity Celebrity Romance

2. Forever with Him: An Opposites-Attract Contemporary Romance

The Berkeley Hills Series - all standalone novels

1. In Trouble with Him: A Forbidden-Love Office Romance (Finn and Annie's story)

2. Second Chance at Us: A Second Chance Romance (Becca and Blake)

3. Falling for You: A Friends-to-Lovers Romance (Isla and Owen)

4. The Spark Between Us: A Grumpy-Sunshine, Firefighter, Brother's Best Friend Romance (Sarah and Braden)

5. Playing for You: A Sports Romance (Tatum and Donovan)

6. No Match for Her - An Opposites-Attract, Friends-to-Lovers Romance (Cherry and Charlie)

San Francisco Strikers Series - standalone novels

1. He's a Keeper: A Grumpy-Sunshine Sports Romance (Molly and Holden)

2. He's a Player: A Second-Chance Sports Romance (Jordan and Tim)

3. He's a Charmer: A Brother's-Best-Friend, Forced-Proximity, Sports Romance (Linnie and Weston)

Buttercup Hill Series - standalone novels

1. Love You More; A Single-Dad, Grumpy-Sunshine Small-Town Romance (Jax and Ruby)

2. Love You Anyway; A Small-Town Billionaire-Next-Door Age Gap Romance (PJ and Colin)

3. Love You Truly; A Fake-Fiancé, Small-Town Romance (Dash and Mallory)

Love You Truly ~ Sneak Peek

A SMALL-TOWN, FAKE-DATING, GRUMPY-SUNSHINE ROMANCE

Chapter 1
Dash

The parking lot at Sunshine Foods market is jam-packed at seven in the evening, which doesn't bode well for getting in and out of the store in a hurry.

And I'm in a hurry.

I'm always in a hurry these days because our family winery is operating in crisis mode.

A competitor, who happens to be a half-brother we just discovered existed, has hired away several of our key growers, and I'm the one in charge of human resources around here. That means I need to replace those folks or find a way to win back the ones who've been lured by higher salaries or perks I haven't thought of yet.

Archer, the oldest of my siblings, raised an eyebrow when he saw me leaving the property in my truck, a pickup that I've lovingly restored from its former junkyard state. Now, painted a deep, shiny blue, it's a source of pride when I drive it through town, even if it still has a rattle deep in its bones.

"I'm going to do some networking," I told Archer in answer to his skeptical look, which turned downright doubtful. His eyes narrowed, and he frowned at me. "The kind of networking you did last week with two different women?"

I shrugged at the intimation because there's no sense in trying to dissuade my siblings from thinking what they want about me. I supposed I come by my reputation as a local heartbreaker and playboy somewhat honestly because I certainly know how to have a good time. But if any of my four siblings bothered to think about it, they'd realize there haven't been any stories coming from my direction. Not in a long time.

But old assumptions die hard. Just like my patience as I scan the lot looking for any available spot. I see none.

My fault for waiting until after work to do my shopping, right alongside every other resident of Napa Valley, apparently. If I hadn't promised to meet my former college roommate, Lucas, at the Duck Blind bar in Calistoga later, I wouldn't be here at this hour. The chances of running into someone are too great, and it's the last thing I need today.

After taking what seems like the last available spot in the parking lot, I weave through the sea of vehicles—pickup trucks and Teslas in equal numbers—and grab a shopping cart.

I know exactly what I need, so it shouldn't take too long.

Tortilla chips, avocado, chicken breasts, white rice, black beans. And a bag of powdered sugar mini donuts.

The donuts have nothing to do with cooking tacos for my family tomorrow night. They have everything to do with a craving after work when I haven't had dinner and probably won't. Splitting a plate of wings at the bar hardly counts as dinner, but Lucas is as predictable as he is insistent that we keep our weekly guys' night ritual going.

I've been meeting him and a group of other guys who are less consistent than us for the past three years. In all that time, neither Lucas nor I have missed a single Wednesday night, and I don't plan to be the one to break our streak. Let him fall for a girl and come crawling, telling me he just has to spend Wednesday night with her.

I'm stubborn enough to win any kind of showdown he throws my way.

Rounding the endcap of the cereal aisle, I try to recall whether I have anything left in my pantry that might qualify as breakfast tomorrow morning. For the past few days, I've slept in and skipped breakfast in order to make it to work on time. Bad habit. Need to change that.

The vast wall of cereal puts me in a temporary trance. Colors dance in front of my eyes as Cap'n Crunch's blue hat merges with the beak of Toucan Sam and morphs into the yellow of a Cheerios box. Organic cornflakes, regular ones… I wonder if they taste any different.

It should be a thoughtless selection. Any kind of cereal will do, especially if I end up skipping breakfast on half the days, but the selection suddenly seems daunting. Raisin bran or maple pecan flakes? Does it even make a difference?

Three days of work problems have left me unable to make a basic decision. I know I should grab a box—any box—and move on, but my feet feel glued to the floor. I stare down the cereal as though I'll find some explanation there for my inertia.

It's why I barely move out of the way until I hear a frustrated "excuse me" beside my shoulder. I feel it more than I hear the words—a lilt against my ear, a subtle hint of jasmine perfume, a warm sweep of air as she moves past me. My senses light up before I even get a look at the woman who nearly sideswipes me with her shopping cart.

I feel the close call with all of my Spidey senses on alert. Same feeling I used to get when I played high school football, and I'd feel someone on my heels before I could see him running to tackle me. It allowed me to dart out of the way more than once and score a touchdown.

But the woman is the one who looks more likely to end up on

the ground. I'm interested enough to follow her form as she careens down the aisle.

Yes, careens. Like a drunk linebacker with a case of vertigo.

Her shopping cart is loaded to the top with box upon box of canned sparkling water and cases of bottled water, and the cart itself seems to have a wonky wheel. The bright flash of her red sweater calls to me like a toreador waving a flag. And I'm the bull, unable to tear my eyes away as her captivating form weaves down the aisle.

The rogue wheel seems to be turning the cart in circles just as the woman fights to keep it moving straight ahead, hanging on for dear life. The problem is that with a hundred pounds of beverages in the cart, she's fighting a losing battle against the laws of physics.

Instead of moving to help her, I stand frozen, watching the impending disaster unfold like a movie. I know it's terrible, but I can't get my feet to budge.

From behind, I watch her long, dark hair sweep from side to side against her red sweater as the shopping cart has its way with her. She wears tight black jeans, her legs long and lean. She works hard to control the cart which nicks a box of Lucky Charms, sending it to the floor.

She swears under her breath, but it's loud enough for me to hear the string of curses and be amused by her choice of words. Bending down to pick up the box, she briefly lets go of the cart, which sweeps in a circle and dead ends into fourteen different kinds of Special K. The weight of the cart keeps them in place, but freeing the cart doesn't look like an easy job.

I can't help but wonder why she has so many drinks in her cart, but that's beside the point. Then I notice a jumbo bag of dog food on the lower rack of the cart. Probably weighs fifty pounds. I feel compelled to tell her that there are delivery services for these things.

Finally unmoored from the linoleum tiles on the floor, and I start moving in her direction. "Hey, can I help you with that?"

She doesn't answer, instead yanking on the shopping cart, which hurls her along with it into the center of the aisle. Digging in with her three-inch heels, she doesn't get much traction, but I admire the effort.

This is why I tell people like my uptight eldest brother that it's important to get out of the office. Seeing people in their natural environments often tells me more about them than a resume packed with qualities they think *I* think are important.

Hitting the gym and watching which guys are all about their own workouts—wearing headphones, refusing to spot someone who's lifting—tells me how they'd fare in a workplace. Seeing someone like this woman, determined to complete her mission, fighting a shopping cart goliath like David in a red sweater, tells me she has grit.

All of these things matter, and since I'm the one in charge of hiring new people to keep our winery afloat, I notice.

"Excuse me?" I try again, thinking she'll turn or respond, but she ferries onward.

I keep going anyway, pushing my own cart after hers, determined to help if she needs it. I'm not being chivalrous; this feels like a public safety issue at this point.

In a few strides, I've caught up with her, but not before she tries to whip the cart to the right to get around the end of the aisle. Big mistake.

The rogue wheel makes the cart overly eager to make the turn, so it cuts too close to the end of the aisle, where an unfortunate pyramid of glass jars is stacked five feet high. Well, it was…

I abandon my cart as hers craters into the jars and she goes with it. Her high heels have no chance of digging in and stopping the cart on the slick supermarket floor, so she slides along like a kite surfer in a tornado.

The cart hits the display so hard that it forces a rebound effect, throwing her backward just as I reach her and put my hands out like it's fourth down and I'm alone in the end zone.

If it were a football game, I'd be the hero. In this case, I'm more like a punching bag, losing my own footing in a sea of pale green pickle juice seeping from dozens of broken jars.

"Whoa…!" she yells, punctuating my string of curses which do nothing to break out fall.

The air reeks of vinegar as both of us slip backward, me holding her against my chest and throwing one hand down in an attempt to break our fall. More pickle juice greets my hand, which slips, dropping me to my back. My arm encircles the waist of the woman in the red sweater as her full weight lands with me on the ground.

I'm aware of how silent and still the air around us feels. It takes a couple moments before other shoppers appear, observing us down their noses like we're odd specimens who don't know how to grocery shop properly. "You guys okay?" A woman in a gray puffer coat down to her knees looks over small round glasses and tilts her head to the side.

Since I'm pretty certain I took the brunt of our fall, I feel confident that the woman is probably okay. But from the way she buries her head against my shoulder, I'm guessing she doesn't want any attention.

"Yup. Fine. Clean up on aisle seven," I say, forcing levity into my tone when I'm halfway certain I've broken a rib. The other shoppers move around our two-cart pile up and go on with their shopping, and I do my best to push up from the floor with one hand.

The pickle juice has its way, however, and I slide sideways before righting myself. Meanwhile, the woman splayed on top of me wriggles out of my grip, but her heels slide in the pickle juice, and she has no luck separating her body from mine.

I have enough wherewithal to appreciate the warm feeling of her form against mine, the softness of her sweater under my hand, and the scent of jasmine, which I now realize is coming from her hair. Long tendrils dance across my face as she fails to push herself away from me.

Finally, I muscle my way to standing, holding tight to her

body so she rises from the floor along with me. She's stiff against my ribcage, and her feet pedal against the floor as she struggles to stand on her own.

"I've got it," she bites out right before slipping and almost taking both of us back down again. I hold on tight, bracing an elbow against a display of paper towels, which stays in place under my weight.

"Not quite, you don't." I push away from the paper towels and test my footing on the slippery floor. I feel steady, but I quickly realize I'm bracing this woman across the swell of her breasts beneath the sweater with my hand. A part of me knows I need to move my hand—and quickly—lest she think I'm trying to grope her. At the same time, I do so very much want to keep my hand right where it is.

When she finally stops fidgeting in my grip, she looks down at where my hand still grips her securely. I move it away gingerly, testing her steadiness before I take a step backward. I feel a whoosh of refrigerated air between us and fight the urge to pull her back against my chest. Then I check myself for the source of that urge.

"Sorry. You okay?"

She nods. "Yeah. Thanks."

I'm not a caveman. I don't have a problem finding women to date, and if I wanted a pair of full breasts to fondle, it wouldn't be hard to find. I'm not bragging. If anything, I wish my reputation as a ladies' man wasn't tattooed quite so insistently across my face.

"Once a man-slut, always a man-slut," my childhood friend Caroline is fond of teasing me when she shows up at the Duck Blind every so often and watches my roaming eye. In some ways, it's an old habit. In other ways, it's just an act, a way to entertain my friends since they seem to expect nothing less from me.

But the real Dashiell Corbett? He wants to be about as far from a man-slut as a guy can get. Old reputations die hard, though, and people see what they want to see.

As if for emphasis, a jar of sweet baby dills teeters on what's left of the display, rolls off the top of the jar below it, and smashes on the ground a few feet away. Glass shards explode in all directions.

The woman sighs and turns around and surveys the damage around us—a dozen or so smashed pickle jars, tiny gherkins as dill slices as far as the eye can see, and the pervasive smell of dill and vinegar. "Bet you didn't expect to become a human pickle when you came here tonight."

But all I can think is that I know this woman. In fact, I've sort of known her half my life, at least enough to recognize her. The fact that we've barely ever spoken is merely incidental. It takes another few seconds for her eyes to sweep from the mess to my face, and I see the jolt of recognition halfway through her next sentence. "You landed hard—are you hurt?"

Her eyes go wide. "Dash."

"Mallory."

It didn't occur to me that the woman careening down the aisle a few minutes earlier was Mallory Rutherford because why would Mallory Rutherford be commandeering a stuffed shopping cart in high heels on a Wednesday night? Doesn't she have some expensive wine industry gala to attend where she can tease some poor vineyard owner into thinking she may sell him a few acres of grapes from her family's sprawling lots?

By all accounts, Mallory Rutherford was a socialite, the daughter of a winery owner on the other end of Napa Valley, and arm candy to any man with a big enough pocketbook. I barely know her, so her reputation is all I have to go on, whether it's accurate or not.

The irony of that isn't lost on me, but what can I do?

Her face is a confluence of expressions and shades of pink. Lips colored with a rosy lipstick, cheeks drowning in scarlet, brow furrowed, eyes squinting. Then wide. Then squinting again.

She opens her mouth and closes it again as her cheeks notch a hue brighter pink.

"Are—are you okay?"

Her expression of concern for my well-being strikes me as almost antithetical to everything I know about Mallory Rutherford—out for herself, only interested in a man if she can flirt her way into a business advantage, and ultimately a spoiled heiress who cares only about herself.

Again, the irony is real.

She looks me over from head to feet, and as she does it, I feel the warmth of her gaze like a feather duster. Immediately, I shake myself back to reality because this is Mallory Rutherford and I don't know whether she's sizing up my health out of concern or because I might make a nice next meal.

My hand goes to my lower back, which took the brunt of my fall backward, but near as I can tell, I haven't broken anything.

"I'm fine. You?"

The embarrassment on her face is taken over by an icy stare. "Fine. She looks at her shopping cart, which has a few jars of pickles sitting on top of the cases of drinks, and begins removing them one by one. She looks around the floor for any jars that haven't broken—and there are a few—and picks those up as well.

I stand there agog, watching Mallory totter around in her heels amid a green layer of pickle juice on the floor. She could easily walk off and flag down a supermarket employee to clean up the mess and be out of the store before the cleanup is finished. Yet, she's trying to put the display back into its pyramid shape herself.

It makes me want to help her, so I chase after the few jars that have rolled the furthest away and stack them back on the display.

"Thanks." Her voice is barely audible, and I can't decide whether it's because she doesn't like to ask for help or she doesn't like me. Which is ridiculous because she doesn't know me.

And it reminds me that she sent me a text last week asking me out. A woman I only know in passing sent me a text with no explanation for her sudden interest in spending time with me. It came from so far out of the blue that I felt the need to discuss it with my siblings and my Duck Blind drinks crew before responding, and it's at this moment that I realize I never did respond.

Which is rude. Which might explain why she's now glaring at me like she hates my damn guts.

Can't say I blame her.

-v-

You can preorder LOVE YOU TRULY now!